MURDER ON THE CELTIC

MURDER ON THE CELTIC

CONRAD ALLEN

THORNDIKE
CHIVERS

This Large Print edition is published by Thorndike Press, Waterville, Maine, USA and by BBC Audiobooks Ltd, Bath, England.

Thorndike Press is an imprint of Thomson Gale, a part of The Thomson Corporation.

Thorndike is a trademark and used herein under license.

A Mystery Featuring George Porter Dillman and Genevieve Masefield.

The text of this Large Print edition is unabridged.

Other aspects of the book may vary from the original edition.

Set in 16 pt. Plantin.

LIBRARY OF CONGRESS CATALOGING-IN-PUBLICATION DATA

Allen, Conrad, 1940–
    Murder on the Celtic / by Conrad Allen.
      p. cm. — (Thorndike Press large print mystery)
      ISBN-13: 978-0-7862-9474-9 (lg. print : alk. paper)
      ISBN-10: 0-7862-9474-4 (lg. print : alk. paper) 1. Celtic (Steamship) —
Fiction. 2. Ocean liners — Fiction. 3. Doyle, Arthur Conan, Sir, 1859–1930 —
Fiction. 4. Dillman, George Porter (Fictitious character) — Fiction.
5. Masefield, Genevieve (Fictitious character) — Fiction. 6. Ocean travel —
Fiction. 7. Large type books. I. Title.
PR6063.I3175M877 2007b
823'.914—dc22   2007000361

BRITISH LIBRARY CATALOGUING-IN-PUBLICATION DATA AVAILABLE

Published in 2007 in the U.S. by arrangement with
St. Martin's Press, LLC.
Published in 2007 in the U.K. by arrangement with the author.

U.K. Hardcover: 978 1 405 64100 5 (Chivers Large Print)
U.K. Softcover: 978 1 405 64101 2 (Camden Large Print)

Printed in the United States of America on permanent paper
10 9 8 7 6 5 4 3 2 1

Murder on the Celtic

ONE

"It's not fair," said Genevieve with a hint of petulance.

"Not fair?" he echoed.

"No, George. Other couples cross the Atlantic as a means of celebrating their marriage, but the moment we step aboard a ship we always have to conceal the fact that we're man and wife."

"It's all in a good cause," said Dillman.

"Is it?"

"Of course. It helps us to do our job properly."

"I still don't like it."

"Neither do I, Genevieve, but work must come first. If we operate as a married couple, then there's a limit to the number of people we can get to know during a voyage. Since we have to be seen together all the time, our movement is restricted. And as private detectives," he argued, "we need

7

the maximum amount of freedom on board."

"I don't want freedom — I want my husband."

Dillman grinned. "I'll come and tuck you in every night."

"It's not enough."

"Then I'll have to add a few refinements."

"I want to travel as Mrs. George Dillman," she said wistfully, "not get divorced every time I walk up a gangway."

They were in their room at a New York hotel, ready to embark on their latest assignment as shipboard detectives. It was a moment that she always hated. Having enjoyed the delights of marriage for over a week, she now had to revert to being Miss Genevieve Masefield once more, a change of name that signaled her altered status. It was quite true that as a single woman she would have more room for maneuver aboard the ship, but she would also be exposed to the inevitable, irksome, unsought male attention with which she always had to contend when sailing, ostensibly alone, across the Atlantic.

"Don't you get jealous?" she asked.

"Jealous?"

"At the way that your wife arouses romantic interest on board."

"Not at all," he said airily. "I rather like it. Whenever I see you hotly pursued by some lovesick passenger, I have the consolation of knowing that you would never succumb to his advances. Besides," he went on, allowing himself a rare moment of vanity, "I, too, have been known to make hearts flutter."

"That's what worries me, George."

"I'm all yours, darling. No other woman could tempt me."

"It won't stop them trying."

"Their efforts will be in vain."

George Porter Dillman was a tall, slim, elegant Bostonian with handsome features and an air of urbanity. He had first glimpsed Genevieve on a crowded railway platform as she was about to catch the boat train to Liverpool. During the maiden voyage of the *Lusitania,* they had been drawn together, and because she had helped him to solve a murder, Dillman had persuaded her to join him as a detective with the Cunard Line. Genevieve was a tall, slender Englishwoman with a natural grace and a remarkable self-possession.

"It's only for a short time," he said, taking her in his arms to give her a warm hug. "Then we have ten whole days together."

"Until we set sail again."

"I thought you liked the work."

"I do," admitted Genevieve. "I love it. I enjoy life at sea and I get to meet the most extraordinary range of people. In a perverse way, I even relish the element of danger. I've had a loaded gun pointed at me so many times now that I no longer feel weak at the knees."

"Then what are you complaining about?"

"You, George."

"Gadding about as a bachelor?"

"And having to pretend that we're complete strangers."

"Only in public," he argued. "I make up for it in private."

"I know," she said, kissing him gently on the mouth, "and those moments are very precious to me. But they're usually few and far between. We always seem to have far too much on our plate during a voyage — murder, theft, blackmail, drug smuggling and so on. We never have time for each other."

"We'll *find* some time."

"If only passengers were more law-abiding."

"The vast majority of them are, Genevieve. We only ever get a small handful of crooks. Who knows?" he said with an optimistic smile. "We may get none at all on the *Celtic*."

"We've never had a trouble-free crossing yet."

"There's a first time for everything."

"You really think we'll have no villains on the ship?"

"Apart from the odd cheat at the card table."

"I can cope with that," she said happily. "What I resent is an endless stream of crimes that form a barrier between us."

"That won't happen on the *Celtic*."

"Do I have your word on that?"

"You can have more than my word," he volunteered.

And he sealed his promise with a long, loving, husbandly kiss.

When the *Celtic* had made her maiden voyage in 1901, she was the largest ship in the world, supplanting another vessel in the White Star fleet, the *Oceanic.* That claim to preeminence was surrendered two years later, and when the *Lusitania* and *Mauretania* were brought into service in 1907, the two Cunard monsters dwarfed the *Celtic.* Yet she remained a fine vessel, sleek, spacious and opulent. She also retained her popularity with passengers who crossed the Atlantic on a regular basis. She was always the first choice for Frank Spurrier and

Joshua Cleves, and they were among the earliest people to go aboard. They did so with an enthusiasm that was not shared by every passenger.

As they stood at the rail they watched a sorry procession making its way to steerage accommodation. Clutching their meager possessions and with their heads bowed in defeat, shabbily clad people were trudging along the pier like so many dogs with their tails between their legs. Joshua Cleves, a big, broad-shouldered American in his early forties, identified the reason at once. After pulling on his cigar, he exhaled a cloud of smoke.

"Turned back at Ellis Island," he decided.

"Why?" asked Spurrier.

"All sorts of reasons, Frank. They could be too old, too ill, too stupid or unable to offer any skills on the labor market. Their papers might have been incorrectly validated or they might not have the required amount of cash on them. We don't just let anyone breeze right in, you know."

"But the United States encourages immigration."

"Sure — as long as we get the right sort of immigrants. New York is handling thousands a day, but many of them are undesirables. They have to be sent back home."

"It must be soul-destroying for them."

"They've sold everything they had simply to get here."

"What have they got to go back to, then?" Cleves gave an expressive shrug. "It's so cruel," Spurrier went on, watching the grim parade below. "They're lured by the mirage of a wonderful new life in a country full of promise and the door is slammed shut in their faces."

"We have to maintain certain standards."

"Look at them — they're like beaten animals."

"Then they'll never make true Americans."

Spurrier did not reply. He was thinking of the westward voyage he had made on the *Celtic.* When they left Southampton, there were well over two thousand steerage passengers aboard, crammed into the lower decks, enduring Spartan conditions and unappetizing food, sustained by a vision of a better existence for them and their families. It had been a wasted journey that left them in despair.

Frank Spurrier was touched by their plight. He was an arresting figure in his late thirties, tall, lean and with an exotic ugliness that women somehow found appealing. He ran a hand across his clean-

13

shaven chin.

"Poor souls! I feel sorry for them."

"You're too soft-hearted."

"Nobody could ever accuse *you* of that, Josh."

Cleves laughed. "I hope not."

"Don't you have any sympathy for them?"

"I save my sympathy for the guys who work on Ellis Island. They're little more than cattle drovers. Just think about it — endless shiploads of miserable wretches from all over the world trekking through that reception hall."

"It must be terrifying for them," observed Spurrier. "Especially if they don't speak any English."

"I'd hate to be in the middle of that chaos," said Cleves, removing his cigar to speak. "Think of the *smell* — many of them stink to high heaven. And the noise — it must be pandemonium in there. No wonder the officials resort to shortcuts."

"What do you mean?"

"Some people can be rejected at a glance, and there are lots more who fail a simple medical examination. If the doctors suspect them of illness, they mark the lapels of their coats with different-colored chalk, coded to indicate a particular disease."

"What happens then?"

"If they're rejected, they're kept on the island in conditions that are even worse than the ones they suffered in steerage. Then they live on a diet of prunes and rye bread until they can be shipped back to wherever they came from."

"You seem to know a lot about it, Josh."

"I had a friend who worked as a medical superintendent there," said Cleves. "He reckoned that he was more like a missionary. In the course of a normal day he might hear twenty different languages being spoken without understanding a word of any of them."

Spurrier gazed across the water. "It must be hell for them," he said, pointing at the distant Statue of Liberty. "Their spirits are raised by the sight of that wonderful statue, then brutally dashed by some anonymous official on Ellis Island."

"We have to be practical, Frank. We can't let infectious disease into the country. It might cause an epidemic. And what use are lunatics, fanatics, epileptics, blind people or cripples?"

"You're too harsh."

"Survival of the fittest. Law of nature."

"Your own family emigrated from Europe, didn't they?"

"That's beside the point," said Cleves irritably, not wishing to be reminded that his parents had left their native Poland almost half a century earlier. "I was born and brought up here. I consider myself to be one hundred percent American and I'm proud of the fact."

"What was your surname before it was changed?"

"I've forgotten."

"Nobody forgets something like that."

"I have."

Joshua Cleves gave him a challenging stare before flicking cigar ash over the rail. His eye then fell on some passengers heading for the first-class gangway. One group in particular caught his attention. A stout elderly man in a top hat and a coat with an astrakhan collar was arm in arm with a dignified old lady in a full-length fur coat and a matching hat. It was the young woman beside them who interested Cleves. Tall, stately and immaculately dressed, she glanced up at the ship and enabled both men to get a clear view of her face under the brim of her hat.

"Now there's a far better subject for study," said Cleves with an admiring chuckle. "A gorgeous English rose."

"She could be American."

"With parents like those? Not a chance,

Frank. They're as English as cheddar cheese."

"But they're not her parents," said Spurrier, noting the way that the old man stood aside and doffed his hat slightly so that the women could go up the gangway before him. "What man would lift his hat like that to his own daughter? Besides, they're too ancient. My guess is that they met in the customs shed. The lady may be traveling alone."

Cleves smirked. "Not for long, if I have anything to do with it."

"She's too young for you, Josh."

"Not in my book."

"In any case, I'm sure that she'd prefer a sophisticated English gentleman like me." Spurrier straightened his tie. "I look forward to getting acquainted with her."

"I saw her first," protested Cleves.

"All's fair in love and war."

"She's mine, Frank. Let's face it — I have more money."

"But I have more charm."

"I've got greater experience with women."

"You'd be out of your depth with a real lady."

"I could have her eating out of my hand in a couple of days."

"It would only take me twenty-four

hours," boasted Spurrier.

"Are you willing to bet on that?"

There was no hesitation. "Of course."

"Even though you're bound to lose?" taunted Cleves.

"Name the stake."

"A hundred dollars."

"Make it guineas," decided Spurrier, warming to the notion of a contest. "We're dealing with an English thoroughbred, after all. A hundred guineas to the first man who makes real headway with her."

Cleves smirked again. "I intend to make much more than headway," he said with overweening confidence, "so you'd better have the money ready and waiting. When you tap on her cabin door at midnight, the chances are that I'll be the person who opens it from the inside." He offered his hand. "You accept the wager?"

Frank Spurrier nodded firmly and shook his hand. The two of them inspected their quarry once more. Far below them, unaware of their intense scrutiny, Genevieve Masefield went up the last part of the gangway and onto the ship.

Nelson Rutherford was a stocky man of middle height, with a black beard adding strength and definition to an already eye-catching face. Standing behind his office desk in his smart uniform, the purser had the look of a ship's captain with a piratical past. George Dillman liked the man at once.

"With a name like yours," he commented, "I suppose that you simply had to go to sea."

"Yes," said Rutherford with a pleasant drawl, "though I wasn't named after Admiral Nelson. It was a family name, handed down from one generation to another. I loathed it at first."

"Why?"

"Kids at school called me Nelly."

"Where are you from?"

"The Florida Keys. I learned to sail before I could even walk properly. The sea is in my blood."

"Then we're two of a kind. My father runs a business in Boston making oceangoing yachts. I spent most of my childhood afloat."

"The *Celtic* is much more than a yacht, Mr. Dillman."

"So I noticed."

They shared a laugh. Dillman had left the hotel before Genevieve so that they could arrive at the harbor separately. Having come aboard early, he had first introduced himself to the purser, whom he found a friendly, capable and helpful character. Rutherford clearly knew about Dillman's excellent record as a shipboard detective and he was curious to meet him.

"I gather that you sailed here on the *Oceanic,*" said Rutherford.

"That's true. We had the doubtful pleasure of traveling in the company of the man who owns the line."

Rutherford was impressed. "J.P. Morgan?"

"Far be it from me to criticize our employer, but I rather hope that his name is not on the passenger list this time."

"It isn't, Mr Dillman. You're quite safe."

"Good."

"The *Celtic* is a fine ship — bigger and better than the *Oceanic,* with room for an additional nine hundred people or more."

"I've seen the specifications — almost three hundred and fifty in first class and a hundred and sixty in second. Over four times that combined number in steerage."

"You've done your homework."

"I like to know what we're up against," said Dillman with a smile, "and so does my partner."

"I thought the two of you would turn up together."

"We make a point of staying apart, Mr. Rutherford. If we're seen together, people might start to connect us and that could hamper the pursuit of any villains aboard.

We do our best to look like ordinary passengers so that we can mix easily with everyone else. That way, we have a chance to catch any criminals off guard."

"We don't get too many crooks on the *Celtic.*"

"How do you know?"

"Because so few crimes ever come to our notice."

"That doesn't mean they're not committed," Dillman argued. "Certain crimes are not always reported — blackmail, for instance — and others are not discovered until passengers have disembarked. It's a rare ship that has no villainy on it at all. I just hope that we have no real problems this time," he went on, remembering his promise to Genevieve. "On the *Oceanic* we had a murder to solve."

"Nothing like that has ever happened on the *Celtic,*" Rutherford told him. "Her problem is that she's been dogged by bad luck."

"In what way?"

"Less than two years after her maiden voyage she collided with a steamer in the River Mersey. Six months later there was a fire in hold number five while she was docked at Liverpool. A cargo of cotton, leather and other merchandise was destroyed. A more worrying incident came on Christmas Day 1905." The purser grimaced at the memory. "It was my first voyage on the vessel."

"What happened?"

"We were hit by a massive wave that sent water into all of the second-class areas. Windows were smashed, doors taken off their hinges and carpets ruined. It was a nightmare."

"I can imagine," said Dillman, knowing how treacherous the North Atlantic could be. "It's difficult to be full of Christmas spirit when you're soaked to the skin."

"The awful thing is that the same thing happened again three years later. I was deputy purser at the time. Huge waves buffeted us on the westward crossing," recalled Rutherford, "and scoured the decks. The wooden railing was torn from the bridge and there was a lot of other damage."

"A real chapter of accidents, then."

"It didn't end there, Mr. Dillman. Last year, when we docked at Liverpool, we had a fire in the hold that burned for two days."

"Thank goodness you were not at sea when it broke out."

"A small mercy, but an important one." He gave a reassuring smile. "I wouldn't want you to think that the *Celtic* has a jinx on it. Most of the time she's a real joy to sail on."

"I'm sure that she is."

"Pleasure to have you and Miss Masefield aboard."

"Thank you."

Rutherford picked up some papers from the desk. "There's a passenger list for each of you," he explained, handing them over to Dillman, "and a diagram of the ship. Not that you'll need to go anywhere near some parts of it."

"Any information about the vessel is welcome."

"Then I'd better warn you about the competition."

"Competition?" repeated Dillman.

"Yes, you and your partner will not be the only detectives aboard. On this crossing we have the honor of carrying the most famous sleuth of them all."

"Really?"

"Look at the list of first-class passengers," advised Rutherford. "One name will jump out at you — that of Sir Arthur Conan Doyle. I daresay you know why he's so famous."

"Yes," said Dillman with interest. "Sherlock Holmes."

Two

No matter how many times she set sail, Genevieve Masefield liked to be at the rail for the moment of departure. There was an excitement that never seemed to dull, an exhilaration at setting out each time on a new adventure. It was a shared experience. The pleasure of being part of a large, elated crowd of passengers was heightened by the presence on shore of so many relatives, friends and well-wishers who had come to wave the ship off. Those who thronged the various decks felt a tingle of anticipatory delight as the vessel pulled slowly away from the pier. Those left behind shouted and cheered with unrestrained gusto, their enthusiasm tempered by a faint sadness as they saw loved ones disappearing for a length of time. The *Celtic* was sailing on a huge tide of emotion.

Genevieve stayed on board until the concerted farewell slowly faded beneath the noise of the engines and the melancholy cries of the gulls. People around her began to disperse to their first-class cabins. She was about to follow them when a man stepped forward to block her way and raised his hat in greeting.

"Miss Jameson?" he said. "Miss Stella Jameson?"

"I'm sorry," she replied. "You've mistaken me for someone else."

"Are you certain?"

"Absolutely certain."

"Then I offer my profound apologies," he said, still gazing intently at her face. "The likeness is uncanny. I could have sworn that you were she. My name is Frank Spurrier, by the way," he went on. "Perhaps I should explain that the young lady whom you resemble so closely once worked for a friend of mine. You could be her twin."

"Indeed?" said Genevieve.

"I should have known that you couldn't be Stella — Miss Jameson, that is — because she, like you, is very beautiful. She must surely be married by now."

"Not every woman chooses to relinquish her freedom."

He was surprised. "Does that mean *you* are still single?"

"As it happens, I am."

"I find that impossible to believe," he continued, smiling at her with candid approval. "You must spend all your time turning down marriage proposals. Before this voyage is over, I daresay that you'll have spurned a few more amorous swains."

"I do not make a habit of it, Mr. Spurrier."

"Do you object to the notion of marriage?"

"That's my business," she said crisply.

Genevieve wanted to move away, but there was something about him that kept her rooted to the spot. Though his gaunt face and protruding nose gave him an almost sinister appearance, his eyes had an appealing glint in them and his voice had a beguiling quality. She found him strangely interesting.

"Have you sailed on the *Celtic* before?" she asked.

"Seven or eight times."

"You're a seasoned traveler, then."

"Business brings me to New York at least twice a year."

"And you always choose the White Star Line?"

"If I can."

"Cunard would get you here quicker."

"It's not only a question of speed," he said

blandly. "Loyalty also comes into it and I've always been a loyal person. What about you?"

"Yes, I value loyalty as well."

"Does that mean you stay faithful to the White Star Line?"

"Most of the time," she said. "To get to New York, I sailed on the *Oceanic* and I've also been on the *Baltic.*"

"Another seasoned traveler, then. Why haven't we bumped into each other before? By the way, you didn't give me your name."

"It's not Stella Jameson, I can assure you of that."

He laughed. "To be honest, I'm rather relieved."

"Why?"

"Because she was not the most intelligent person on the planet," he explained. "No disrespect to her. Stella was gorgeous to the eye but she had very little conversation — unlike you."

"How can you say that when you hardly know me?"

"Instinct. It never fails."

"Does that mean you've had plenty of practice at accosting unaccompanied young ladies?"

"Not at all," he said, hearing the note of censure in her voice, "and I hope that you don't think that's what I was doing. One can sense things about people. That's all I meant. And I sense that I'm talking to someone who can hold her own in any situation. That was not the case with poor Stella."

"Then why did you approach me with such readiness if you believed that I was she?"

"A familiar face is always welcome on a voyage."

"True."

"Unless the face is as unprepossessing as mine, of course." He gave her a smile of self-deprecation. "It does at least have the virtue of being unique. Nobody has ever mistaken me for someone else."

Genevieve knew that he was fishing for a compliment that she was not prepared to give him. Torn between curiosity and caution, she could not make up her mind about Frank Spurrier. To travel in first class and to wear such expensive clothing he had to be at least moderately wealthy, and he had the easy sophistication of a man of the world. But something about his manner rang a distant warning bell. She decided to reserve judgment on her new acquaintance.

He stood back. "I'm holding you up, I'm afraid."

"Yes, you are."

"Am I forgiven for thinking you were someone else?"

"There's nothing to forgive, Mr. Spurrier." She gave him a farewell nod and walked past him. "I suggest we forget it."

"You didn't tell me your name," he complained.

She paused. "That's right — I didn't."

"Ah, I see — I'm to be kept in the dark."

"I cherish my privacy."

"In that case, I shall call you Stella."

"Then you'll be well wide of the mark."

"Will you not even give me a hint?"

"You'll have to excuse me," she said pleasantly. "I have to unpack my trunk."

"Good-bye, Stella."

"Good-bye, Mr. Spurrier."

As she walked toward the nearest door, she was conscious that his eyes followed her every inch of the way. Genevieve was mystified. Her first impression of a person was usually so clear, but not in this case. Polite, unthreatening and engaging, Frank Spurrier nevertheless worried her and she could not understand why. Nor could she explain why she had held back her name from him. Of only one thing was she firmly convinced — that there was no such person as Stella Jameson.

Many of the people in steerage had never been on a vessel of any kind before, still less on a liner that would sail over three thousand miles across a vast ocean. They had crowded the rail eagerly and watched the familiar sights of New York starting to diminish in size before their eyes. A first visit to England — or to Europe — was, for them, a thrilling venture that held all kinds of possibilities. For others, however, the voyage was a form of death sentence, returning them to countries that held only poverty and unemployment for them, a misery they had tried desperately to escape. Instead of pleasure, they felt only pain. Instead of a surge of hope, they were weighed down by a sense of abject failure. Having gone to extraordinary lengths to reach America in order to embrace its opportunities, they had been deemed unfit as citizens in some way. Rejection was more than a violent shock to them. It was like a physical blow that left them stunned.

Nobody was suffering more than Leonard Rush. While other emigrants huddled together on deck in groups, or moped in their cramped cabins, Rush sat alone in the dining saloon, deep in contemplation. He was a tall, wiry man in his fifties with stooping shoulders and a face pitted by a life of drudgery. Beneath his tattered overcoat he wore his only suit, frayed at the cuffs and worn at the elbows. His cap concealed a balding head that was covered by livid blue scars. There were other visible mementos of a working life spent down a coal mine. Two fingers were missing from his left hand and he had lost an eye when a piece of vengeful anthracite had shot up into it.

But it was the invisible wounds that smarted the most. His first two children had been stillborn, a tragedy that he ascribed to God's disapproval of him. Rush gave up drinking, attended church regularly and tried to curb his tendency to violence. When a third child was eventually born — a healthy daughter — he believed that he had achieved some sort of redemption. It was short-lived. The girl died of diphtheria before her first birthday, plunging her parents into dejection. Rush began to drink again and get involved in brawls. There were no more children.

"It was not to be," said a voice beside him.

Rush looked up. "What's that?"

"I saw you on Ellis Island. You were turned away, just like us."

"Yes."

"Maybe it's all for the best."

"The *best?*"

Rush could not believe he had heard the word. Nor could he believe that the old man who had spoken it could do so with such philosophical calm. There was an air of gentle resignation about Saul Pinnick. Wearing a moth-eaten black overcoat and a battered bowler hat, Pinnick was a small, shrunken individual in his late sixties with a wizened face fringed with a silver beard. While Rush was in a state of anguish at what had happened, the other man seemed able to shrug it off as a minor disappointment.

"We had family in America," said Pinnick, "but that didn't matter. The doctors still wouldn't let us through. Miriam, my wife, is almost blind and I'm afflicted with all kinds of ailments. They chalked something on our lapels, and that was that." He gave a hollow laugh. "We were turned away from the gates of paradise." He sat down beside Rush. "What about *you,* my friend?"

"Me?"

"Did they give you a reason?"

"No," replied Rush.

"They must have offered some explanation."

"They didn't."

"Well, they should've," insisted Pinnick. "Nobody can be rejected on the whim of an official. Were your documents in order? Did you have enough money? And what about your medical examination — did you pass that?"

"What does it matter?"

"It matters a great deal. You deserved a reason."

"It's all over now."

"But you've been badly treated, my friend."

Rush became aggressive. "Why should you care?"

"I'm only showing an interest."

"You're poking your nose in where it's not wanted."

"There's no need to get upset," said Pinnick, spreading his arms in a gesture of conciliation. "We're on your side. Miriam and I are in exactly the same position as you."

"No, you're not," said Rush, getting abruptly to his feet. "Now, leave me alone. I don't want your sympathy."

Turning on his heel, he stalked out.

Though he had seen many photographs of the famous author, George Dillman realized that none of them had captured the essence of the man. In the flesh, Sir Arthur Conan Doyle was tall, well built, and straight-backed, retaining, now that he had turned fifty, more than a few vestiges of an athletic youth. With his heavy eyelids, ruddy complexion and drooping mustache, he looked like a benign walrus. When he exchanged a handshake with him, Dillman felt the firmness of his grip.

"It's good of you to come so promptly," said Conan Doyle.

"I had a note from the purser to say that you wanted to see me, Sir Arthur. You can always expect a swift response."

"Thank you, Mr. Dillman."

"Is there a problem of some sort?"

"There may be — in due course. But that's not the only reason I asked to meet one of the ship's detectives. I was curious to see what you looked like and I'm reassured to learn that you are nothing at all like a certain Mr. Sherlock Holmes."

"I lack his brilliance and his deductive powers."

"I'm sure that you have compensating virtues," said Conan Doyle, sizing him up. "The purser spoke very highly of you. He tells me that you once worked as a Pinkerton agent."

"That was how I learned my trade, Sir Arthur."

"And you learned it well."

"I had to — my life sometimes depends on it."

"Well, your life is not at risk here. Indeed, there's no danger involved at all. My request is very trivial, I fear. I need to ask a favor."

"Granted before you put it into words."

"That's very obliging of you, Mr. Dillman," said Conan Doyle, "but you haven't heard what it is yet."

What Dillman had heard was the nervous, halting voice with its clear echoes of Conan Doyle's Scottish upbringing. From such a forthright man, the detective had expected more confidence. They were in the author's stateroom, one of the most luxurious on the ship, and Dillman was delighted to have such an early opportunity of making the acquaintance of Conan Doyle. The last thing he had allowed for was the man's slight diffidence.

"Fame sits rather heavily on my shoulders at times," confided the author. "I'm the first to admit that I enjoy its trappings, and my wife and I made the most of them on our lecture tour around your country. But the truth is that I'm not, by nature, gregarious. I hate being at the mercy of my admirers."

"You'll find lots of those on board, Sir Arthur."

"That's my fear and it leads me to my request. If you see me being helplessly besieged in one of the public rooms, I'd be most grateful if you could come to my rescue."

"Of course."

"Find some excuse to call me away and I'll be eternally grateful. My wife is an able bodyguard, but I'm sometimes ambushed on my own. At times like that, I need a friendly intervention."

"Say no more. I'll be standing by."

"Casual conversation with a few people is not a problem," said Conan Doyle. "It's when I get mobbed by a dozen or more ardent readers that I begin to feel uneasy."

"I understand, Sir Arthur."

"I knew that you would."

Dillman returned his smile. He had taken an instant liking to the man. Conan Doyle was affable, approachable and entirely without affectation. With his burly frame and red cheeks he looked more like a head gardener than a renowned author. After a lengthy tour of the eastern states he seemed rather tired, yet there was still a merry twinkle in his eye.

"I have a second favor to ask, Mr.

Dillman," he said with mock seriousness. "I want you to promise me that your choice of profession was in no way inspired by any of my detective stories."

"It was not, Sir Arthur."

"That's a relief."

"I've read them, naturally, and enjoyed them immensely, but I have to confess a preference for *The White Company.*"

"How wonderful!"

"There's real detection at work there," said Dillman. "You must have done the most enormous amount of research before you could even lift up your pen. You must have looked for clues, collected facts and sifted evidence carefully before reaching your conclusions."

"I did, indeed," said Conan Doyle, pleased with the approbation. "*The White Company* is very dear to my heart — as are all my historical novels. But they'll never get the attention that they deserve, alas. They're doomed to be eclipsed by a gentleman in a deerstalker who has some rather peculiar habits."

"Peculiar but endearing."

"Not when he takes over your life, Mr. Dillman."

"Is that what's happened?"

"I'm afraid so," said the other wearily.

"Sherlock Holmes casts a giant shadow. There are times when I regret that I ever created him. But," he went on quickly, "I always remind myself how much I owe to him. I'm loath to acknowledge this, but the fact remains that I'd never have been invited on a lecture tour in America on the basis of my being the author of *The White Company*." He stifled a yawn. "I do beg your pardon. Travel has rather exhausted us."

"Then I'll get out of your way and let you rest, Sir Arthur."

"My wife is already taking a nap," said Conan Doyle, indicating the bedroom, "and I may do the same. But I did want to engage your services during the voyage. And don't worry," he added. "There's no need for Jean — for Lady Conan Doyle — to know that you are the ship's detective. Anonymity is vital in your job. I respect that."

"Thank you. It's the reason I never wear my deerstalker."

Conan Doyle chuckled.

"I'll keep an eye out for you in the public rooms. We don't like any of our passengers to be pestered, whatever the reason. Incidentally," he said, moving to the door, "I take it that you've put any items of value in the ship's safe?"

"Indeed, we have, Mr. Dillman. My wife

handed over her jewelry box as soon as we came aboard."

"Good. Not everyone understands the importance of security. You've no idea how careless some people are with their valuables — then they complain like mad when they're stolen."

"Even though it's their own fault."

"Why tempt Fate?" asked Dillman. "It's so foolish."

"I hope that you have no crimes to solve on the *Celtic*."

"So do I, Sir Arthur. I have a good feeling about this ship. Something tells me that we're going to have a relatively quiet voyage for once. With luck," he said, opening the door, "the only thing I'll be called upon to do is to save you from your adoring fans."

The purser was so busy dealing with requests from various passengers that it was some time before Genevieve Masefield was able to catch him alone in his office. When she introduced herself, she put a smile of surprise onto Nelson Rutherford's face.

"You're the last person in the world I'd suspect of being a detective," he said, waving her to a chair. "I'm sure that goes for everyone else aboard."

Genevieve sat down. "It's a big advantage,

Mr. Rutherford. It's one of the reasons why George persuaded me to become his partner. He said that I'd be invisible."

"Invisible yet highly conspicuous."

"I suppose that I'm something of a paradox."

"You have the perfect disguise," said the purser. He became more businesslike. "Now, has Mr. Dillman given you the passenger lists?"

"He slipped them under my door."

"There was a diagram of the ship as well, though I'm sure that you're used to finding your way around ocean liners."

"It's a necessary skill that I've had to acquire."

"Then you may well need to put it to the test, Miss Masefield."

"Oh?"

"We may have a real problem aboard," he said, reaching for a piece of paper on his desk. "Earlier on, when I met your partner, I assured him that the *Celtic* never had any serious trouble from its passengers. I spoke too soon."

"Did you?"

"Five minutes ago the wireless operator brought me this."

"What is it, Mr. Rutherford?"

"A warning from the New York Police

Department. They were on the trail of a wanted man named Edward Hammond — there's a brief description of him here — but he gave them the slip. They believe that he sneaked aboard this ship to escape them." He passed the message across to her. "He could be armed and dangerous."

"What is he wanted for?" asked Genevieve.

"Murder."

THREE

Dinner on the first evening was a comparatively informal affair, but there were always those who believed in dressing up for the occasion. Amid the smart suits and pretty frocks in first class, therefore, was a scattering of men in white tie and tails. They escorted ladies in long evening dresses with an unashamed display of jewelry. On the second day at sea, such attire would be the norm. Until then, passengers like Frank Spurrier took advantage of the more relaxed dress code. He was astounded to see that Joshua Cleves had not done so. When they met in a corridor, Spurrier blinked in astonishment. His friend was resplendent in one of the curtailed dinner jackets that were becoming fashionable in some quarters, and he was sporting diamond cuff links. His hair had been brushed neatly back.

"Hello, Frank," he said, eyeing his suit.

"You remind me of that story about King Edward and the man in the Norfolk jacket."

"Do I?" asked Spurrier.

"Yes, it was at a formal garden party at the Palace. Someone had the temerity to violate the dress code, so the king sauntered across to him and said, 'Good afternoon, Simpson. Going ratting?' I guess that put him in his place."

"It's obvious that *you're* not going ratting, Josh."

"I suppose that I am involved in a hunt of some sort."

"I've never seen you in formal wear on a first day before."

"I've never been invited to dine with the aristocracy before."

"Aristocracy?"

"Lord and Lady Bulstrode," explained Cleves, baring his teeth in a grin of triumph. "A charming couple. By the end of the evening I expect to be on first-name terms with them — Rupert and Agnes. It's nice to rub shoulders with real quality."

"I thought you were a republican."

"All societies must have their patrician element."

"What about royalty?"

"I'd draw the line at that, Frank. We don't recognize kingship in the United States. We fought to throw off that particular yoke." He adjusted his black tie and pulled down his black waistcoat. "I meant to ask you if you'd managed to get anywhere near the young lady about whom we spoke earlier on."

"As a matter of fact, I did," said Spurrier, spying a chance to boast about the progress he had made. "We had a long chat on deck just after we set sail. At close quarters she's even more beautiful."

"Really?"

"Have you spoken to her?"

"Not yet."

"Then I've stolen a march on you, Josh."

"What's her name?"

"Ah, that's the one thing I didn't find out."

"Then let me save you the trouble," said Cleves, savoring his moment. "She's called Miss Genevieve Masefield and she's returning from a visit to friends in New York."

Spurrier was nonplussed. "How on earth did you find that out?"

"By the most effective means, Frank. While you rushed in too recklessly, I did a little research by ingratiating myself with Lord and Lady Bulstrode. They were the couple we saw talking to Miss Masefield when she came aboard. They found her delightful."

"I see," said Spurrier through gritted teeth.

"In fact, they were so taken with her that they invited her to join them for dinner this evening." He beamed. "And I'll be sitting at the same table with them."

Spurrier was fuming. Having congratulated himself on achieving a brief but revealing conversation with Genevieve, he was shocked to learn that his rival would actually be dining with her. Envy began to rise inside him but he hid it behind a nonchalant smile.

"Congratulations, Josh," he said. "First blood to you."

"You may as well hand over the money now."

"Contriving a meeting with her is not the same as conquest."

"But it's a necessary part of the process."

"Only if she's susceptible to your dubious charms," observed Spurrier, "and that remains unlikely. I've met her already, you must remember. Miss Masefield is a lady with high standards. She's also irredeemably English and that means she views any American with a degree of circumspection."

"You're forgetting something, Frank."

"Am I?"

"My first wife was English."

"Only for the short time you were married to her."

"We were happy enough while it lasted."

"What about your second wife?"

"Martine was French — lovely, elegant and full of Gallic passion. The five years we had together were idyllic. Between them, my wives rubbed off all my rough edges. That's why I have no qualms about consorting with lords and ladies. I know the rules."

"You mean that you learned to hide your true self."

"Isn't that what we always do with women?"

Spurrier was disparaging. "You're too cynical, Josh."

"I prefer to call it being realistic."

"Is that how you hope to ensnare Genevieve Masefield?"

"I'll use a combination of blandishments to reel her in."

"I think you'll find that you've met your match in her," warned Spurrier. "She has great poise and self-assurance."

"In other words, she kept you at arm's length."

His friend was piqued. "That's not true at all!"

"Where you failed," said Cleves complacently, "I'll succeed. Move aside, Frank. You had your turn up on deck. This evening, over dinner, it's my turn."

"I wish you good luck."

"That's very noble of you."

"I have no worries about the dining arrangements. The young lady will be chaperoned by Lord and Lady Bulstrode. They have a right to expect your attention, Josh." He wagged a finger. "You won't be able to leer at Miss Masefield throughout the meal."

"That was never my intention."

"No?"

Cleves beamed afresh. "I'm not giving away any trade secrets," he said. "Watch and wonder, that's my advice. And don't be stupid enough to issue another challenge to me where women are concerned. Because you'll lose every time." He indicated the way. "Shall we go to dinner?"

No dress code was ever observed in steerage because some of the passengers had only the clothing that they were actually wearing. Seated in serried ranks at long wooden tables, they occupied chairs that were bolted to the floor to prevent movement when the ship rolled. Since there were so many mouths to feed, the stewards did not stand on ceremony. Speed of delivery

47

was the order of the day and they went briskly up and down the aisles unloading food from their trays. The noise was deafening, amplified by the clatter of plates, the clash of cutlery and the deep, rolling thunder of the engines. Family arguments occasionally broke out and crying children added to the pandemonium. The cavernous dining saloon was a huge echo chamber that threatened to burst any sensitive eardrums.

Though her husband was right beside her, Miriam Pinnick had to raise her voice to be heard above the tumult. She was a gray-haired old woman with a skinny body, skeletal hands and an emaciated face. She squinted badly.

"It's even louder than when we came," she said.

Saul was tolerant. "Two thousand people make a lot of noise," he said, popping a piece of bread into his mouth. "You'll get used to it, Miriam. It will only be until the end of the week."

"That's more than long enough."

"Try to make the most of the voyage."

"I hate the sea."

"And cheer up a little, my love."

"How can I?" she protested. "I thought that we'd be living in Brooklyn with Isaac by now, but we never even set foot on the

48

mainland. It's a disgrace, Saul. At the very least, they should have let us see your cousin. Isaac must have wondered what was going on."

"He'll have got my letter by now."

"It's still a disgrace."

She munched her food disconsolately and did her best to ignore the din caused by a fight between two small boys. Dragged apart by angry parents, they continued to yell taunts at each other until a few hard slaps apiece brought the argument to an end. Their howls of pain reverberated throughout the dining saloon. Miriam shuddered, but Saul was more interested in the figure of Leonard Rush hunched over a table nearby, somehow isolated in a crowded room.

"Maybe I should speak to him again," he said.

"Who?" asked his wife.

"That man I told you about. He's suffering, Mirry."

"We're *all* suffering. Do you want to know what suffering is?" she went on, her hands gesticulating. "It's spending your last farthing on the fare to America, then finding they don't want you because you're too old, too poor, too weak and half-blind."

"So — we go back to the East End. We have friends there."

"Yes," she said bitterly, "and we told them that we were going to better ourselves. Instead, we have to crawl back. It will kill me, Saul. I can't do it anymore. I can't work for fourteen hours a day sewing dresses. It made me ill. It ruined my eyes."

"We'll manage, my love."

"How? We have no house to go back to."

"Others are worse off than us, Mirry."

"I don't care about anyone else."

"Well, I do," he said, watching as Rush got up from the table, coughed loudly several times, then shuffled toward the exit. "Him, for instance. I could see it in his face. The poor man is in torment."

"So am I," she complained.

Unlike his wife, Saul Pinnick was not given to self-pity. He accepted his fate without complaint. More than forty years earlier they had fled from a pogrom in their native Russia. It had been the first of many hopeful journeys to a different country. Each time they had had to find housing, search for work and learn a new language. When they settled in London — and changed their surname so that English tongues could pronounce it — they thought that they had reached the end of their nomadic existence. Then some relatives emigrated to America and urged them to follow. Since their children had long since flown the nest, the old couple elected to sell their little house in Whitechapel and sail after a dream. It had proved to be an illusion. Yet Saul was not disheartened. To him, it was just one more mistaken turning off the road of life. They were still alive. They were still together. That was all that mattered to him.

Leonard Rush had aroused his interest.

"I wonder if he's the one," he speculated.

"What one?"

"Have you forgotten what happened on the voyage to America?"

"How can I when I was in agony all the way?" she demanded, jabbing a finger at her chest. "I remember every last minute of that ordeal. It was terrible."

"Someone died down here in steerage," Saul reminded her. "A sick woman passed away before she even reached America. Think how her husband must have felt. The two of them set out together, but only one of them survived. The wife was buried at sea." His brow was furrowed in sympathy. "Imagine the horror of that, Mirry."

"I've got enough horror of my own," she said bluntly.

"Show a little sympathy, woman."

"I've none left to spare."

"It could be him," decided Saul. "In fact, I'm sure it must be. No wonder he was so sour with me. He's hurting badly inside."

"And you think I'm not?" she challenged.

"Calm down, Mirry."

"Then stop going on about a complete stranger."

"But he's not a stranger — that's the point. He's one of us. They rejected him as well. It was his voice, you see. That woman who died came from Yorkshire and he talks like someone from up North. He's not from London, I know that." He wheezed quietly. "I ought to speak to him again. I ought to offer comfort." He glanced at his wife. "Did you hear what I said, Mirry?"

But her gaze was fixed immovably on the remains of his dinner.

"Are you going to eat that food?" she said covetously. "Because, if you're not — let *me* have it."

Since they had not met since coming aboard, George Dillman made a point of calling at Genevieve's cabin on his way to the first-class dining saloon. After a warm embrace, they compared notes. Dillman, too, had heard about the possibility that there was a fugitive on the *Celtic.*

"It would help us a lot if we had a more

detailed description of the man," he observed.

"We know his name, his nationality, his age, his height, his hair color and his distinguishing facial features."

"But we don't, Genevieve."

"Didn't the purser show you the second message he had from the police?" she asked. "It told us much more about him."

"An optical illusion."

"How can you say that?"

"Because I know how easily criminals can disguise their appearance. According to the police, he has a beard — do you think he'll be careless enough to leave it on? As for his name, he'll certainly have changed that. He came aboard on a false passport."

"We still know that he's in his thirties, of medium height and has curly brown hair. That's something, George."

"It is," he agreed. "Unfortunately, it's a description that fits several people. I've counted nearly ten so far in first class alone. Not that he's likely to be here."

"Why not?"

"Put yourself in his position."

"What do you mean?"

"Well, if you want to conceal your identity on a ship, you'd find it much more difficult in first class where everyone is on show. The most obvious place to go to ground is in steerage."

"Safety in numbers."

"Exactly," he said. "There'll be hundreds of men there who are the same age, height and coloring as Edward Hammond. Much easier for him to avoid detection."

She smiled. "You should have been a criminal, George."

"I've just learned to think like one."

Genevieve was rather deflated by what he had said, but she saw the logic of his argument. The wanted man would be even harder to find than she had imagined — if, that is, Edward Hammond was actually aboard. All that the police could say was that there was a likelihood of his being on the *Celtic.* Had it been an incontrovertible fact, and had the ship not sailed so far before the telegraphed messages were received, the captain might have considered going back to port so that the police could come aboard and institute a search. He would not make such a momentous decision on the strength of a mere possibility. With or without Hammond, they had sailed on.

Dillman was wearing a well-cut navy-blue suit and a sober tie, but Genevieve had opted for more dramatic attire. Her silk evening dress had a turquoise hue and displayed her figure to advantage. She wore the opal necklace that her husband had bought her in Australia and an opal dress ring set in gold. Brushed up at the back, her hair was held in place by a large silver slide. Genevieve had used cosmetics frugally but artfully to enhance her beauty.

"This is what comes of hobnobbing with the aristocracy," said Dillman, appraising her. "You have to dress the part."

"Lady Bulstrode is a stickler for decorum."

"Then I'd not pass muster."

"They were kind enough to invite me to dine with them, so I had to make the effort. How do I look?"

"Irresistible," he said, reaching out for her.

"One moment, George," she told him, pushing him gently away. "We're still on duty as ship's detectives."

Dillman grinned. "I was thinking of a husband's duties."

"Wait for a more opportune time," said Genevieve, brushing his cheek with a kiss. "We have to be patient. Besides, you haven't told me whom you've befriended since you've been on board."

"Oh, nobody of importance," he said casually. "An English couple — you've probably never even heard of them."

"Who are they?"

"Sir Arthur and Lady Conan Doyle."

Genevieve gaped. "You've *met* them?"

"I've met Sir Arthur. His wife was taking a nap when I called on him earlier. He's not at all as I expected," said Dillman. "Literary gentlemen can be rather pompous at times, but not him. Sir Arthur is refreshingly down-to-earth."

"How did you bump into him?"

"He sent for me, Genevieve."

Dillman explained why he had been summoned to meet the celebrated author, then he fielded a stream of questions from Genevieve. She had been fascinated to learn that Sir Arthur Conan Doyle was on the *Celtic* and had hoped to catch a glimpse of him at some point. Dillman had actually befriended him.

"I'm insanely jealous of you, George," she said.

"And I of you, darling," he countered. "I may have made the acquaintance of a knight, but you're on intimate terms with a baron."

"With his wife, to be more exact. It was Lady Bulstrode who decided to take me under her wing."

"Lord Bulstrode will not complain when

he sees you looking like that. You'll be the center of attention in the dining saloon."

"Oh, I hope not," she sighed, taking a last critical look at herself in the mirror. "I don't want anybody else to dance attendance on me."

He was intrigued. "You've gained a first admirer *already?*"

"I think that's what he is."

"Surely you know."

"I don't, George. I wish I did. I couldn't fathom him somehow. He was inscrutable. He invented an excuse to talk to me on deck and was very courteous, but there was something about him that was vaguely disturbing."

"Disturbing?"

"I couldn't quite put my finger on what it was."

"But it was no chance encounter."

"Oh, no. He was lying in wait for me."

"So why did you find him unsettling?"

"Heaven knows," she said with a shrug. "Nothing untoward happened between us — we only spoke for a few minutes. And he made no attempt to arrange a meeting with me."

"Yet you sensed something?"

"I did, George. I'm well used to male attention and quite adroit at dealing with it as a rule. But I didn't get the feeling that he was really interested in me as an individual. What I felt was this sense of calculation. And it was faintly unnerving."

"What was his name?"

"Spurrier," she said. "Frank Spurrier."

Frank Spurrier had sailed on the *Celtic* so many times before that he took the sumptuousness of its first-class areas for granted. He was no longer impressed by the splendor of the dining saloon with its magnificent dome of stained glass and its lavish decoration. It was left to the couple opposite him at the table to express delight at the luxurious surroundings. Once introductions had been made, Jane Lowbury gazed around the room with awe.

"I just love all this extravagance," she said, exhibiting perfect teeth in a smile. "It's like being in a fancy hotel."

"That's why I chose White Star," explained her husband.

"It's wonderful, David!"

"No more than you deserve."

Jane Lowbury was a shapely young woman in her twenties with an almost doll-like prettiness. Her bright blue eyes were alight at the wonder of what she saw. Seated beside her, David Lowbury was a more phlegmatic character, older than his wife, more sophisticated and more inclined to measure his words before speaking. Of stocky build and with close-cropped hair, he had the quiet confidence of a moneyed man. From the way that he and his wife kept referring to each other by name, and touching each other, Spurrier surmised that they might be on their honeymoon.

When they discovered that he was English, he was assailed by questions about London and he answered them readily. David and Jane Lowbury were pleasant company, though Spurrier would much rather have been at the table where Genevieve Masefield was sitting. From time to time he glanced across to see how his rival was getting on with her. But he was unfailingly polite to his new acquaintances.

"This is your first visit to England, then?" he said.

"Yes," replied Jane, "and we're so excited about it, aren't we, David? Actually," she continued, lowering her voice as if confiding a secret, "we're going to Paris as well."

"A magical city — you'll enjoy Paris."

"You know it, Mr. Spurrier?"

"Very well."

"What should we see?"

"Everything."

"That sounds like good advice," said Lowbury with an easy smile. "May I ask what line you're in, Mr. Spurrier?"

"I run an auction house in London."

"Antiques and paintings?"

"Anything that commands a good price, Mr. Lowbury. Or, to put it more succinctly, anything of real beauty." He smiled at Jane. "If she were not married, I'd be tempted to put in a bid for your wife."

Jane responded with a giggle of appreciation and Lowbury seemed pleased with the compliment. He squeezed his wife's arm with affection, then turned back to Spurrier.

"Is that why you came to New York — looking for items to buy?"

"It is, indeed," said Spurrier, "and I had quite a good haul this time. It's safely stored in a crate in the hold."

"What did you acquire?"

"Furniture, china and a couple of paintings. But the most exciting purchase on this visit was a selection of rare books."

Jane was intrigued. "You mean second-hand books?"

"These have been through many hands, Mrs. Lowbury."

"Yet they still have value? That seems crazy to me."

"The books in question belonged to a man who collected works by French authors. He had first editions of Montesquieu, Voltaire and so on. The real gem was a copy of Montaigne's *Essais*. It was published in 1580, so it will fetch a high price."

"If this man was so fond of his books," said Lowbury, puzzled, "why did he agree to part with them?"

"He didn't," said Spurrier. "It was his widow who sold them to me. When her husband died she had no need of the library and so she contacted me. It was a happy coincidence."

"Coincidence?"

"Yes. I'd actually sold two of the books at auction in London to this particular collector. His wife had my business card. I was able to buy back the two books — both by Diderot, as it happens — along with several others. That library was a treasure trove."

"I had no idea there was so much money in old books."

"The older, the better," Spurrier told him, "though they don't necessarily have to be centuries old. The trick is to spot an author who has great promise early in his career. Then you lay down first editions of his work like fine wine and wait for their value to grow. Look at Charles Dickens, for instance," he said, warming to his theme. "Anyone with a copy of *The Pickwick Papers* in its original serial form would be able to sell it for vastly more than was paid for it when the magazines first came out. Good authors are excellent investments."

"So it seems," said Lowbury, genuinely interested. "I started out as a stockbroker and I thought I knew the market, but it never occurred to me to put money into books. I always went for a quicker return. But you say that the profit margins are attractive?"

"Very attractive — if you pick the right books."

"Such as?"

"You've a perfect example on this very ship," said Spurrier, looking around. "Somewhere in here is the famous British author Sir Arthur Conan Doyle."

"I've never heard of him," admitted Jane.

"Yes, you have," corrected Lowbury. "Sherlock Holmes."

"Oh, did he write those books?"

"And lots of others," said Spurrier. "He has an international reputation. The early Sherlock Holmes stories were published in *The Strand Magazine.* Copies of those editions have already appreciated markedly in value. Sir Arthur's work is a target for collectors now."

"You live and learn," said Lowbury. "Thank you, Mr. Spurrier. If you have your business card on you, I'd be grateful to have one. It may be that Jane and I can visit your auction room while we're in London. Not that we're interested in old French books, mind you," he added with a smile, "but china is a different matter."

"We always have plenty of that," said Spurrier, taking a card from his waistcoat pocket and handing it over. "In ten days' time, everything that I bought in New York will be auctioned. It would be rather ironic if you bid for something that had already crossed the Atlantic once."

"Oh, we aim to settle in England in due course."

"Yes," added Jane. "One of the reasons we're going is to look for a house where we can live one day. David is used to it, but I find New York so brash and crowded. I come from a small town in Connecticut."

"Jane fell in love with those paintings by Constable," said her husband fondly. "I keep telling her that it may not actually be like that in Suffolk, but she insisted that we at least take a look."

"You won't be disappointed," said Spurrier.

Throughout the meal, conversation between the three of them ebbed and flowed. Frank Spurrier spoke to the people on either side of him — David and Jane Lowbury also chatted with their immediate neighbors — but the Englishman always returned to the people directly opposite him. He found Jane quite charming, if a trifle gauche, and thought her husband an interesting character. Having studied the stock market keenly for years, Lowbury had made some lucrative investments on his own account. Instead of selling stocks and bonds, he explained, he had gravitated upward to become a financier. He was now on the board of a number of companies. Yet he remained modest about his achievements. Spurrier took to the man. They had a mutual interest in making money.

When the meal was over and people were starting to drift out of the saloon, Spurrier glanced once more at the table where Genevieve Masefield had been sitting with Joshua Cleves. His friend was still there and so were Lord and Lady Bulstrode, but there was no sign of Genevieve. Spurrier was annoyed that he had missed the opportunity to exchange at least a few words with her. Excusing himself from the table, he picked his way across the room. Seeing him approach, Cleves got to his feet.

"Good evening, Frank," he said. "Delicious meal."

Spurrier nodded. "I always enjoy good food."

"Lord and Lady Bulstrode, allow me to present Frank Spurrier."

Cleves made the introductions as if the elderly couple were old friends of his and not simply recent acquaintances. Lord Bulstrode was a corpulent man of seventy with rheumy eyes and a pudgy face that was further enlarged by two bushy white side-whiskers. His florid complexion suggested a fondness for alcohol. His wife, by contrast, was a slim, pale, birdlike creature, bowed with age yet possessing an undeniable air of distinction.

"Frank owns the best auction house in London," said Cleves.

Lord Bulstrode elevated an eyebrow. "Really?"

"That's how we met. I bought some antiques from him."

"It's all that you seem to do these days, Josh," said Spurrier, trying to score a point off him. "Since you became a member of the Idle Rich, you've dedicated your life to indolence."

Cleves laughed. "And to getting richer!"

"In England, fortunately, wealth is not the only criterion by which we judge a person."

"Quite so," agreed Lord Bulstrode, jowls wobbling. "Breeding comes into it — decisive factor, in my view — and standards, of course. I judge a man by the standards he sets himself."

"So do I, Rupert," said Cleves.

Spurrier winced to hear that his rival was already on first-name terms with Lord Bulstrode. If he had insinuated himself into their good graces, Spurrier feared, he might also have done the same with Genevieve Masefield. After going through the conversational niceties, Lord and Lady Bulstrode went off to have an early night. Spurrier was left alone with Joshua Cleves.

"Well?" he asked.

"Well what?"

"How did you get on with Miss Masefield?"

"A gentleman does not talk about such things."

"Oh, come on, Josh. Don't be so irritating."

"I'm serious," said Cleves with condescension. "It would be quite wrong to breach confidentiality."

"You dined in a public room — what's confidential about that?"

"You wouldn't understand, Frank."

"Did you speak to the lady?"

"Of course."

"Then what was said?"

"It was more a question of what was not said."

"That doesn't make sense."

"It does to a true huntsman," Cleves told him. "Looks, smiles and gestures can be far more eloquent than words."

"So what did you divine from them?"

"I told you — I'm not prepared to discuss it."

"I think you're bluffing," decided Spurrier. "Miss Masefield kept you at arm's length. If you and she established such a bond, why did she leave the table so early?"

"I'll ask her tomorrow."

"Tomorrow?"

"Yes," said Cleves smugly. "It's the one thing I am prepared to disclose. Genevieve and I will be having breakfast together."

Frank Spurrier felt as if he had been kicked in the stomach.

FOUR

When dinner was over, most of the passengers made their way either to the public rooms or to their respective cabins. A few ventured out on deck, but a stiff breeze deterred all but the really determined and the hopelessly romantic. Nelson Rutherford stood outside the door of the first-class dining saloon so that he could be seen and recognized by those who went past. Like anyone who held the post, he felt it was important for the purser to be a visible presence on the voyage. Rutherford had an extraordinary memory for faces, and people he had already met in the course of the first day were hailed by name. Some stopped to chat, others merely gave him a nod of acknowledgment. Inevitably, he had to listen to a few minor complaints. As the mass exodus slowed to a dribble, George Dillman sauntered across to the purser.

"Good evening," he said.

"I haven't spotted him yet," admitted Rutherford.

"Who?"

"The wanted man — Edward Hammond."

"He may not be aboard."

"That's my fervent hope, Mr. Dillman."

"And even if he is, he won't necessarily be traveling first class."

"True."

"We've the best part of three thousand passengers on the ship," said Dillman. "That makes the job of finding him much more difficult."

"What do you suggest?"

"That we wait until he shows his hand."

"I don't follow."

"Remember that first telegraph message, Mr. Rutherford? It said that the murder was committed during a burglary at the victim's home. Hammond went to that house in order to steal something, not to kill anyone. He's a professional thief. If he *is* aboard the *Celtic,* I don't think he'll be able to resist practicing his trade."

"In his place, I'd just want to hide."

"Oh, he probably thinks he's safe now that we're afloat," said Dillman. "I fancy that the temptation will be too strong. There are a lot of wealthy people on this ship, and not all of them have the sense to keep their valuables in a safe. If Edward Hammond is here, then sooner or later we'll know about it."

"I take your word for it, Mr. Dillman."

"The main thing is that nobody else is made aware of the fact that we may — just may, of course — have a killer aboard. If it became common knowledge it would unsettle everyone."

"I agree," said Rutherford, breaking off to exchange greetings with the last of the diners. He turned back to the detective. "Well — so far, so good."

"We've a long way to go yet, Mr. Rutherford."

"I accept that but I remain sanguine." They strolled away from the dining saloon. "Did you enjoy your meal?"

"Very much."

"We pride ourselves on the quality of our cuisine."

"Quite rightly," said Dillman. "It was delicious. Though I wasn't there to appreciate the skills of your chefs. Like you, I'm always on duty. That's why I chose a table near the far wall and sat with my back to it. While talking to those nearest me, I could also keep an eye on the whole saloon."

"Did you see anything of interest?"

"A great deal."

"Such as?"

"Well, it's always intriguing to watch people forming into groups early on. Some are traveling with friends, or as part of larger parties, but the majority are not. It's amazing how quickly they make new acquaintances and create bonds. At the start of the meal," Dillman recalled, "it was fairly subdued in there. By the end of the evening there was a constant babble. A good sign."

"Did you notice Sir Arthur and Lady Conan Doyle?"

"At his request, I paid particular attention to them. Sir Arthur asked for some assistance if I saw him surrounded by over-eager admirers at any stage."

"Yes," said Rutherford with a sigh. "Fame can be a real problem at times. We've carried celebrated writers, actors and politicians before, and some of them do get besieged."

"I don't think that will happen to Sir Arthur somehow. Most of the passengers will not even know who he is. Sherlock Holmes is far more famous than the man who actually brought him to life. On the other hand," Dillman continued, "Sir Arthur has just completed a long lecture tour. His photograph will have been in many American newspapers. Someone will recognize him."

"As long as they don't pester him unnecessarily."

"I'll be on hand to make sure that doesn't happen."

"Did you meet Lady Conan Doyle?"

"No, she was resting when I visited their stateroom."

"A charming lady," said Rutherford, "though quite a bit younger than her husband. I understand that she's his second wife."

"She is," confirmed Dillman. "His first wife died after a long illness. He seems very happy with the new Lady Conan Doyle. In fact, when they came into the dining saloon, that was the first thing that struck me about them."

"What was?"

"They had a wonderful air of contentment, as if quietly delighted in each other's company. It was rather touching. They looked like the perfect advertisement for marriage."

Sir Arthur Conan Doyle had been pleasantly surprised over dinner. Once he had yielded up his name to the people opposite them at the table, he braced himself for the usual questions about Sherlock Holmes, but, miraculously, they never came. His dinner companions clearly knew who he was, but they spared him any interrogation about his work and deliberately introduced neutral topics of conversation.

"I was reminded of the first time we met," he said as he and his wife entered their stateroom. "I had the identical sense of relief then. It was at an afternoon tea party on March 15, 1897."

Lady Conan Doyle smiled nostalgically. "Do you think I'll ever forget a date like that?"

"As with this evening, I thought I'd have to deal with the same tedious cross-examination about my work. Instead, you asked me if I'd seen the exhibition of photographs of Nansen's expedition to the Far North. It was the last question I expected."

"I knew that you'd once sailed to the Arctic on a whaling ship, so I assumed that you'd be interested in Nansen's voyage."

"I was fascinated by it. That's why I went to hear him lecture at the Albert Hall where he received a medal from the Prince of Wales. The remarkable thing is that *you* were there as well."

"Pure coincidence."

"Oh, it had a deeper significance than that, Jean."

"But we didn't know each other then."

"We were destined to meet. We were drawn together."

"Well," she said, giving him a kiss on the cheek, "I won't argue with that. What I can tell you is that, when I went to hear Nansen at that meeting of the Royal Geographical Society, it never crossed my mind for a second that I would one day end up as your wife."

"Do you have any regrets?"

"None at all, Arthur."

"Neither do I, my darling."

"Good."

Lady Conan Doyle was a striking woman in her thirties with a pretty face framed by curly dark-blond hair. Her bright green eyes shone with intelligence and he had discovered at that fateful first meeting how quick-witted and well read she was. The former Jean Leckie had been trained as a mezzo-soprano. When he heard her singing Beethoven's Scottish songs, he had been enchanted. The fact that her family claimed lineal descent from Rob Roy, one of the nation's greatest heroes, was another powerful source of attraction for him.

"I always feel proud when I walk into a room with you on my arm," he confided. "It was a joy to have you with me on the tour."

"Thank you."

"I hope you weren't too bored, having to listen to me spout on."

"Not at all," she said. "Besides, you didn't only talk on literary subjects. You gave lectures on spiritualism as well and we share a profound interest in that."

"I just wish that the schedule had not been quite so full."

"People wanted to hear you, Arthur," she said. "That's why so many different venues had to be fitted in. Now that we're on the way home, you'll have time for a nice rest."

"So will you." He slipped off his coat and put it on the back of a chair. "What do you make of the *Celtic?*"

"She's luxurious."

"Much more so than the *Elbe,* the German ship I sailed on the first time I came to America."

"I thought you sailed on the Cunard line."

"No," he explained, "that was on the return voyage to Liverpool. The ship was the *Etruria* — nowhere near as large and lavish as this."

"Which lecture tour did you prefer?" she asked, turning her back so that he could unhook her necklace. "The first or the second?"

"Oh, this one, without a doubt."

"Why?"

"You were with me, for a start. Last time, I was very lonely. I had nobody to look after me."

"Is that the only reason you brought me?" she teased. "So that I could act as your nursemaid?"

"Of course not," he said, holding the necklace in the palm of his hand. "You inspire me, Jean. You know that." As she turned to face him, he gave her the necklace. "When you're beside me, I feel complete."

"What a lovely compliment!"

"And I didn't just want your companionship. I was desperately keen to show off America to you, like a child showing off a new toy."

She laughed. "A rather large toy!"

"You know what I mean."

"I do, Arthur, and I'm so grateful that you brought me. It was an education from start to finish."

"I wouldn't have come without you."

"I wouldn't have *let* you come." She kissed him again, then put the necklace down on a small table and began to remove her earrings. "What are we going to do on the voyage?"

"Sleep, for the most part."

"We're neither of us suited to hibernation."

"Then we'll enjoy the facilities of the vessel. There's a whole program of events, including a concert tomorrow afternoon. You ought to be singing in that, Jean."

"I've retired from public performance."

"As long as I can still have private ones," insisted Conan Doyle. "I love to hear your voice."

She stifled a yawn. "Oh, I do beg your pardon!"

"You're tired. Go to bed."

"What about you?"

"I thought I might just stay up for a little while."

"You want to write something, don't you?" she said with an understanding smile. "I know that look in your eye. When you have a new idea, you're burning to put it down on paper."

"I've trained myself to write whenever inspiration strikes, and in whatever circumstances. I'm not the kind of author who locks himself away in an ivory tower to wait for the prompting of his Muse. I can work almost anywhere," he said, opening a bag to take out a sheaf of paper. "If we'd stayed any longer in the dining saloon, I'd have reached for the menu and started writing on the back of it."

"What's this idea for, Arthur — a short story or a novel?"

"Wait and see."

"As long as you don't stay up too late."

"I'm a slave to the creative flow, Jean."

"You also need your sleep as much as I do," she warned. "You'll have plenty of time to write on this voyage. If you confine it to daylight hours, it will be much easier on both of us."

But her husband was not listening. Seated at the table, he was already jotting down the first few lines that had come into his mind. His wife did not protest. She knew how much his work meant to him. Leaving him to it, she withdrew quietly into the bedroom.

Genevieve Masefield rose early the next morning and glanced through the porthole. It looked as if they were blessed by a fine day. Bright sunshine was already burnishing the sea. On the horizon she caught a glimpse of another liner. After having a bath, she dressed and made her way to the dining saloon for breakfast. Before she could enter the room, Frank Spurrier materialized at her elbow.

"Good morning, Stella," he said.

"Oh," she replied, startled by his sudden appearance. "Good morning. But, as I told you, my name is not Stella Jameson."

"I know. It's Miss Genevieve Masefield."

"How did you find that out?"

"I have my spies."

"I don't like being spied on, Mr. Spurrier," she said firmly.

"Then you shouldn't be such an object of fascination," he said with a disarming smile. "You turned a lot of heads over dinner last evening. I was by no means the only man who wondered who you were and what your name was. Since you were dining with Lord and Lady Bulstrode, you were even more conspicuous."

"I can see that your spies have been working hard."

"In truth, there's only one of them, Miss Masefield. I suppose that you might call him an unpaid informer."

"Oh? And who might that be?"

"Your other dinner companion — Joshua Cleves."

"You know the gentleman?"

"We've done business on many occasions," said Spurrier, producing a card from his waistcoat pocket and handing it to her.

"We've bought from each other."

"An auction house," Genevieve noted, studying the card. "It must be a successful one if you cross the Atlantic so often in first class." She slipped the card into her bag. "Mr. Cleves was very personable."

"Yes, Josh can be very charming when he wishes to be."

"Do I detect a note of disapproval?"

"Not at all," he said blandly. "We're old friends. I'm very fond of him. It's just that — like the rest of us, I suppose — he does tend to suppress certain facts about himself."

"You mean that he has a dark secret?"

"There's nothing sinister in his past — as far as I know, anyway. Though he dislikes being reminded of the fact that he's the child of Polish refugees. I'll wager that he made no mention of it over dinner."

"None at all, Mr. Spurrier."

"That's typical. It's almost as if he wants to pretend that his parents didn't exist. He changed his name to Cleves to disguise his heritage — and to make the name easier to pronounce, of course."

"I don't see any harm in that."

"There is a whisper of ingratitude about it, I feel."

"Ingratitude?"

"Yes," he said, eyes locked on hers. "Josh's father came from humble origins yet went on to build up a chain of delicatessens in New York that eventually sold for millions of dollars. If I'd inherited that kind of money, I'd have felt obliged to keep the family name."

"Why are you telling me all this?" asked Genevieve with growing suspicions. "You claim to be a friend of Mr. Cleves, yet you're highly critical of him."

"I just wanted you to understand the sort of person he is. Josh has many virtues — he's cultured, forthright and strong-willed. And although he's quintessentially American, in the best sense of the word he has an excellent knowledge of Europe — particularly of France, but that's only natural."

"Is it?"

"His second wife was French," he told her. "The first, oddly enough, was English. Josh has a soft spot for English ladies."

"What about you, Mr. Spurrier?"

"Me?"

"Do you prefer English ladies?"

He beamed at her. "Every time."

"Yes," she said with a slight edge, "I had the feeling that I wasn't the first one to catch your eye."

Her comment wiped the broad smile from

his face. Nonetheless, once again, Genevieve felt at a slight disadvantage. She wanted to take her leave of Frank Spurrier but something held her back. By sheer force of personality he kept her anchored to the spot. Over dinner the previous evening, Genevieve had been acutely conscious of the interest that Joshua Cleves was showing in her, and of the effort he was making to be on his best behavior. What puzzled her was why Spurrier was now deliberately trying to influence her view of Cleves.

"We've obviously got off on the wrong foot this morning," said Spurrier, anxious to make amends for upsetting her, "and I do apologize. Perhaps I might buy you a drink at some stage by way of recompense."

She was noncommittal. "Perhaps."

"Or perhaps not. I leave the decision to you."

"Thank you, Mr. Spurrier," she said crisply. "As your friend, Mr. Cleves, may have told you, I do like to make my own decisions."

"I admire decisiveness."

"Then you'll excuse me if I make the decision to have breakfast."

"Of course."

As he stood politely aside for her, David and Jane Lowbury bore down on them.

They greeted Spurrier effusively. Genevieve was introduced to the American couple.

"Oh, I'm so pleased to meet you," said Jane, beaming at her. "I just adored that dress you were wearing last night."

Genevieve was surprised. "You noticed me in that crowd?"

"You'd stand out anywhere, Miss Masefield," said Lowbury.

"There you are," observed Spurrier. "Independent witnesses. I'm not the only person to be entranced."

Jane sighed. "I wish I was tall enough to carry off an evening dress like that," she said. "It was gorgeous."

"So are you, honey," Lowbury assured her as he slipped an arm around her waist. "What do you think of the *Celtic*, Miss Masefield?"

"I'm very impressed," said Genevieve.

"So are we. She's like a floating hotel."

"As long as we don't run into bad weather."

"She feels pretty stable to me."

"She is," said Spurrier, "but the North Atlantic is the most dangerous ocean in the world. If we get hit by a squall, we'll certainly know about it."

"I hope that doesn't happen." Lowbury smiled at Genevieve. "Did you know that a famous English author was on board?"

"No," she said, feigning ignorance. "Who is it?"

"Sir Arthur Conan Doyle."

"Really?"

"I wonder if we could persuade him to read one of those Sherlock Holmes stories to us. He'd get a huge audience."

"I'd certainly be part of it, Mr. Lowbury."

"So would Jane and I."

"Unfortunately," said Spurrier, "it's unlikely to happen. Sir Arthur has the reputation of being a very private man. The only way to secure his interest is for one of us to commit a crime."

"A crime?" said Genevieve.

"Yes — then we could send for Sherlock Holmes to solve it."

Leonard Rush stood on deck in the stern of the ship and stared at the massive triangle of white foam left in her wake. The wind had picked up, and the sun had vanished behind some clouds, but he seemed quite unaware of the cold. Saul Pinnick felt it keenly even though he wore a scarf, overcoat and hat. He watched Rush for a few minutes before crossing over to him.

"Good morning," he said.

The other man looked at him but gave no

sign of recognition. Rush's face was pale, his remaining eye lackluster. There was such an air of dejection about him that Pinnick's compassion was stirred.

"We spoke yesterday," he went on. "My name is Saul — Saul Pinnick. What's yours?"

"What does it matter?"

"I like to know who I'm talking to."

Rush considered the request for a long time before speaking.

"My name is Rush," he said at length. "Len Rush."

"And you were a miner, weren't you?"

"I spent the best part of forty years down the pit, starting as a lad. I come from a mining family."

"Whereabouts?"

"Yorkshire."

"There!" said Pinnick. "That's what I told Mirry."

"Mirry?"

"My wife, Miriam. I had this feeling that you might be the man who suffered that terrible tragedy on the voyage to New York." Rush turned away. "I'm so sorry, Mr. Rush. I grieve with you."

It was patently a subject about which Rush did not wish to speak. He was still trying to cope with the loss of his wife, and the mention of her death had caught him on the raw. Pinnick was annoyed with himself for raising the topic. He took a different tack.

"I was a tailor in the East End of London," he said. "I made suits for workingmen. Ironic, really — a Jew like me, making suits for people to wear to church on Sunday. I've never even been in a church," he added with a cackle. "Saturday is our Sabbath. Mirry and I go to the synagogue, regular as clockwork. Everything was fine until I got arthritis in both hands." He held them up for inspection, but Rush took no notice of him. "That put paid to my tailoring. It was the same with my wife. She was a seamstress until her eyes started to go. Still, we can't complain, can we? It's not as if our lives were ever in danger. Yours must have been, down the mine. You hear of the most terrible accidents." He moved to his right so that he could see the side of the other man's face. "Were you ever involved in an accident down the pit, Mr. Rush?"

Rush nodded. "Twice."

"I'm glad that you lived to tell the tale."

"Others didn't, Mr. Pinnick. I lost a lot of good friends."

"Yet you continued to work down the pit."

"What else could I do?" demanded Rush

with a flash of truculence. "Every man in the village was a miner. Nowt else to do." He looked at the old man properly for the first time. "Why did you want to go to America?"

"I have a cousin there. Isaac told us to come and join him. We had a house to go to and a relative to look after us, but it made no difference. They wouldn't let us in."

"They herded us like animals in that reception hall."

"There were so many of us — thousands a day."

"It were my chest that did for me," confessed Rush.

"Was it?"

"Bad lungs. Going down a pit is unhealthy. You're breathing in coal dust all the time. They've got this fancy name for it but what it comes down to is bad lungs. That's why it hurt so much."

"What did, Mr. Rush?"

"Ellen, dying like that. I were the invalid, yet my wife was the one who died on the voyage. Not fair, is it? I mean, it's cruel."

"Life very often is," said Pinnick with a fatalistic shrug.

There was a long silence, but the old man made no attempt to break it. Having made a little progress, he was ready to settle for that. Rush was far too preoccupied with his own misery to talk readily to a stranger. When he realized that Pinnick was offering him friendship, he might, in time, respond. For the moment, he needed to be left alone to brood. After giving him a farewell pat on the shoulder, Saul Pinnick adjusted his hat and walked slowly off down the deck.

George Dillman made a point of getting to know as many people as possible on a voyage. Spending time with new acquaintances was a form of camouflage for him. Nobody ever guessed that the debonair American, who claimed to work in the family business of building yachts, was really the ship's detective. Befriending people was not without its perils. As he headed toward the promenade deck that afternoon, Sophie Trouncer accosted him. She and her mother had sat opposite him at dinner and she had spared Dillman nothing of her history. Sophie was a handsome, full-bodied Englishwoman in her early forties with a distinct whiff of prosperity about her. Widowed two years ago, she and her equally full-bodied mother had been to visit relatives in New York.

"Mr. Dillman!" she cried with delight. "How nice to see you!"

"Good afternoon, Mrs. Trouncer."

"I was just on my way to the library."

"I understand that they have a good stock of books."

"Mother favors light romance," she revealed, her smile broadening with each word, "but I prefer a novel with real passion. What about you?"

"I have very catholic tastes."

"Catholic, as in Roman?"

"Catholic, as in wide-ranging."

"Ah, I see," she said, clutching her hands to her bosom.

Sophie Trouncer's manner was almost girlish. In the course of dinner she had been drawn more and more to Dillman, watching him shrewdly, plying him with questions and making noises of approval at everything he said. Like her mother, she was an educated woman who was at ease in any conversation.

"Mother will be so sorry that she missed you," she said, "but she always likes to lie down after luncheon. I'm the opposite, I'm afraid. I get very restless. My husband used to say that I had far too much energy, but I see it as a virtue — don't you?"

"Very much so."

"One has to keep oneself active."

"I agree, Mrs. Trouncer."

"As one gets old, the more important it becomes."

"Nobody could ever accuse you of getting old," he said gallantly.

"Oh, Mr. Dillman!" Her eyelashes fluttered for a second. "I'll cherish that remark."

"It's well deserved."

"Thank you."

"But you'll have to excuse me. I'm on my way to meet a friend." He moved away. "Do give my regards to your mother, won't you?"

"Of course."

"And happy hunting in the library."

With a brittle laugh, she waved him off. Dillman was glad to escape. He had met her type before. Sophie Trouncer was a merry widow, a rich woman who had come out of an extended period of mourning to take an interest in the opposite sex once again, eager to make up for lost time. She had already hinted that she might invite him to her house in the Surrey countryside, and he was careful not to commit himself. She had many good qualities, but she was too possessive for Dillman. If he let her get close to him, she would severely hamper his work on the *Celtic.*

When he came out on the promenade deck, he took a deep breath. Then he strolled toward the prow of the ship.

Wrapped up warmly, dozens of people were about. The man who interested him most was standing at the rail gazing out to sea. With his bowler hat and his long overcoat, Sir Arthur Conan Doyle looked like an off-duty bailiff. Dillman did not want to disturb him, but as he walked past, the writer turned and saw him.

"Hello, Mr. Dillman," he said with obvious pleasure.

"Good afternoon, Sir Arthur. No need of my services, I see."

"Not yet."

"I hope that it continues that way — though I doubt it."

"So do I, alas."

"Once the word spreads that you are on board, you're bound to be stared at by all and sundry. You may even be at the mercy of autograph hunters. It's an occupational hazard for an author. When I sailed on the *Baltic* last year," said Dillman, "Bernard Shaw was aboard. Unlike you, he enjoyed being recognized. In fact, he went out of his way to court public attention."

Conan Doyle grinned. "Just like GBS!"

"Needless to say, he did not seek my protection."

"Actually, I may need rather more than that."

"Oh?"

"Yes," said the other. "There's a possibility that we may have to report someone to you for obtaining money by false pretenses."

"And who might that be, Sir Arthur?"

Conan Doyle raised a palm. "Let's not prejudge the case. Everyone is innocent until proven guilty, so this lady should be given the benefit of the doubt. Until I've met her, I can't be sure about her. My wife, however," he went on, "has reservations and her instincts are rarely wrong."

"What seems to be the trouble?"

"We have a medium aboard."

"Someone who conducts a séance?"

"Exactly, Mr. Dillman. Knowing of our interest in spiritualism, she made contact with my wife and invited us to join her at a séance."

"At a price, I suspect."

"That's what alerted me. Not that she's charging us, mark you," said Conan Doyle. "We were offered free entry. But the other people will have to pay. This lady is a professional."

"Do you intend to go?"

"Of course. She could have genuine gifts."

"Is that often the case, Sir Arthur?"

"Frankly, no. There's a large amount of fraudulence and I've been able to expose it in some instances. I'm sure that you can guess the kind of thing — hidden wires, mirrors, cunning effects. At a séance we attended in Cornwall once," he remembered, "I dragged out the man who was concealed behind the curtains. He'd been speaking into a megaphone with a ghostly voice."

"But some people have genuine gifts, you say?"

"No question of it. They act as gatekeepers to the other world."

"What do you know of this particular lady?"

"Nothing beyond what my wife told me," said Conan Doyle. "She's English, middle-aged and very plausible. She claims to have held many successful séances in America, but we only have her word for that. On the face of it, the lady is above reproach."

"Lady Conan Doyle, however, has doubts about her."

"Yes, Mr. Dillman. That's why I wanted to warn you."

"I'll be interested to hear how you get on, Sir Arthur. I've dealt with every imaginable crime in my time but I've never encountered this kind of thing. If she is indeed a fraud," promised Dillman, "then she'll be arrested for obtaining money by deception."

"The secondary charge carries more

weight in my book."

"Secondary charge?"

"That of willful cruelty."

"I don't understand."

"That's because you've never been to a séance. People who do take part place the utmost faith in the medium. They open themselves up, Mr. Dillman, and bare their souls. They are so desperate to make contact with loved ones who have passed on," said Conan Doyle, "that they render themselves open to exploitation. They are often utterly defenseless. To take advantage of such vulnerable people is more than cruelty," he added solemnly. "It's downright brutality."

FIVE

The concert that was held in the first-class lounge that afternoon was a forerunner of a number of performances that would be offered to passengers in the course of the voyage. Featuring the resident orchestra, it was a small-scale event that provided pleasant entertainment on their first full day afloat. Concerts being held simultaneously in second and steerage class relied strongly on the more homespun talents of the passengers or crew and a motley selection of would-be conjurers, impressionists, musicians, comedians, monologuists and singers who competed for applause. The concert in first class was largely a musical affair and it drew a sizable audience. Genevieve Masefield was among those who took their seats. Her companion was Lady Bulstrode, complete with lorgnette and a small box of chocolates.

"Rupert is not fond of music," said the

old lady, surveying the room through her lorgnette. "I have a dreadful job persuading him to go to the opera with me. He's partially deaf, you see, and his eyesight is a trifle impaired, so he misses a great deal."

"What a pity!"

"That's why I'm so grateful to you, Miss Masefield. It's so vital to have agreeable company at such events as this."

"It's I who should thank you, Lady Bulstrode. Had I come on my own," said Genevieve, "I might have felt far less comfortable."

"You'd not have been alone for long."

"I know."

"Something about the sea air seems to bring out the philanderer in some men," said Lady Bulstrode with a confiding smile. "They cannot help themselves. I noticed it when we sailed to New York. As they enter a public room, certain men immediately look around to see if there are any attractive unaccompanied young ladies on board. Some of those same ladies, of course," she added in a hoarse whisper, "may not be at all what they seem."

Genevieve did not need to be told that. During her years as a detective she had identified more than one high-class prostitute, who traveled on liners in order to pick up wealthy clients. Other women, working with a male confederate, had lured gullible men into compromising positions for the purposes of blackmail. Genevieve had also been called upon to apprehend an occasional female thief or pickpocket on board. Crime was by no means limited to the male sex.

"Rupert is playing chess with that nice Mr. Cleves," said Lady Bulstrode. "I have to confess that I tend to find Americans a little too assertive for my taste, but Mr. Cleves is the exception to the rule. He has such exquisite manners."

"Yes," agreed Genevieve. "I liked him."

"A happy coincidence in both cases."

"I don't understand, Lady Bulstrode."

"Well, I met you in the customs shed and discovered that we had mutual friends back in England. When my husband first chanced upon Joshua Cleves, he not only found someone who is as addicted to racing as he is. Rupert also acquired a fellow chess player."

"Common interests do draw people together."

"They're the basis of civilized society, my dear."

Genevieve had not made a deliberate attempt to befriend the couple. While they chatted in the customs shed, however, Lady Bulstrode had mentioned someone whom Genevieve had actually known. It then transpired that they had other mutual acquaintances among the minor English aristocracy. What Genevieve did not explain was that she had met those people as a result of her engagement to a young man who was set to inherit his father's title. Unforgivable behavior by her fiancé had compelled her to break off the engagement, but she was certainly not going to entrust the details of that episode to Lady Bulstrode. They belonged firmly in her past.

"What did you really think about him?" asked the old lady.

"Mr. Cleves?"

"Yes."

"I found him friendly, interesting and knowledgeable."

"Nothing else?"

"I didn't have much conversation with him, Lady Bulstrode. Over dinner last night — and breakfast this morning — he spent most of the time discussing, with your husband, race meetings he'd been to in England. He's been to the Derby three times."

"Rupert hasn't missed a Derby in fifty years."

"I've only been to one," confessed Genevieve.

"You might well improve on that score, Miss Masefield."

"How?"

"By being invited to attend this year's race," said Lady Bulstrode with another smile. "You may have thought that Mr. Cleves was more interested in horses than anything else, but I believe that he's conceived another passion as well."

"For what?"

"For *you*, my dear. Unless my intuition has deserted me, Joshua Cleves is smitten." Opening the lid of the box, she offered the chocolates. "May I tempt you?"

"No, thank you."

"I can't resist them."

While her companion chewed away, Genevieve reviewed her two meetings with Joshua Cleves. There had been a glint of admiration in his eyes on both occasions, but she was accustomed to that reaction from men. Because he had not tried to monopolize her, she had assumed that Cleves was not overly interested in her. Then she remembered the conversation that morning with Frank Spurrier and the disparaging remarks he had made about his American friend. Like Spurrier himself, she decided, Cleves would need to be watched.

The concert started with a Rossini overture that was followed with piano selections from Beethoven, Chopin and Liszt. A lighter note intruded when one of the senior officers gave a rendition of Stephen Foster songs in a pleasing tenor voice. The orchestra took over again, to be followed by a member of the crew who was a competent amateur ventriloquist. But the real surprise of the afternoon was the appearance of Nelson Rutherford. Accompanied by the piano, the purser revealed himself to be a gifted clarinetist, delighting the audience with a variety of popular melodies.

After the chairman had made his closing remarks, a collection was taken for a seamen's charity, then the concert ended with the playing of "The Star-Spangled Banner" and "God Save the King." The applause was sustained and well earned. Genevieve clapped as enthusiastically as anyone while Lady Bulstrode took the opportunity to slip another chocolate into her mouth. Eventually, they rose to leave. It was only when she turned around that Genevieve realized with a start that she knew the man who had sat directly behind her.

"Did you enjoy the concert, Miss Masefield?" he asked.

"Very much," she replied.

"Me, too."

Frank Spurrier gave her a meaningful smile.

Sophie Trouncer's face was distorted by an expression of disbelief.

"You missed the concert this afternoon?" she said.

"I'm afraid so," Dillman admitted.

"Then you missed an absolute treat. Didn't he, Mother?"

"Oh, yes," May Hoyland confirmed with a roll of her eyes. "It was wonderful — especially the purser on his clarinet."

Dillman was astonished. "Mr. Rutherford took part?"

"He was the star of the whole show."

Never having met a musical purser before, Dillman found the notion rather difficult to envisage. Playing the clarinet was something that he would never have suspected Nelson Rutherford of doing, but he was prepared to accept the word of two witnesses. They were at their table in the first-class dining saloon, and since formality had taken over, the room was filled with a dazzling array of evening dresses and jewelry. Like the rest of the men, Dillman had donned his white tie and tails. Seated opposite him at the table were Sophie Trouncer and her mother, though, since the latter had taken such great pains with her appearance, May Hoyland could almost pass for an elder sister. Now approaching seventy, she had the manner and carriage of a much younger woman. The resemblance between them was very close. Mother and daughter had the same features and the same unquenchable vivacity.

"Did *you* see the concert, Mr. Gaffney?" asked Dillman, turning to the man beside him. "Or am I the only one who missed it?"

"No," said Gaffney. "I missed it as well."

"Are you still having trouble?"

"Yes, Mr. Dillman."

"Speak to the ship's doctor. Perhaps he can help."

"I've tried every remedy there is. None of them works."

Liam Gaffney was a taciturn man of Irish descent in his forties who suffered from seasickness. Though he made the effort to come to the dining saloon for meals, he refused far more than he ate and never touched a drop of alcohol. He was a short, skinny, anxious man making his first trip across the Atlantic and having second thoughts about the wisdom of undertaking the voyage.

"Next time we have a concert," Sophie warned, "I'll insist on taking you, Mr. Dillman."

"That depends when it is," he said guardedly.

"Entertainment is there to be enjoyed — isn't it, Mother?"

"Yes," said May, tapping the table for effect. "You must take full advantage of it, Mr. Dillman. The same goes for you, Mr. Gaffney."

"I'm not well enough to do so, Mrs. Hoyland," said Gaffney. "I wish I were. I just can't seem to find my sea legs."

Dillman was sympathetic. "It takes time."

"Yes," said May cheerily. "I had a nephew who used to work for Cunard and he was a martyr to seasickness. You don't think of merchant seamen having that problem, but they often do. The first day of a voyage was always a trial for Donald, then it seemed to ease off."

"He found that wearing earplugs somehow helped," said Sophie.

"And a glass of rum. Be sure to have one this evening."

"To be honest," said Gaffney, "I'm not in a mood for anything. I just felt that I had to be here. I hoped that all the activity would somehow distract me." He put a hand gingerly to his stomach. "So far, I fear, it hasn't."

When the first course arrived, he waved it politely away, then lapsed into a prolonged silence. Sophie Trouncer and her mother did not complain. It allowed them to concentrate on Dillman. Taking it in turns, they fired so many questions at him that he wondered if they had rehearsed them beforehand.

"Why have you never married?" said May.

"I've never had the time, Mrs. Hoyland."

"The time or the inclination?" Sophie pressed.

"Neither."

"But you have no objection to the institution of marriage?"

"None at all, Mrs. Trouncer."

"That's encouraging to hear," said May, beaming.

"It is," said Sophie. "Married life is a joy. I recommend it."

"I'll bear that in mind," Dillman promised.

While maintaining a conversation with the two ladies, he kept the rest of the room under surveillance. Genevieve, he observed, was dining with Lord and Lady Bulstrode again, seated beside the fleshy American whom she had described to him. Sir Arthur and Lady Conan Doyle also had the same dinner companions as before and all four were having an animated discussion about something. Dillman had not forgotten Edward Hammond. Though he doubted that the wanted man would be in first class — if, indeed, he was actually aboard — he kept scouring the tables for possible suspects. The description given by the police could fit a number of men in the saloon. Dillman tried to whittle the total down by eliminating potential suspects.

The meal was exceptional and even Gaffney was tempted to try the main course. They were halfway through it when Sophie Trouncer broached a new subject.

"Do you believe in spiritualism, Mr. Dillman?" she asked.

He was tactful. "I'm not entirely sure."

"Will you accept that some people have psychic powers?"

"I can't say that I've ever met any of them, Mrs. Trouncer."

"But you don't mock such claims, do you?"

"Not at all," he said.

"There you are, Mother," said Sophie, as if scoring a point.

"I think they're charlatans," said May robustly, "and until I'm proven wrong, I'll go on thinking that. I've seen too many stage mediums and they're always cheats. They've usually been trained as magicians, so they know all the tricks for deceiving the eye."

"You can't deceive the eye if someone is sitting right next to you." Sophie flicked a glance at Dillman. "Don't you agree?"

"Up to a point," he said cautiously.

"Not every medium is an impostor. I've met at least two who had extraordinary psychic powers."

May was scornful. "All they had was a talent for deception," she said briskly. "And you were one of their victims."

"That's unfair, Mother."

"They cheated you, Sophie."

"How do you know? You weren't *there.*"

"I had more sense."

"You'll just have to agree to differ," said Dillman, trying to calm them down before the argument got out of hand. "From what I've heard, the facts are inconclusive. Many condemn spiritualism, yet its worth is attested by some extremely intelligent people."

"Intelligent people should know better," May declared.

"We do," said Sophie. "That's why we spurn your taunts."

"They're not taunts. They're fair comments."

"Maybe we should leave it at that," Dillman suggested.

"Why don't you be the judge?" asked Sophie.

"The judge?"

"Yes, Mr. Dillman. As it happens, we have a medium aboard and she's holding a séance in her cabin after dinner. I've agreed to go," she said, ignoring the muffled protest from her mother. "Come with me and see for yourself, Mr. Dillman. You decide if Mrs. Burbridge is genuine or a fake." She reached across the table to touch his hand. "I'd respect your opinion."

It had taken Saul Pinnick a long time to coax him to join them for the meal, but Leonard Rush had eventually agreed. He was introduced to Pinnick's wife, and in listening to Miriam's mournful complaints about the treatment meted out to her he was able to take his mind off his own troubles. The three of them were part of the huge army of diners in steerage and they ate their food amid the usual tumult.

"Did you take part in the tug-of-war, Mr. Rush?" asked Miriam.

"No," he said.

"Why not? A miner like you must be very strong."

"I'm past that kind of thing, Mrs. Pinnick."

"I was past it the moment I was born," said Pinnick with a throaty chuckle. "I was always too short and too scrawny to be any good at sports. But it was fun to watch the tug-of-war on deck this afternoon. Even Mirry enjoyed it."

"Yes," she said. "They really put their backs into it."

"We had a tug-of-war team at the pit," Rush recalled, "and I was part of it at one time. We used to challenge other collieries or take on local pub teams."

For the first time since they had met, Pinnick saw a look of pleasure on the man's face. It vanished in a second but it had shown that his life as a miner in the Yorkshire coalfield had not been one of unrelieved toil and distress. Pinnick probed for detail.

"Did you have a football team as well?" he asked.

"Football, darts and skittles," Rush answered. He coughed uncontrollably for a few moments, then patted his chest. "I was hopeless at soccer but I captained the darts team for years. We played in a league and won the cup three times."

"You must have had a lot of skill."

"It depended on how much beer I'd had beforehand."

Rush grinned for the first time, exposing a row of small dark teeth. Then, as if catching himself out in a forbidden activity, he lowered his head guiltily and addressed himself to his meal. Miriam picked a fishbone from her mouth and set it down on her plate.

"The food is better than on the way here," she decided.

"It's much the same, Mirry," said Pinnick. "We have the same cooks we had before and the same sort of menu. What do you think, Mr. Rush?"

"I've had worse," grunted the other.

"So have we."

"A lot worse," said Miriam, seizing on her cue. "When we lived in Poland, we'd go for days with no food at all. There was one winter when we lived on potatoes and nothing else. I don't know how we got through it. But the worst time was in Germany."

Miriam went on a rambling journey through the various countries in which she had lived, listing the various privations they had endured. Rush was not really listening — and Pinnick had heard the recitation so

109

often that he ignored it — but that did not check her. She was determined to unburden herself of her tribulations.

"That's what Isaac kept saying in his letters," she went on. "Isaac is Saul's cousin and he lives in Brooklyn. The food is wonderful, he told us. The vegetables were bigger, the fruit was sweeter and the kosher meat was the best he'd ever eaten. All the way across the Atlantic I thought about the tasty meals we'd have in America. But they sent us back. Why?" she demanded. "They let in older people than us. They let in poorer people. Why did they reject us?"

"You know why, Mirry," said her husband patiently.

"It's a scandal."

"We took a chance and we failed."

"Someone should be made to pay for it, Saul."

"It wasn't just us. Thousands of people were refused entry."

"Who cares about them?" She blurted out the words before she could stop herself. Pinnick's nudge reminded her that they had company. "I was just thinking about us," she went on, "and about Mr. Rush, of course. I'm sure he feels the same as me."

"What's that?" asked Rush, looking up.

"We're all victims."

"Are we?"

"They should have given us more respect."

"There's no point in going on and on about it, Mirry," said Pinnick gently. "We have to look to the future. We'll get by somehow."

"You always say that, Saul."

"I have faith."

"Faith," said Rush dully. "What's that? How can you have faith in a God that does such terrible things to us?" He pushed his plate away. "I've got to go."

"There's more to come yet."

"I've had enough."

"Then we'll see you in the lounge afterward."

"I'll be out on deck, Mr. Pinnick. I spend the night there."

Pinnick was horrified. "You sleep on deck?"

"I share a cabin with three other men," Rush explained. "When I lie down, I start to cough. I'd keep the rest of them awake."

"But you've paid for a bunk and you're entitled to it. Sleeping out there in the cold will make your cough even worse."

"I take a blanket with me."

"Speak to the steward. See if he can find you another cabin."

Rush stood up. "I prefer my own company."

"You'll freeze to death out there," said Miriam.

"So?"

He gave them a curt nod of farewell and marched off. Miriam watched him picking his way between the tables, then she turned accusingly on her husband.

"You should have stopped him, Saul."

"What can I do?"

"Talk to him. Reason with him."

"I've tried, Mirry. He just won't listen to me."

"Sleeping on deck in this weather? It's suicide."

Pinnick sighed. "What does he have to live for?"

Throughout dinner, Joshua Cleves had been far more attentive toward Genevieve than hitherto, but he never strayed beyond the bounds of decorum. Pleasant and companionable, he told several amusing anecdotes about previous voyages he had experienced. Lord and Lady Bulstrode clearly approved of him, and Genevieve, too, found him increasingly likable. Yet he did not give the slightest indication that he was in any way enamored of her. When they left the table, however, he made sure that he stayed close to her.

"What are you going to do when you reach London?" he said.

"Catch up on a lot of unfinished business," she replied.

"Will you be staying in the city?"

"Part of the time, Mr. Cleves."

"And what about the rest of it?"

Genevieve was evasive. "I'll be visiting some friends."

"Where?"

"Here, there and everywhere."

"I'd like to think I was on your list, Miss Masefield," he said smoothly. "I'll be staying at the Ritz. They serve an excellent luncheon there. Perhaps you'd be able to sample it with me one day."

"I'm not certain about that."

"Take time to think it over."

"Thank you. I will."

"I won't press you on the matter," he said courteously. "I've no right to do so. After all, we're merely shipboard acquaintances at this point. But that situation may change when we get to know each other better. Just remember that my invitation stands."

"I'll remember, Mr. Cleves."

Genevieve had no intention of accepting his offer, but the fact that he had put the idea to her showed that he did have a deeper interest in her. Her memory was jogged.

"I believe that you know a gentleman called Frank Spurrier."

He beamed. "Yes, Frank and I are old sparring partners."

"He told me that you were good friends."

"We are, Miss Masefield, though we have occasional disputes. Frank is always trying to buy things for less than they're worth and sell them for far more. How do you come to know him?"

"We had a casual encounter on deck."

"I doubt very much if it was accidental," said Cleves with a grin. "Almost everything he does has a distinct purpose. That's the sort of man Frank is. He likes to plan carefully in advance. I don't think he's ever done anything spontaneous in his life." They came out through the doors of the saloon and stopped. "What did he say about me?"

"Very little," she lied.

"Whatever it was, you'd be wise to disregard it."

"Why is that?"

"The truth is that Frank has always been rather envious of me. I inherited wealth and increased it by sound investments. He still has to work for a living and he finds that irksome."

"I got the impression that he was very happy in his work."

"He'd be even happier without it," said Cleves. "Then he could do what I do and devote himself to cultural pursuits. Well," he added, glancing toward the staircase. "I'm off to enjoy a cigar. Thank you again for the pleasure of your company, Miss Masefield." He offered his hand and she shook it. "I do admire the way you're so at ease with the aristocracy. Rupert and Agnes clearly adore you."

"You get on well with them yourself."

"Wealth is a great leveler."

"There's rather more to it than that."

"Of course," said Cleves, producing his most radiant smile. "But I'm not going to tell you what it is — not here, anyway. Come to the Ritz with me and I may be more forthcoming."

The first-class smoking room was a popular venue after a meal and several people were already there when the two men came in. Settling into one of the luxurious leather armchairs, Frank Spurrier took out a silver cigarette case, flicked it open and offered it to David Lowbury.

"Thanks, Mr. Spurrier," said the American, extracting a cigarette and slipping it

115

between his lips. "Beautiful case you have there."

"Yes," Spurrier agreed, selecting a cigarette before snapping the case shut. "Solid silver. Would you like to see it?"

"Please." Lowbury took it from him to examine it. "Inscribed with your initials, I see. What does the O stand for?"

"Osborne. Francis Osborne Spurrier."

"You're a man of real taste."

"If you smoke as many cigarettes as I do, you might as well have a decent case in which to keep them."

"This is much more than decent." Lowbury laid it on his palm to feel its weight, then passed it back. Spurrier slipped it into his inside pocket. When their cigarettes were alight, they inhaled deeply, then added more smoke to the fug that was already gathering in the room.

"What I really want to ask you about is books," said Lowbury. "I didn't wish to bring this up over dinner because it might sound a little mercenary, and, in any case, Jane had warned me not to badger you on the subject."

"I'm always happy to talk about books, Mr. Lowbury."

"Is there really such a good profit margin?"

"In antiquarian books, certainly."

"Supposing I had first editions of, say, Edgar Allan Poe or Herman Melville? Would they be valuable?"

"You'd have no difficulty selling them to collectors, I know that. Price would depend on the condition of the books. If they were in good condition, you'd get far more for them. If, of course," said Spurrier with a smile, "you had copies that were autographed by the authors, then the price would shoot up even more."

"I'll remember that."

"What you really need at an auction is to have two or three people bidding against each other and sending the price artificially high. Last year, we had rival bidders who were keen to get their hands on a first edition of *The History of Tom Jones, a Foundling.*"

"Pardon my ignorance, but who wrote that?"

"Henry Fielding," said Spurrier, "way back in 1749. It's one of the greatest novels in the English language. Not that everyone approved of it at the time. Samuel Johnson was very critical, so were Richardson and Smollett. Yet none of them wrote a novel that could touch *Tom Jones.*"

"And there were rival bidders after the book?"

"Three of them, each one determined to win. When a bid was finally accepted, it was over four times the reserve price we'd set."

"Jack London is my favorite author," Lowbury volunteered. "I guess that his books wouldn't fetch quite so much."

"No," said Spurrier. "He's still alive. If he'd been dead for a hundred and fifty years, like Fielding, it would be a different matter."

"Yet you told us that Sir Arthur Conan Doyle's books were worth a lot and he's still with us."

"First editions of his early work are prized by collectors."

Lowbury chuckled. "Maybe I should ask him if he's got any to spare." He pulled on his cigarette. "How did you first come into this business, Mr. Spurrier?"

"Through my father. He was a buyer for a London auction house and decided to set up on his own. The firm prospered. He taught me all I know and I'm eternally grateful to him for that." He looked at his companion through the swirling smoke. "What about you?"

"Oh, I just drifted into a job as a stockbroker. I always had a good head for figures. And I learned quickly — that helped."

"How did you meet your wife?"

"Quite by accident," said Lowbury with a fond smile. "Jane had come to New York on a shopping trip and we started talking to each other while waiting for service in a store. The conversation is still going on."

"She's a charming lady. You're a lucky man."

"Thank you."

"Mind if I join you?" asked Joshua Cleves, lowering himself into the armchair opposite the two men. He leaned forward and stretched out a hand to Lowbury. "I don't believe I've had the pleasure, sir."

"David Lowbury," said the other.

"My name is Josh Cleves."

"Gentleman of leisure," Spurrier explained.

"I've been called worse, Frank."

"I'm sure that you have."

"I enjoy life to the hilt," said Cleves blithely. "What's wrong with that? I was saying as much over dinner to Rupert and Agnes — that's Lord and Lady Bulstrode," he added for Lowbury's benefit. "In England, you need a title to have the edge over everyone else. All it takes in America is money."

"I'm very happy with that situation," said Lowbury.

"Then we speak the same language, my

friend." Cleves drew on his cigar before emitted a cloud of aromatic smoke. "By the way, I've got a bone to pick with you, Frank."

"Over what?"

"Miss Genevieve Masefield."

"Isn't that the lady I met?" asked Lowbury.

"Yes," said Spurrier. "I introduced you to her."

"Once seen, never forgotten."

"I've had the good fortune to dine with her twice," boasted Cleves, "along with Rupert and Agnes. I discovered this evening that Frank had been telling her all kinds of lies about me."

"That's not true, Josh," said Spurrier quickly. "I made a few observations about you, that's all."

"Unkind observations, by the sound of it."

"Is that what Miss Masefield told you?"

"No, but I could read it in her eyes."

"And damned fine eyes, they are!" Lowbury commented.

"Did she tell you that we went to the concert together?" asked Spurrier, trying to goad his rival. "We discussed it at length afterward. I was surprised you weren't there, Josh."

"I was too busy playing chess against Rupert."

"You preferred *that* to an afternoon with Miss Masefield?"

"Of course. I knew that I'd be sitting beside her again this evening — and it won't be the last time that we break bread together."

"Really?"

"When we get to England," said Cleves, striking a proprietary note, "Genevieve and I have arranged to have luncheon at the Ritz." He deposited some cigar ash in the tray nearby. "It's the sort of thing we gentlemen of leisure do."

It was quite late before George Dillman met up with the purser again. After dinner the detective had wandered down to the second-class area of the ship so that he could take stock of the men in the public rooms. Though they were fewer in number than in first class, he was able to identify over half a dozen who might conceivably fit the description of Edward Hammond. None of them wore a beard, but he was certain that it would have been the first thing to be removed by the wanted man. In the convivial atmosphere of the lounge and smoking room, it was difficult to believe that a killer was lurking. Yet he could well be part of the immaculately dressed assembly, and where violent crime was concerned, Dillman had long ago learned to discount nobody.

He finally caught up with Nelson Rutherford in his office.

"Congratulations!" he said. "I hear that you excelled yourself in the concert this afternoon."

Rutherford laughed. "I was only there as comic relief."

"That's not what I heard. By all accounts, you played the clarinet like a trained musician."

"I did my best, Mr. Dillman."

"I hope to hear you perform again at some point."

"I daresay I will," said the purser jovially. "Well, everything seems to be going very smoothly so far."

"That was my impression."

"No calls for help from Sir Arthur Conan Doyle?"

"None at all," said Dillman. "People seem to be respecting his privacy. If he does encounter a problem, it will come from another source altogether."

"Oh?"

"Sir Arthur had a quiet word with me earlier. It seems that he and his wife have been invited to attend a séance this evening. Knowing of their interest in such things, Lady Conan Doyle was approached by a Mrs. Thoda Burbridge, who claims to be a medium."

"It's a world I know little about," admitted Rutherford. "Except that it does attract fraudsters."

"Sir Arthur has unmasked one or two of them in his time."

"Does he think this lady is a fake as well?"

"He hasn't met her yet," said Dillman, "so he's giving her the benefit of the doubt. If she is a bogus medium, tricking money out of people, he'll report her to me at once."

"And if she's genuine?"

"Then I won't hear a word from him."

"My guess is that you won't," said Rutherford confidently. "Indeed, I think you'll have very little to do on this voyage beyond staying on patrol. The *Celtic* has a tradition to uphold, Mr. Dillman. We've never had a serious crime committed on board."

"Don't forget Edward Hammond."

"I've stopped worrying about him."

"Why?"

"Because the police were misled. I don't believe that he's on the ship at all. I remember what you told me about him."

"What was that, Mr. Rutherford?"

"That a professional thief like Hammond just couldn't resist the rich pickings on a White Star liner. He'd have made his first strike by now, surely?"

"He could simply be biding his time."

"I doubt it," said the purser breezily. "I think we can forget about Edward Hammond — and about any other criminal, for that matter. The only turbulence we'll get on this crossing will come from the Atlantic Ocean. We're completely safe, Mr. Dillman."

Letting himself into the stateroom, the man switched on the light and began a thorough search. It did not take him long to find what he sought. He concealed the object under his coat and went back to the door. Inching it open, he saw that nobody was in the corridor outside. Within seconds he had vanished down a companionway.

SIX

The theft did not come to light until the following morning. It was immediately reported to the purser and he dispatched George Dillman to investigate. The detective was invited into the stateroom occupied by Sir Arthur and Lady Conan Doyle. They were clearly upset.

"I blame myself," said Conan Doyle, shaking his head dolefully. "I should have had it locked safely away with my wife's jewelry box instead of leaving it in here. It never occurred to me that anyone would actually steal the book."

"That's all that was taken?" asked Dillman. "A single book?"

"It's not just any book, Mr. Dillman," explained Lady Conan Doyle. "It's the one Arthur quotes from during his lectures. It has the most enormous sentimental value for him."

"What about its pecuniary value?"

"I should imagine that it would fetch a high price."

"It was a copy of *A Study in Scarlet,*" said its author sadly. "That was the story that introduced Sherlock Holmes to the world by means of the reminiscences of his friend, Dr. Watson."

"I know, Sir Arthur. I've read and enjoyed it."

"It first appeared in 1887 in *Beeton's Christmas Annual,* with a rather garish illustration on the front cover. I was thrilled when it was published in book form the following year by Ward, Lock and Company."

"I had the American edition from Lippincott."

"That came out in 1890 and won me a lot of welcome attention in your country. Magazine publication is important, but it doesn't give anything like the intense satisfaction you get from seeing your work between the hard covers of a book."

"The stolen copy, I assume, was a first edition?"

"Naturally."

"Did it have your signature on the flyleaf?"

"Yes, Mr. Dillman," said Conan Doyle. "It also had pages of notes inserted in chapters I read to my audiences — jottings that would be incomprehensible to anyone but me."

"Nevertheless," Dillman pointed out, "they would certainly add to its value. What we are talking about is a unique edition of the book, signed by the author and containing his notes on the text. It would be eagerly sought after by certain collectors."

"But they'd be handling stolen goods," said Lady Conan Doyle with exasperation. "That book is my husband's property. Nobody else has the right to touch it."

"I agree."

"It must be recovered as soon as possible."

"I hope that it will be, Lady Conan Doyle."

"We know that it's on the ship somewhere," she said with a sweeping gesture. "You must search every cabin until you find it."

"Mr. Dillman will have his own methods," said Conan Doyle with a hand on her arm. "We mustn't presume to tell him his job."

"That book has great symbolic importance, Arthur."

"I'm well aware of that."

"The thief must be caught and punished."

"I'm sure that he will be, Jean." He smiled at the detective. "And I'm equally sure that Mr. Dillman will know the procedure to follow."

"I do, Sir Arthur," said Dillman, "though I should warn you that I lack the deductive powers of Sherlock Holmes. I'd like to be able to tell you that the thief was a red-headed Scotsman with a squint, a fondness for quoting Balzac in the original French and three fingers missing from his left hand, and that he had recently retired from the British army after seeing service in India, where he met and married a Parsi princess educated in Switzerland." He gave a shrug. "The truth is that I have very few clues to assist me."

"You must have reached some conclusions."

"Only the obvious ones. The probability is that the thief is traveling in first class because it's unlikely that other passengers even know that you're on board the *Celtic*. Also, of course, they're forbidden access to this part of the vessel."

"That's a start, Mr. Dillman. What else do you deduce?"

"The man is not a professional criminal."

"He must be," protested Lady Conan Doyle. "How else did he get in and out of here so easily?"

"That remains to be seen," said Dillman, looking around. "The simple fact is that, having gained entry, he only stole a single item when there are many other things he might have taken."

"There's no money or jewelry in here."

"Perhaps not, Lady Conan Doyle, but there's expensive clothing, souvenirs from your lecture tour, leather suitcases, writing materials and so on. Thieves will take anything that can be resold for a profit. In that sense, you've been fortunate."

"I don't feel it, Mr. Dillman," she said with a slight shiver. "It's very distressing to be robbed like this. We feel invaded."

Dillman nodded sympathetically. "That may be so," he said, "but you'd feel even more aggrieved if, for instance, someone had taken that fur coat and hat I saw you wearing on deck earlier this evening."

"And I'd have been mortified if someone had stolen this," said Conan Doyle, opening a satchel to take out a sheaf of papers. "These are notes for a new book. I had the inspiration for it aboard this ship." He waved the papers. "These are irreplaceable."

"Then it's just as well the thief was unaware that they existed because he came specifically in search of work by a famous British author." Dillman indicated three books on the table. "He had no interest in those written by someone else."

"They're books on spiritualism that we

bought in Boston."

Dillman's ears pricked up. "That's my hometown, Sir Arthur," he said. "Where did you stay?"

"At the Parker House."

"I know it well. Number sixty, School Street, one block north of Boston Common. It was built on the site of the original Latin School founded in 1635."

"They told us it was the oldest public school in America."

"That's what you'd call the oldest state school in England. Public schools are actually private ones in your country. It's one of the many peculiarities of the English language I could never quite comprehend. Coming back to spiritualism," he went on, "I need to ask you what happened at the séance last night."

"That's hardly relevant, Mr. Dillman," said Lady Conan Doyle.

"You never know. It could be. The simple fact is that someone entered this stateroom when you were elsewhere."

"They could have done that while we were having dinner."

"They could, indeed," Dillman conceded, "but I have my doubts. Cabin stewards are at their busiest during dinner. Yours would have come in here to turn down the beds

130

and been responsible for adjacent state-rooms as well. A thief would be more likely to choose a time when fewer people were about. And since he may well be a first-class passenger," he continued, "he would have been eating his own dinner at the same time as you. No, I fancy that the theft may have occurred while you were visiting Mrs. Thoda Burbridge."

Conan Doyle blinked. "You're surely not suggesting that she was in any way implicated in this?"

"No, Sir Arthur. There's no evidence to suggest that. But it's possible that the thief was aware that the séance was taking place. How many of you were involved?"

"Five, including the medium herself."

"Mrs. Trouncer was one of them, I believe."

"That's true," said Conan Doyle. "The fifth person around the table was an American gentleman from Chicago. Mr. Agnew. Philip Agnew." He raised a quizzical eyebrow. "But how did you know that Mrs. Trouncer was there?"

"She sat opposite me at dinner and mentioned the fact that she'd be attending the séance. Her mother, with whom she's traveling, was very skeptical about the whole notion."

"Yes, we heard about Mrs. Hoyland."

"Would she have remained skeptical, had she been there?"

"Probably."

"Why is that, Sir Arthur?"

"Because very little happened," replied Conan Doyle. "You cannot expect successful results from every séance. The spirit world is not something you can reach instantly with a telephone call. Contact can only be made under strict conditions."

"Were they lacking last night?" asked Dillman.

"So it would appear."

"And what was your opinion of Mrs. Burbridge?"

"The lady has unmistakable gifts."

"There's no question about that," said his wife. "She's a member of the Society for Psychical Research and has written many articles for its journal. Mrs. Burbridge had been to Philadelphia to attend an international conference on psychic phenomena."

"So she was not a fraud?"

"No, Mr. Dillman."

"We'd have spotted any trickery," said Conan Doyle.

"Tell me about Mr. Agnew. What sort of person is he?"

"Brash, larger than life and about my own age."

"Did you discover his occupation?"

"He owns a menagerie of some sort and is going to Europe in search of animals to buy. The other thing we learned about him is that Philip Agnew is most definitely not a reading man."

"How do you know?"

"Because he'd never even heard of my husband," said Lady Conan Doyle with slight irritation. "I thought that extraordinary. *Everyone* knows the creator of Sherlock Holmes."

"Apparently not."

"I found it rather refreshing," said Conan Doyle. "He treated me as a complete stranger. I was able to be anonymous for once."

"You were certainly not anonymous to the thief," said Dillman. "He either stole *A Study in Scarlet* in order to sell it for a good price or to cherish it as the work of a favorite author."

"Whatever the truth, I feel duly humbled."

"Do you, Sir Arthur?"

"Yes. When I sit down at my desk, I can solve the most complicated crimes with ridiculous ease. Now that I'm confronted with a real mystery, I'm completely baffled.

I wouldn't know where to start."

"Where will *you* start, Mr. Dillman?" asked Lady Conan Doyle.

"With your steward. He'll be able to give me precise times when he was either in here or in the vicinity. I'll want to know if he saw any sign of disturbance when he came in."

"Then what?"

"I'll speak to the other stewards on this deck in case any of them noticed something that aroused their suspicions. After that, I may well have a word with Mr. Philip Agnew."

"What about Mrs. Burbridge?"

"Oh, I'll leave her to my partner," said Dillman. "She's far more adept at interviewing women."

Conan Doyle was curious. "You have a female partner?"

"A highly effective one, Sir Arthur. I'll make sure that she speaks to Mrs. Trouncer as well. If I did so, I'd have to reveal that I'm actually employed by the White Star Line and I'm very reluctant to do that. I try to lower my mask as little as possible."

"I understand."

"What I'm trying to establish is who knew that you'd both be at that séance. Mrs. Burbridge may inadvertently have mentioned in company that you and your wife would be joining her in her cabin. That information would have given the thief his opportunity."

"I find this so disturbing," confessed Lady Conan Doyle. "I hate the idea that we've been watched and stalked."

"We'll find the culprit," said Dillman.

"But everyone in first class must be considered a suspect," said Conan Doyle. "It will take you ages to work through them all."

"No, Sir Arthur. Many people can be discounted immediately. Those who've never heard of you would hardly steal one of your books. And there'll be dozens of others whom we can eliminate straightaway. We'll soon narrow it right down."

"How?"

"By sifting patiently through the evidence we gather."

"Isn't there a quicker way?" Lady Conan Doyle wondered. "Why not do what I advocated earlier and search every cabin in first class?"

"For a number of reasons," said Dillman. "First, we'd never get permission to do so. Second, it would, in any case, take a long time and cause an immense amount of disruption. Third — and most telling of all, in my opinion — it would be a complete waste of time."

"Why?"

"Because the thief wouldn't risk leaving the stolen item in his cabin. He'd either find a hiding place elsewhere or simply carry the book with him. It could easily be concealed in the pocket of an overcoat. No, Lady Conan Doyle," he added, "at this stage of the investigation there's only one assumption that is sensible for us to make — *A Study in Scarlet* is still on this ship." He distributed a smile between them. "My partner and I will start looking for it."

It was a cold morning with a fresh breeze, but many of the first-class passengers ventured out to play deck games, to take a bracing stroll or simply to watch the icebergs that floated menacingly nearby. David and Jane Lowbury stood at the rail in their coats, scarves and hats. Frank Spurrier still recognized them instantly from behind. Lowbury's arm was around his wife's shoulders and their romantic pose seemed to confirm that they might well be on their honeymoon.

"Good morning!" said Spurrier, stopping beside them.

As they turned to exchange greetings with him, Lowbury instantly detached his arm from his wife. Jane seemed a little unhappy to be interrupted, but her husband showed more cordiality.

"Nice to see you again, Mr. Spurrier," he said warmly.

"The pleasure is mutual."

"By the way, what exactly was going on last night?"

"Going on?"

"Yes, you and that friend of yours, Mr. Cleves, seemed to be baiting each other about Miss Masefield."

"Oh, it was just harmless fun," said Spurrier.

"It sounded pretty serious to me."

"Josh and I always cross swords like that."

"He was trying to rile you."

"David told me about it," said Jane, taking an interest. "He had the feeling that you and your friend were involved in some sort of contest. Is that true?"

"Nothing could be further from the truth, Mrs. Lowbury," said Spurrier with a brittle laugh. "Since you've met the lady in question, you can see why our curiosity has been aroused."

Lowbury grinned. "Not just curiosity, I'd say."

"David!" scolded his wife.

"Well, she's a beautiful woman, you have to admit that. Not that she compares with you, of course," he added hastily. "Nobody could do that. Besides, those English ladies are always so cold and reserved. You can never really get close to them."

"I don't *want* you getting close to them."

"No danger of me ever doing that, honey. I don't have time for *any* other women."

"Good."

"One is enough for any man and I was lucky enough to pick the best of the bunch. Right, Mr. Spurrier?"

"We're all very jealous of you," said the other, looking at Jane.

"Thank you, kind sir." She gave a titter of appreciation at the compliment. "You're very generous."

"Observant, that's all."

"I guess you need a good eye in your trade," Lowbury noted.

"My father taught me how to pick out real quality. That's a wonderful asset in my profession." He glanced from one to the other. "How long have you known each other?"

"Long enough," said Lowbury contentedly.

"And how long would that be?"

"A year or so."

"I had a feeling that it hadn't been all that long."

"Why?"

"Because you haven't acquired the sorts of habits that married couples always lapse into after a while. You have a delightful sparkle about you, as if you're still discovering new things about each other."

"We are, Mr. Spurrier."

"Every day brings a lovely surprise," said Jane.

"That's good. Have you ever heard of Walter Pater?"

She shook her head. "No, I'm sorry."

"Is he in the auction business as well?" asked Lowbury.

"Hardly!" Spurrier exclaimed. "The poor man died well over a decade ago. Pater was a distinguished British author and art critic. He wrote such books as *Marius the Epicurean.* But that's beside the point. What I always remember is the warning he gave in three words."

"And what was that?"

"Habit is failure."

Jane was puzzled. "What exactly did he mean?"

"That the moment something becomes a habit, it loses its real point. It becomes dull and meaningless repetition. We should always strive for freshness and novelty, for something that spurs us on."

"We try to do that," she said, "don't we,

139

David?"

"We always will," Lowbury vowed.

"That's why we never get bored."

"Never."

There was a brief pause as they stared longingly at each other. Lowbury took hold of her hands. Jane beamed up at him. They seemed to have forgotten that somebody else was standing there.

"I get the feeling that I'm rather in the way," said Spurrier, taking a step back. "If you'll excuse me, I'll continue my stroll around the deck."

"No, no," said Jane with a restraining hand on him. "Please forgive our rudeness. Don't let us frighten you away."

"Join us for morning coffee," Lowbury urged. "I'd like to hear much more about how you price antiques at auction. Listening to you has been a revelation, Mr. Spurrier."

"In that case," said the other, "I'll be glad to instruct you."

"I'm hoping you'll let us into your little secret as well."

"What secret?"

"The one that involves Miss Genevieve Masefield."

Spurrier's laugh had a hollow ring to it.

■ ■ ■ ■

Genevieve was sorry to hear details of the theft and anxious to recover the stolen book as soon as possible. After she had discussed the crime with Dillman, she went off in search of the woman who had held the séance. Thoda Burbridge was in her cabin, writing letters to the various friends she had made during her time in America. She was surprised when Genevieve called on her and introduced herself as one of the ship's detectives.

"Have I done anything wrong, Miss Masefield?" she asked.

"No, Mrs. Burbridge."

"Has there been a complaint about me?"

"None at all," said Genevieve with a reassuring smile. "I just wondered if you might help me, that's all."

"Of course. Do come in."

Thoda Burbridge was a plump middle-aged woman with a double chin that quivered as she spoke. Her gray hair was brushed back from her high forehead and she had a motherly face. She wore a dress of dark red velvet. After indicating a chair, she sat opposite her visitor and peered through wire-framed eyeglasses. Her manner was so warm and open that Genevieve felt as if she were visiting a favorite aunt.

"What seems to be the trouble?" said Thoda.

"Before I go any further," replied Genevieve, "I must ask you to keep everything that passes between us to yourself. I speak in the strictest confidence."

"This is beginning to sound serious."

"Can I have your word that you'll be discreet?"

"Utterly discreet, Miss Masefield."

"Thank you." Opening her purse, she took out a pad and pencil. "Yesterday evening — perhaps during the time that you were holding a séance in here — something was stolen from the stateroom occupied by Sir Arthur and Lady Conan Doyle."

"Dear me!"

"Although the only item taken was a book written by Sir Arthur, it's caused them a lot of distress."

"I can imagine."

"Knowing that someone has searched your belongings makes you feel very uncomfortable. I've been in that position myself, so I can sympathize with them. Because Sir Arthur treasures that book, we wish to recover it promptly."

"I don't see how I can be of any assistance, Miss Masefield."

"He and his wife spent the best part of two hours in this cabin last night. We believe that the crime may have been committed during that period. What I'd like to know is who would have been aware that they were involved in the séance?"

"Nobody beyond those who were actually here."

"Are you sure?"

"Yes," said Thoda, nodding so vigorously that her chins bounced up and down like rubber balls. "Most people are inclined to be very critical of the notion that contact can be made with the spirit world. Over the years I've had to cope with a lot of hostility. It's the reason I never discuss my work in public," she admitted. "I'd only expose myself to mockery."

"How did you choose people for this particular séance?"

"They chose themselves, Miss Masefield. When I went to the ship's library, I met Sophie Trouncer in there, poring over a book on spiritualism. We fell into conversation and I discovered that she'd been to a couple of séances in the hope of making contact with her late husband. When she described what had happened," Thoda went on with a grimace, "I could see that she'd been the victim of fraud. The medium whom she trusted was patently a fake."

"Did you tell her that?"

"No, it would only have caused unnecessary anxiety. When I explained who I was, and that I'd be holding a séance on board, she implored me to let her take part."

"For a fee?"

"People pay me nothing unless they are completely satisfied with the way in which everything has been conducted," said Thoda, meeting her gaze. "I don't look upon séances as a source of income, Miss Masefield. They are shared experiences that allow me the privilege of putting people in touch with loved ones whom they have lost."

"You approached Sir Arthur and Lady Conan Doyle, I believe."

"Only because I knew of their interest in the subject."

"What about Philip Agnew?"

Thoda smiled. "He was the most unlikely person I've ever had at one of my séances," she said. "On the surface, Mr. Agnew is such a forceful, down-to-earth person. He's the sort of man I'd have expected to sneer at people like me."

"But he didn't, obviously."

"No, Miss Masefield. We sat next to each other at dinner on the first evening. All that he could talk about was his love of animals. When I argued that, if he loved them that much, he wouldn't keep them in cages, Mr. Agnew was quite sharp with me. Afterward, however," she recalled, hands clasped in her lap, "he sought me out to apologize. Beneath that hard exterior, I realized, was a fairly sensitive man. He asked me why I'd gone to America in the first place."

"I was told that you were attending a conference."

"It was on psychic phenomena and I was one of the speakers."

"Is that what you explained to Mr. Agnew?"

"Of course," said Thoda. "I always give an honest answer to a direct question. He was amazed. Instead of being scornful, he pressed me for details of my work, then he more or less insisted on joining the séance." She gave a shrill laugh. "We had an incongruous group seated around that table last night."

"I can see that," said Genevieve, writing something on her pad.

"Apart from my four guests, I told nobody about the séance. My profession is like yours, Miss Masefield."

"In what way?"

"Confidentiality is essential."

"You may not have advertised the event, Mrs. Burbridge, but someone else did. I have it on good authority that Mrs. Trouncer talked about it in public, and it may be that Mr. Agnew did the same. They could easily have been overheard."

"I'd no means of preventing that."

"Granted." Genevieve jotted down something else before putting her pencil and pad away. She studied the other woman. "May I ask how you got involved with spiritualism in the first place?"

"I realized that I had a gift, Miss Masefield."

"You believed that you could contact the spirit world?"

"No, no," said Thoda, "that came much later — after I'd developed my gift. I was always able to sense things about people, you see. At first I just thought it was mere intuition, but it went well beyond that. Whenever I meet someone for the first time, I have a knack of spotting something about them that they try to keep hidden."

"Could you give me an example?"

"As long as you don't think me impertinent."

"Why should I do that?"

"Because I sensed something about you the moment you sat down," said Thoda, glancing at Genevieve's left hand. "You don't wear a wedding ring, yet I believe you're married. Is that correct?"

Genevieve was startled. "It is, actually."

"Why you choose to pass yourself off as a single woman is your business and I wouldn't dare to press you on the matter." She screwed up her eyes in concentration. "But I do get another sensation from you, Miss Masefield. Your husband might well be aboard."

"How on earth did you know that?"

"I told you — it's a gift."

"An extremely valuable one, Mrs. Burbridge."

"I'm sure that you have gifts of your own." She stood up. "I'm sorry that I wasn't able to be of more use to you."

"On the contrary," said Genevieve, getting to her feet, "you've been very helpful and I'm grateful to you."

"I do hope you manage to find the stolen book."

"We'll do everything in our power to catch the thief."

Thoda smiled knowingly. "You and your husband, you mean?"

"Am I so transparent?"

"Only to someone like me, Miss Masefield."

"Do you intend to hold another séance on board?"

"Of course," said Thoda. "After dinner this evening. The very same people will be here. You'd be most welcome to join us."

Genevieve pondered. "Thank you, Mrs. Burbridge," she said at length. "I might well take up that invitation."

Wilfred Carr was a short, neat, fussy Englishman in his forties with bushy hair flattened into submission and carefully divided by a center parting. Looking spruce in his uniform, he was proud of the fact that he was the cabin steward to some of the most important people aboard. Dillman caught him when Carr was having a rare moment off duty. The steward was outside the laundry enjoying a quiet cigarette. When he learned whom he was talking do, he stubbed it out on the sole of his shoe. Dillman told him about the theft of *A Study in Scarlet.*

"Well, it was there when I left," said Carr defensively.

"How can you be certain of that?"

"Because it was on the table with the other books. It was the one with slips of paper sticking out of it. Sir Arthur's name was on the spine." He drew himself up to his full height. "I notice things like that,

148

Mr. Dillman."

"What else did you notice yesterday evening?"

"Nothing unusual."

"No passengers wandering along the corridor?"

"They were all at dinner, sir."

"What about members of the crew?"

"The only ones who had any business to be there were the cabin stewards like me."

"How many keys are there to Sir Arthur's stateroom?"

"Three, sir, apart from those held by the passengers. I have one, the chief steward has a master key to all the first-class cabins and so does the purser. And before you ask," he went on, patting his pocket, "my key never leaves my person."

"What time did you finish your work last night?"

"It would have been around nine o'clock."

"Sir Arthur and Lady Conan Doyle didn't return until nearly eleven. That means the thief had a fair amount of time in which to operate."

"How did he get in? That's what I want to know, sir."

"So do I," said Dillman reflectively. "By nine o'clock, then, you and the other stewards had left that area altogether?"

"Yes," said Carr, "but we remained on duty. You never know when you might be called upon. One of the stewardesses was hauled out of bed in the middle of the night because a lady was terrified that she had a spider in her cabin."

"And did she?"

"No — it was all a dream."

"Were you summoned by any of the passengers last night?"

"No, I was lucky. I did my usual patrol and that was that."

"Your patrol?"

"Yes," explained Carr. "I always stroll past the cabins I look after around ten or ten-fifteen. It's the time when some of the passengers are turning in and I like to be on hand in case they need me."

"So at approximately ten-fifteen, you'd have walked past the stateroom belonging to Sir Arthur and Lady Conan Doyle?"

"That's right, Mr. Dillman."

"Did you notice anything out of the ordinary?"

"Not a thing, sir. They were obviously inside."

"They couldn't have been," Dillman argued. "Sir Arthur was very precise about the time of their return — nearly eleven."

"There was a light under the door, that's

all I know."

"Perhaps you left it on."

"I'd never do that, sir," said Carr indignantly. "I follow a strict routine every evening and I never leave lights on. Somebody else must have been in there." As the truth dawned on him, his eyes tried to escape from their sockets. "It was that bleeding thief, wasn't it?"

Saul and Miriam Pinnick braved the wind to walk arm in arm around the main deck. Though he tried continuously to cheer her up, his wife remained resolutely miserable. Even the sight of another tug-of-war contest between two teams of brawny passengers did not attract more than a cursory glance from her.

"We've another concert this afternoon," said Pinnick.

"What use is that?"

"It's good entertainment to while away the time."

"I don't want concerts," she said bitterly. "I want to spend my old age in America. I've worked hard all my life. I *deserved* it."

"You did, Mirry."

"We both did. They betrayed us."

"I felt the pain as much as you," he said, "but there's no point in going on about it.

We've been turned away before where our faces didn't fit. We simply go somewhere else and carry on our lives."

"We don't *have* lives, Saul."

"Of course we do."

"No," she moaned. "We just exist."

"Then we'll exist side by side, Mirry, as we've always done. You won't hear me complain about that. I count my blessings."

She frowned. "I've got none to count."

"You've got more than some people."

"Who?"

"Him, for instance."

Coming to a halt, Pinnick indicated the man at the rail in the stern of the ship. Leonard Rush cut a sorry figure. Hunched up against the wind, he gazed intently down at the sea as if searching for something. There were numerous passengers on the deck, but he was cut off from all of them, imprisoned in a private world that nobody else could enter. Pinnick and his wife went across to him.

"Good morning, Mr. Rush," said Pinnick. There was no reply. He touched the man on the shoulder. "Good morning to you."

Rush spun round as if he'd been struck and bunched his fists as if to protect himself. When he recognized the others, he lowered his arms and relaxed slightly.

"It's only Mirry and me," said Pinnick. "You're among friends."

"I thought it was him again," Rush muttered.

"Who?"

"The man who tried to steal my blanket last night."

"You shouldn't have slept on deck," said Miriam.

"I had to, Mrs. Pinnick. It's the only place for me. I was woken up when I felt someone tugging at my blanket. I had to hit the man hard to get rid of him."

"There must be somewhere else you can sleep," said Pinnick.

"There isn't. I have to keep a vigil."

Miriam was perplexed. "Whatever do you mean?"

"I know what he means," said her husband softly. "Mr. Rush lost his wife on the voyage to America. She was buried at sea."

"It was wrong," protested Rush. "Ellen deserved a proper grave, not to be dumped into the water like a sack of rotten potatoes. I should have done more for her. I should have got her some respect."

"She was given respect. I was at the funeral along with hundreds of others, and we were all moved by the dignity of the service. We shared your grief, Mr. Rush. We wept with you. It may have seemed cruel to bury your wife at sea, but it was the right thing to do." Pinnick spread his arms in a vivid gesture. "Did you really want to arrive in New York with her body in a coffin?"

"They'd never have let you bury her there," said Miriam.

"Would you *want* her laid to rest in a foreign country?"

"No," confessed Rush.

"There you are, then."

"I should have taken her back to England. It was my duty."

"No man could have been expected to undergo that suffering, my friend. Think how dreadful it would have been for you, knowing that your wife's body was somewhere down in the hold. And, of course," Pinnick reminded him, "costs would have been involved."

Rush nodded and withdrew into his shell. When he and his wife had set out from Southampton, their resources had been limited. He had been relying on getting some menial work once they were allowed into America. But his wife had died of pneumonia somewhere in the mid-Atlantic and he had neither the money nor the presence of mind to hold out for a proper funeral on land. Saul Pinnick was right about one thing. Though quite short, the burial service had been conducted with great reverence and a host of strangers had turned up in a collective show of sympathy.

At the time, Rush had been deeply moved. On reflection, however, he felt that he had let his wife down and he was consumed with guilt. Brushing a tear away with the back of his hand, he turned to stare out across the waves again.

"I'll find it sooner or later," he promised.

"Find what?" asked Miriam.

"The place where they tipped my wife overboard."

"You can never do that, Mr. Rush."

"I must. It's the least I can do for Ellen."

"Try to put those thoughts out of your head," Pinnick advised. "I know that it's hard because we've lost loved ones ourselves — far too many of them. But you have to think of yourself, Mr. Rush. Whatever your despair, life must go on."

"Not when it's so pointless."

"But it's not. There's always some hope, however faint."

"No, Mr. Pinnick. I'm not interested in hope. All I can think about is doing right by Ellen. When we reach the place where her body was dropped into the sea, I'll know it for sure."

Pinnick was alarmed. "Then what will you do?"

"I'll join her," said Rush.

SEVEN

In order to discuss the progress of their investigation, they forsook luncheon in the first-class saloon that day and met in Dillman's cabin. Referring to her notebook, Genevieve gave a detailed account of her visit to Thoda Burbridge and explained that she had been invited to attend the séance that evening.

"I've always wanted to see what goes on at one of those things," she said, "and now I have the opportunity."

"I'm glad that you accepted. Sophie Trouncer tried to persuade me to join her at the séance but I thought better of it."

"Why?"

"To be honest, I don't wish to get any closer to Mrs. Trouncer."

She was amused. "Do you think she has designs on you?"

"I don't want to be in a position where I might find out."

"You'd enjoy meeting Thoda Burbridge. She's an interesting character. I'm usually dubious about people who claim to possess psychic gifts, but not in her case. She really does have strange powers. She saw right through me."

"It must have come as something of a shock."

"It did, George. I wonder what else she divined about me."

Dillman smiled. "She was obviously too polite to tell you," he said. "But she's given you the perfect camouflage for talking to Sophie Trouncer. Instead of confiding that you work for the White Star Line, you can approach her as someone who'll be sitting around the table with her in Mrs. Burbridge's cabin."

"Yes," said Genevieve. "And because Philip Agnew will be there as well, I'll be able to kill two birds with one stone."

"I'd still like to have a chat with him myself."

"He's not the thief, George. I can vouch for that."

"He could still be the person who unwittingly passed on details of the séance to the thief. I talked to the steward who looks after Sir Arthur and Lady Conan Doyle's stateroom. The theft almost certainly occurred

158

while they were with Thoda Burbridge."

"What else did you learn?"

"Only that the crew are trained to take security very seriously. If they have the slightest suspicion about anything," said Dillman, "they report it immediately to the chief steward. Wilf Carr — the man I spoke to — was very disturbed to hear that something had been stolen from a stateroom that he looked after. It's never happened before. He took it as a personal insult."

"Did you talk to anyone else?"

"I questioned all the stewards who work on that deck, male and female. Every one said the same. They saw nothing."

"Were there any possible suspects among them?"

"No, Genevieve," he said firmly. "They struck me as a dedicated body of people. To work in first class, they have to be highly efficient and trustworthy. Besides, what would any of them want with a copy of *A Study in Scarlet*? If there was a thief in their ranks, he'd steal something far more valuable than a single book."

They broke off to eat some of the sandwiches that Dillman had had sent to the cabin. Tea had also been provided. He poured two cups and passed one to Genevieve.

"Luncheon would have been more tempting than this," he said.

"Yes, George, but it would come with certain dangers."

"Are you still being hounded by Joshua Cleves?"

"He doesn't really hound me," she replied, "that's the trouble. He's effortlessly polite and scrupulously well behaved. He knows just how far to go. Nevertheless," she added, stirring sugar in her cup, "I have a few worries about him."

"If he becomes a nuisance, let me know."

"Oh, I have no qualms about handling him."

"What about your other suitor?"

"I don't have any suitors," she said with a laugh.

"I was thinking about Frank Spurrier."

"Ah, now he's a little more problematical."

"I had a feeling that he might be," said Dillman.

"He keeps popping up when I least expect him. I told you about the way he sat directly behind me at the concert yesterday afternoon. He also intercepted me as I went into the dining saloon last night, and he did the same this morning."

"So he was waiting in ambush for you?"

"It didn't seem like that, George," she said. "Mr. Spurrier was just there. He has this uncanny knack of appearing out of nowhere." She took a first sip of her tea. "Then there's the other thing."

"What other thing?"

"The way he always makes critical remarks about Mr. Cleves."

"He obviously views him as a rival," Dillman observed, "and is trying to warn you off. What about Cleves? Does he snipe at his friend in the same way?"

"On the contrary, he speaks well of him."

"Does he realize he's being traduced by Spurrier?"

"Oh, yes. He rather enjoys it."

Dillman was taken aback. "*Enjoys* it?"

"Apparently," said Genevieve. "He takes it in his stride. And he makes no attempt to hit back — I admire him for that. He's a model of restraint and he has definite charm. It's the reason he gets on so well with Lord and Lady Bulstrode. When it comes to friends, they're very selective."

"That's why they chose to share a table with you."

"They'll have to miss me today — I had a better offer."

He blew her a kiss. "Thank you."

"As for Frank Spurrier, I'll try to dodge

him in future. He's turned up once too often for my liking."

"Didn't you say that he runs an auction house in London?"

"Yes," said Genevieve, "and he's a very astute businessman, according to Mr. Cleves. He's an expert on furniture and china, but his real love is for . . ." She paused as she realized the import of what she was about to say. "His real love is for rare books and modern first editions. Heavens!" she cried. "I should have thought of him before. He'd know the true value of a book."

"How much would he pay for *A Study in Scarlet*?"

"Where are you staying in London?" asked Joshua Cleves.

"At the Savoy Hotel," said David Lowbury.

"You'll like it there. Excellent food. Make sure they give you a room overlooking the river. The great thing about the Savoy is that it has far more bathrooms than the average hotel."

"You've stayed there?"

"Two or three times. It's where I first met Frank Spurrier."

"I can never make out if you two love or

hate each other."

"A bit of both, I guess," said Cleves with a chuckle.

They were sitting in the first-class lounge after luncheon and it was beginning to fill up as other passengers came in from the dining saloon. Cleves waved to Lord and Lady Bulstrode as they went past. Lowbury acknowledged a few people with whom he had become acquainted. He turned back to his companion.

"He's an odd fellow, isn't he?"

"Who?"

"Frank Spurrier," said Lowbury. "I mean, if I had a face like that, I'm sure that I'd scare the ladies away. Yet he doesn't seem to do that. They're drawn to him. Jane — my wife, that is — went so far as to say that he's almost handsome in a perverse sort of way."

"He lives up to his nickname."

"What's that?"

"John Wilkes."

Lowbury shrugged. "The name means nothing to me."

"Nor to me at first," confessed Cleves. "It turns out that Wilkes was a political firebrand in the eighteenth century. He was also a member of parliament until he fell foul of George the Third — but, then, we

Americans didn't exactly see eye to eye with the king either."

"Where's the link with Mr. Spurrier?"

"I'm coming to it. Among his many talents, Wilkes was very fond of the ladies, in spite of the fact that he was rumored to be the ugliest man in England."

"Did he have any success with them?"

"A tremendous amount, from what I hear," said Cleves with a grin. "He was a real libertine. He boasted that he could talk away his face in half an hour. Frank is the same — hence the nickname."

"Does he like it?"

"No, Mr. Lowbury. He detests it."

"I can understand why."

"He gets very touchy if you call him John Wilkes."

"I'll be sure to remember that." He glanced toward door. "Talk of the devil — here he is!"

Frank Spurrier had just entered the lounge and was looking around in every direction. As he got level with them, Cleves put out a hand to stop him.

"She's not here, Frank," he announced.

"How do you know I was searching for someone?" said Spurrier.

"Because you have the concentrated expression of a hunter on the trail of his quarry. But the bird has flown. Miss Masefield didn't even turn up for luncheon today."

"I noticed that," said Lowbury.

"She must have got fed up with sitting beside you, Josh," said Spurrier, lowering himself into a chair. "And who can blame her?"

"Lady Bulstrode did," Cleves answered. "She missed her badly."

"Anyone would miss a woman like Miss Masefield," said Lowbury with admiration. "I've watched her. She has real class. If I wasn't already spoken for, I might even join you two in this little competition of yours."

"What competition?"

"Come off it, Mr. Cleves. I'm not blind. The pair of you have set your sights on Miss Masefield and you're both chafing at the bit."

"That's a rather inelegant way of putting it," said Spurrier.

"But it's near enough to the truth."

"No, Mr. Lowbury."

"We're just having some fun at each other's expense," said Cleves. "We always do that if we sail on the same liner. It adds a bit of spice to the trip. Isn't that so, Frank?"

"Yes, Josh," Spurrier agreed.

"All that we admit to being is interested observers."

"Well, I've been doing a spot of observing myself," said Lowbury, "and I know a contest when I see one." Before they could speak, he raised both palms to silence them. "No need to protest. Believe me, I don't blame you for trying. I wish you good luck. The way to add a bit of real spice to the trip is to entice Miss Masefield into your cabin for a spot of hanky-panky."

"Do you have to express it quite so vulgarly?" said Spurrier with evident disapproval. "In your position, I'd have thought you'd be far too preoccupied with your wife to worry about any other woman."

"Oh, I'm not worried about *her* — only about the two of you."

"What do you mean?"

"That neither of you stands a chance."

Cleves was purposeful. "We'll see about that, Mr. Lowbury."

"Would you put money on it?"

"Yes, I would."

"You're sounding like much more than an observer now."

"That's none of your business!"

"I just wanted to offer you some friendly advice, that's all," said Lowbury, relishing the hostility he had aroused. "She's way

166

beyond your reach, gentlemen, and always will be. Find someone else to add to your list of conquests."

Spurrier was stung. "This conversation is starting to get very unseemly," he complained. "I've no wish to continue it."

"Then I'll gladly withdraw," said Lowbury, rising to his feet. "But don't forget what I said. Neither of you will claim the prize. You're both courting rejection. Why? To put it bluntly," he went on, looking down at Cleves, "you're much too old for her."

"Damn you, sir!" exclaimed Cleves.

"And as for you, Mr. Spurrier," he said with a provocative smile at the other man, "this is one occasion when you won't be able to talk your face away like John Wilkes. Good day, gentlemen."

David Lowbury left the pair of them fuming.

Genevieve had no difficulty in recognizing Sophie Trouncer. The latter's appearance was very distinctive and Dillman had given a very accurate description of her. Sophie was in the library, reaching down a book from the shelf so that she could leaf through it. Genevieve was pleased that nobody else was there that afternoon. It meant that they could talk in private.

"Mrs. Trouncer?" she began.

"Yes," replied Sophie, looking up. "That's me."

"My name is Genevieve Masefield. I believe that we have a mutual acquaintance on board."

"Oh, who might that be?"

"Mrs. Burbridge."

"Yes, I know dear Thoda!" said Sophie, her face lighting up. "In fact, this is the exact spot where I first met her. I came in search of books on spiritualism."

"That's precisely why I'm here. Mrs. Burbridge was kind enough to recommend a couple of books that she said I'd find here."

"Do you have an interest in the subject as well?"

"Yes," said Genevieve. "I'll be joining you at the séance tonight."

"Wonderful!"

Genevieve had liked the woman on sight and Sophie clearly accepted her without any reservation. They were soon chatting amiably. Genevieve indicated the chairs.

"Why don't we sit down for a moment?"

"Good idea." They sat at either side of a table. "Oh, I'm so glad to have the chance to meet you, Miss Masefield. Mother and I both noticed that dress you wore at dinner last night."

"It does seem to have caught the eye."

"It's the person wearing it who does that," said Sophie. "Even at your age, I would never have dared to wear anything like that. I lacked both the figure and the courage."

"You don't strike me as a woman who's short of courage," said Genevieve. "You have such an air of determination about you. Once you set your mind on something, I'll wager that you're bold and single-minded."

"I am, Miss Masefield, and always have been. I had to be bold to undertake this trip in the first place. Mother and I have traveled thousands of miles on our own, you know. And we did so without a tremor," she said proudly.

"Good for you."

"But you're even more courageous."

"Am I?"

"If, as it appears, you're sailing on your own."

"One soon makes friends on a ship, Mrs. Trouncer. It's one of the pleasures of crossing the Atlantic. But tell me what happened last night," she said. "I understand that the séance was something of a disappointment."

"Not to me. I was so privileged to be there."

"Were you?"

169

"Thoda is such an extraordinary person. As we sat around the table with her, I could feel the power she had. Sir Arthur and Lady Conan Doyle were there as well," she said, "and they had the same impression as me. Thoda is a true medium."

"What about the other person involved?"

"Mr. Agnew?" She wrinkled her nose. "I can't say that I took to the gentleman. He was too loud. Americans sometimes are, I fear."

"Not all of them," said Genevieve, thinking of her husband.

"He didn't like it when Thoda demonstrated her gift."

"Yes, I had a demonstration of that as well."

"Mr. Agnew took exception to it. Luckily, it was before Sir Arthur and his wife joined us, and the argument was over by then."

"Argument?"

"Thoda can sense things about people. She knew facts about me that I'd long forgotten and I was quite shaken when she disclosed them. But I didn't deny that they were true," she said. "Mr. Agnew thought it was all a trick. At one point, he got quite defiant."

"Why?"

"He more or less challenged Thoda to tell

him something hidden in his own past. Yet when she did, he refused to admit that the facts were accurate."

"What sort of facts?"

"That he grew up in Utah as part of a Mormon community. Thoda was even able to name the town where he was born, but Mr. Agnew refused to discuss it. If you want my opinion, Miss Masefield," she said, wagging an index finger, "that was what ruined the séance. Mr. Agnew had created the wrong atmosphere. Sir Arthur and his wife were unaware of it but I wasn't. The evening was spoiled by that noisy American."

"I'm afraid that Philip Agnew will be there again tonight."

"Then I hope he behaves himself. Thoda was a saint. She was so tolerant with him. She let him rant on, then apologized for making a mistake about his past. But I don't think it *was* a mistake."

Genevieve knew why the medium had not mentioned the incident to her. Thoda Burbridge had been as good as her word. Confidentiality was maintained. Genevieve's respect for the woman increased. She had not only coped with the protesting Philip Agnew and the ebullient Sophie Trouncer, she had never lost her composure while doing so. The prospect of being present at the next séance took on an additional interest for Genevieve. She felt that it could be a memorable experience.

"I was hoping that *he* might join us," said Sophie.

"Who?"

"A handsome gentleman we've befriended. He's the kind of refined American who could almost pass as an Englishman. Mother adores him and he certainly makes my heart flutter. He's the complete antithesis of Mr. Agnew."

"Really?"

"He's kind, considerate, well mannered and highly educated. I invited him to come this evening, but unfortunately he's too busy." A dreamy look came into her eyes. "I'd have loved to walk into Thoda's cabin with George Dillman beside me. He's so good-looking."

Genevieve stifled a comment.

Later that afternoon, George Dillman tracked him down in the first-class smoking room. Philip Agnew was one of the few people still there, stubbing out the remains of a cigar in the ashtray. He was a big, heavy man in his fifties with a weatherbeaten face and a balding pate. When the detective approached, Agnew was reading a magazine.

"You're missing the concert," said Dillman.

"On purpose."

"Don't you like entertainment?"

"Not when amateurs are involved," said Agnew, tossing the magazine aside. "Why are you dodging it?"

"For much the same reason. When I crossed on the *Oceanic,* I had to sit through an accordionist, a man who recited humorous monologues and two people who did bird impressions."

"Then I'm glad I wasn't there. I care about birds."

"Mind if I join you?"

"Be my guest, sir," said Agnew, indicating the chair beside him.

The detective offered his hand. "George Dillman."

"Philip Agnew."

They shook hands, then Dillman took a seat. He noticed that the discarded magazine had a picture of a lion on the front of it.

"Are you interested in animals, Mr. Agnew?"

"I have to be — it's my job."

"Oh?"

"I own a menagerie on the outskirts of

Chicago. We're in the process of extending it so that we can have more species on display. That's the main reason I'm going to Europe."

"I would have thought Africa would be the best place."

"No, I've got all the big cats I need and a couple of hippos. Last year I bought a rhino from a zoo in Michigan. What I'm really after on this trip are birds and small mammals."

"Where will you get them from?" asked Dillman.

"All over the place. I deal with zoos, private collectors, breeders. In most cases, I pay cash, but some folk prefer to trade."

"You've brought animals with you?"

"Native American species," said Agnew. "Any animal that could be transported in a cage without making too much noise or stinking the whole ship out. That's why I drew the line at coyotes and skunks."

Dillman smiled. "We're all grateful to you for that."

"What do you do, Mr. Dillman?"

"Exactly what I'm doing at the moment — I sail. We have a family business in Boston making oceangoing yachts. I get to put them through their paces before we sell them."

"That means you're a good sailor. I envy you."

"Do you have trouble with seasickness?"

"Only on the first day."

"So how have you been passing the time on the *Celtic*?"

"Eating plenty, drinking even more. And I do a lot of walking," said Agnew. "When I'm on a ship, I'm like an animal in a cage. I'm always on the prowl."

"Exercise is important. I've been round the deck dozens of times each day. It's been a very enjoyable voyage so far. The weather's been kind to us and I've met some nice people. The person I'd really like to meet, however," he said artlessly, "is that famous British author."

"Which one?"

"Sir Arthur Conan Doyle."

"Save yourself the trouble. I know him. He's nothing special."

"But he created Sherlock Holmes."

"I've got no time for writers."

"Why not?"

"I only respect a man who does a real job, Mr. Dillman."

"Then you ought to respect Sir Arthur. Before he became an author he was a qualified doctor. At one stage, I believe, he acted as a ship's surgeon on a whaling boat so that he could get some money to continue his medical studies."

"Yes," said Agnew with a sneer. "He mentioned that. It was one of the reasons I took against the man."

Dillman was shocked. "You object to his being a doctor?"

"What I object to is the random killing of animals. Sir Arthur actually harpooned a whale himself and he helped to club dozens of seals to death. That was brutal," he said with feeling. "I keep seals in my menagerie. They're lovely creatures. Only a cruel man would want to kill them."

When they had met, Conan Doyle had struck Dillman as a gentle, considerate man, but he did not say so to Agnew. The latter was clearly passionate about the care of animals. He had contempt for hunters of any kind. A writer who had been involved in killing animals aroused particular disgust. Agnew's cheeks became inflamed.

"And now," he said with scorn, "he leads the life of a country squire. That means he goes hunting, shooting and fishing. I know that we all have to eat and that certain animals have to be slaughtered, but anyone who kills for sport should be arrested."

"How did you meet Sir Arthur?"

"At a séance."

"Here on the ship?" said Dillman, feigning surprise.

"Yes. There's a woman on board called Thoda Burbridge. She claims to be a medium. But I didn't see any proof of it last night." He looked Dillman in the eye. "Do you believe in spiritualism?"

"I try to keep an open mind on the subject."

"I thought it was all nonsense, and that the people who tried to make contact with the dead were fools. Then my wife passed away," Agnew recalled with a sigh, "and I began to take it more seriously. I had a friend in the same position as me and he swears that he spoke to his late wife at a séance. That set me thinking."

"I can see how it would."

"When I met this woman on board who just happens to be a medium, I began to wonder if it was more than a coincidence."

"Is that why you decided to go to the séance?"

"Yes, Mr. Dillman. My wife was everything to me. If I could reach her in any way, however briefly, I'd be overjoyed. Mrs. Burbridge seemed quite genuine when we spoke, and she obviously has powers of some sort. So I asked if I could join in."

"But the event was a failure."

"I thought so," said Agnew, "but maybe I was expecting too much. One of the people there — Mrs. Trouncer — reckoned that it was an honor just to be present, but I didn't feel that."

"What did you feel, Mr. Agnew?"

"Well — that I'd been sort of cheated."

"Did the medium ask for a fee?"

"No. In fairness, she didn't. Mrs. Burbridge only takes money from people who get what they want."

"And you were not happy with the way things went?"

"Not at all."

"Would you attend another séance?"

"I don't think so," said Agnew. "I agreed to go back again this evening, but I won't bother. I couldn't face that kind of letdown again, and I don't really want to sit shoulder to shoulder with a man like Sir Arthur who kills dumb animals. No," he added with a grim smile, "from now on, I'll get all my spirits out of a bottle."

Like most of the people in first class, Sir Arthur and Lady Conan Doyle decided to attend the concert that afternoon. As they filed into their seats, his mind was still on the lost book.

"It's like looking for a needle in a haystack," he said.

"I thought you had faith in Mr. Dillman."

"I do, Jean, but I quail at the size of his task."

"How would Sherlock Holmes solve the crime?"

"If he was looking for a needle, he'd burn down the haystack."

"That's rather impractical when there's a book inside," said Lady Conan Doyle. "I'm so sorry, Arthur. I know how much that book means to you, and I can remember the thrill I felt when I first read it."

"Did you ever imagine that you'd one day marry the author?"

"That would have seemed like an absurd fantasy."

"And now?" he asked.

She squeezed his hand by way of reply. Other people came to sit beside them, so their conversation became more neutral, but both of them still kept thinking about the copy of *A Study in Scarlet.* It was not long before the chairman took charge and the concert began. Although the artistes were drawn primarily from the passengers and the crew, the standard of performance was fairly high. A talented pianist was the first to delight the audience, then one of the engineers told a series of hilarious nautical anecdotes. After two young girls had done their tap dance routine, Nelson Rutherford reappeared to play a medley of tunes on his clarinet.

Three vocalists were featured, but in the opinion of Conan Doyle, not one of them could match the beauty of his wife's singing. It was toward the end of the concert that the real surprise came.

"And now," announced the chairman, "we bring you something quite different. Nobby Ruggles is one of the barbers on the *Celtic.* He's also a master of the monologue. Please give Nobby a warm welcome as he recites the stirring ballad 'Corporal Dick's Promotion.' "

A round of applause came, but Conan Doyle did not contribute toward it. The poem chosen was one of his own, written for a collection called *Songs of Action,* an anthology of narrative ballads about soldiers and sportsmen. He wondered why that particular poem had been selected. Dressed in army uniform, Nobby Ruggles marched into view and saluted to the audience as he halted. He was a stocky man of medium height with the face and manner of someone who had seen military action. When he launched into his recitation, he did so with immense gusto.

"The eastern day was well-nigh o'er
When, parched with thirst, and travel sore,
Two of McPherson's flanking corps
Across the desert were tramping.
They had wandered off from the beaten
   track
And now were wearily harking back,
Ever staring round for the signal jack
That marked their comrades camping."

What made the performance so compelling was the way the ballad had been dramatized. By using graphic gestures, clever movements and endless changes of voice, Ruggles brought the story alive for them. He delivered the lines as if declaiming a Shakespearean soliloquy and he fully deserved the ovation that followed. He cut it short by semaphoring wildly.

"No, no, ladies and gentlemen," he said with patent humility. "I merely brought the message to you. The person to applaud is the man who actually wrote it, and he's sitting in this very room. A generous hand, please, for the creator of 'Corporal Dick's Promotion,' " he went on, "Sir Arthur Conan Doyle!"

Cheers rang out and everyone turned in the direction to which Ruggles pointed. Many passengers had not even realized that the author was on board the ship, and those who did had not seen very much of him. Much to his discomfort, Conan Doyle was forced to rise to his feet in acknowledgment of the applause. It was only when the clapping began to die down that Nobby Ruggles saluted him and marched off. Conan Doyle gratefully resumed his seat. His hopes of traveling in comparative anonymity had been shattered. When the concert eventually came to an end, everyone close to him wanted to congratulate him. Few of them had known that the man whose name was inextricably linked with Sherlock Holmes was also a poet.

As the crowd began to thin out, he pulled a face. "I knew that it was a mistake to come," he said ruefully.

"You weren't to know what would happen, Arthur," said his wife. "Besides, I thought he performed it very well."

"Far too well, Jean. When he revealed my name, I felt as if I had a dozen searchlights trained on me. It was gruesome."

"Noblesse oblige."

"I suppose you could put it that way."

All he wanted to do was to steal quietly away to the safety of their stateroom, but they were not allowed to do so. As soon as they stepped out of the room, Nobby

Ruggles confronted them. He had changed back into the white coat and dark trousers he wore when on duty as a barber. The glow in his eyes was akin to hero-worship.

"Norman Ruggles — at your service, Sir Arthur!"

"You did extremely well, Mr. Ruggles," said Conan Doyle. "I've never heard that ballad given such a stirring recitation before."

"Thank you, Sir Arthur." He turned to Conan Doyle's wife. "Your husband is a genius, Lady Conan Doyle."

"I don't need to be told that, Mr. Ruggles," she said with a smile.

"He and I have met before. Sir Arthur won't remember me, but I remember him. We all did, every last man of us."

"Did you by any chance serve in the Boer War?" asked Conan Doyle. Ruggles stood proudly to attention. "Good for you, my man. I tried to enlist myself, but they turned me down on the grounds of age. I was determined to get to South Africa somehow, so I became part of a medical unit."

"And you did sterling work, Sir Arthur," said Ruggles. "I was in Bloemfontein when that typhoid epidemic broke out. I helped to recapture the water pumps from the Boers."

"We must have ridden out together in that freezing weather."

"The night before the battle was the coldest I'd ever known. Shall I tell you how I kept myself warm, Sir Arthur?"

"How?"

"By reciting your poems to myself. They inspired me. The one about Corporal Dick was my favorite. Still," he said, stepping aside, "I won't hold you and Lady Conan Doyle up any longer. I just wanted you to know that we appreciated what you did for us. Your book on the Boer War was the best thing ever written about it."

"Thank you, Mr. Ruggles."

"If you ever want a free haircut, you know where to come."

The barber gave a final salute before walking away. Conan Doyle led his wife down the corridor, glad to be alone with her at last but pleased to have made contact with the former soldier.

"Ruggles was one of the lucky ones," he said.

"Was he?"

"Yes — he survived. Bloemfontein was a hellhole. The epidemic went on for a month. At the height of the contagion they were burying sixty men a day in shallow graves."

"How horrible!"

"We set up our hospital in the pavilion of the Ramblers' Cricket Club and erected marquees all over the playing field. Our men suffered hideous deaths. That's why I was so keen to write a book about my experiences in South Africa."

"The army did come in for a lot of criticism at the time."

"I defended them, Jean. They deserved it."

"At least one old soldier appreciates what you did."

"Yes," said Conan Doyle. "It was rather touching. I just wish that he hadn't exposed me in public like that this afternoon. It was excruciating. Next time he stands up in front of an audience," he decided, "I'll insist that he recite Rudyard Kipling instead."

Sophie Trouncer was at her most animated over dinner that evening. Delighted to have another opportunity to talk to Dillman again, she was also highly excited at the prospect of another séance.

"Something dramatic will happen tonight," she predicted.

"Yes," said her mother dryly. "You'll discover that the medium is nothing but a well-bred confidence trickster."

"That's not true. Mrs. Burbridge has

amazing powers."

"I've heard that," said Dillman.

"Then you heard correctly," said Sophie. "The first time I met her she told me that I'd been born in London during a thunderstorm. How could she possibly have known that?"

"A wild guess," said May Hoyland.

"She *sensed* it, Mother."

"She also sensed that you could easily be taken in. If this lady has such wondrous powers, why did nothing happen last night?"

"I blame Mr. Agnew for that."

"You always make excuses, Sophie."

"It's not an excuse, it's an explanation."

"Ha!"

The two women bickered throughout much of the meal and allowed Dillman to survey the room at regular intervals. There was a much more settled feel to the saloon now. After the first tentative dinner, when most people were strangers to one another, friendships had been formed and an air of familiarity prevailed. Genevieve was chatting to Lord and Lady Bulstrode as if she had known them for years, and so relaxed was he in their company, Joshua Cleves might have been a neighbor of theirs. Sir Arthur and Lady Conan Doyle had now become more conspicuous and Dillman noticed how many people glanced in their direction. The disapproving Philip Agnew was not among them. He spurned the British author.

Anxious to get to the séance, Sophie was the first to leave the table, ignoring the prickly remark that her mother made by way of a farewell. When her daughter was out of earshot, May looked across the table at Dillman. She became contrite.

"You must think it's beastly of me to taunt her like that," she said, "but I'm doing it for her own good."

"You and your daughter must agree to differ, Mrs. Hoyland."

"Sophie just won't see how silly it all is."

"It's wrong to condemn something that you've never experienced yourself," said Dillman. "You've dismissed it out of hand."

"But I haven't, Mr. Dillman. That's the trouble."

"Oh?"

"I'm not that narrow-minded," she said, leaning forward. "For all I know, there may very well be something in spiritualism. But I still don't want my daughter to be involved in it."

"Why not?"

"Because it's silly — and it's also unhealthy."

"I don't see why."

"The dead are dead, Mr. Dillman. We have to accept that. I don't think it's right to try to get in touch with someone beyond the grave." She shivered involuntarily. "It's eerie. It's unhealthy. It's not right."

"That's a matter of opinion, Mrs. Hoyland."

"Would *you* want to speak to someone who'd passed away?"

"Probably not," he admitted.

"Neither would I. Life is for the living. That's what upsets me about Sophie. It's silly to look back all the time. She had a happy marriage that came to an untimely end. A period of mourning was only proper. But," she continued, "my daughter should be turning her eyes to the future now. Geoffrey was a devoted husband to her, but he's not the only man in the world."

"No, there are a lot of us about."

"That's what I keep telling her. She must do what I did."

"You, Mrs. Hoyland?"

"Yes," she said, fixing him with a stare. "My first husband died of smallpox when we'd only been married for two years. I was stricken down with grief. But I learned a valuable lesson from that ordeal, Mr. Dillman."

"Did you?"

"The way to get over the loss of a first husband is to marry a second one. That's exactly what I did. My second husband was Sophie's father and — yes, she was right — she *was* born in London during a thunderstorm. I want her to follow my example while she's still young enough to do so." Her gaze intensified. "Sophie is a very attractive prospect in every way."

May Hoyland tried to prod him into making flattering comments about her daughter, but Dillman was too adroit. Since he might be one of her targets, he was quite content for Sophie Trouncer to seek a reunion with her late husband rather than search for his replacement. The last thing the detective needed was pursuit by an eager female with aspirations to marriage. Now that May Hoyland had shown her hand as a self-appointed matchmaker, Dillman had no conscience about manufacturing an excuse and withdrawing from the table.

The first place he went to was the lounge so that he could continue the search for the stolen book. Following a process of elimination, he had already discarded most of the names from the list of passengers. By meeting new people, if only casually, he could soon decide if they were potential thieves.

Aware that a female hand could have spirited Conan Doyle's book away, he was as interested in the women as the men. By the time he had finished chatting to various people, he had crossed another dozen names off his list.

After spending a productive hour in the lounge he elected to call on Nelson Rutherford in his office to apprise him of developments. The purser was pleased to see him. Having shown off his musical talent at the concert that afternoon, he was now in uniform and back on duty. He rubbed his hands together.

"How are things going, Mr. Dillman?" he asked.

"Slowly but surely."

"Do you have any suspects yet?"

"A handful of them," said Dillman. "When I get down to the last three, I'll let you know who they are."

"Sir Arthur is desperate to get that book back again."

"Understandably."

"I keep telling him that he must put his trust in you."

"And in my partner. There are two of us, remember."

"Yes," said Rutherford. "A man and a woman make a good team. You can go places where Miss Masefield cannot, and vice versa. That way, you have access to anywhere on the ship."

"In this case, our activities will be confined to first class."

"What about Edward Hammond? It must have crossed your mind that he may turn out to be the thief."

"Not for an instant, Mr. Rutherford."

"No?"

"The one thing we do know about the man is that he's a professional criminal. He stole a small fortune from the house that he burgled in New York. If you get away with a hundred thousand dollars in cash and jewelry," Dillman argued, "are you going to be bothered about a copy of *A Study in Scarlet*?"

"I suppose not."

"My feeling is that he's not even on board. We'd have been aware of him if he was. No, I think you can rule out Hammond right now."

"That's a relief," said the purser. "The thought that we had a killer on board was rather unnerving. Someone who simply takes a book is very different. We've no reason to fear him." There was a loud knock on the door. "Come in!" he called.

The door opened and Jane Lowbury burst

in. She was in such distress that she did not even notice Dillman there. Panting for breath, she went across to the purser's desk.

"I need your help, Mr. Rutherford," she gasped.

"Of course," he said. "What's the problem?"

"It's my husband — he's disappeared!"

"That sounds highly unlikely. Could I have his name, please?"

"David — David Lowbury."

"What makes you think he's disappeared, Mrs. Lowbury?"

"In the middle of dinner he went back to the cabin to get something for me and he never returned. I've searched everywhere for him. And before you tell me that he might be playing a game with me," she said, "I can assure you that he's not. David would never do that." She took a handkerchief from her purse and dabbed at her eyes. "We're on our honeymoon, Mr. Rutherford. We've never been apart for more than a few minutes." She suddenly became conscious that Dillman was standing behind her. "Oh, excuse me. I didn't see you there."

"This is George Dillman, the ship's detective," said Rutherford, motioning him forward. "You can speak freely in front of him."

"How long has your husband been missing?" asked Dillman.

"Well over an hour."

"It wouldn't take him that long to go to your cabin and back."

"That's what alarms me, Mr. Dillman. I looked for him in all the public rooms but there was no sign of him." Jane wrung her hands. "It's so unlike David to go astray. He's always so reliable."

"What did you send him to get?"

"Some pills that I forgot."

"And were they in the cabin when you went back there?"

"No," she replied. "They were gone. David obviously got that far."

"I'm sure there's a perfectly simply explanation for all this," said Rutherford, trying to soothe her. "We've never lost a passenger on the *Celtic* yet. Take heart, Mrs. Lowbury. Your husband simply must be on the ship *somewhere*."

"He's not," she wailed, tears streaming down her cheeks. "I know it. Something terrible has happened to him. David has vanished."

Eased over the gunwale, the body fell swiftly through the darkness until it hit the water with a splash. The noise went unheard beneath the insistent roar of the engines and the repeated smack of the waves. Unaware that she had just lost a passenger, the *Celtic* steamed on regardless into the night.

EIGHT

The first thing they tried to do was to calm Jane Lowbury down. She was shaking all over and sobbing uncontrollably. Her shoulders were hunched. Her pretty face was distorted by pain. Dillman eased her into a chair and crouched solicitously beside her.

"Can I offer you a drink, Mrs. Lowbury?" asked the purser, taking a bottle from a drawer in his desk. "A drop of brandy works wonders sometimes."

"No, thank you," she said.

"A glass of water, perhaps?"

"Nothing at all, Mr. Rutherford."

"This must have come as a terrible shock."

"It has, believe me."

"We'll do everything we can to help."

"Thank you." She made a visible effort to steady herself. "I just want to know what's happened to my husband."

"We'll institute a thorough search," Dillman assured her. "I know that you've looked for him yourself, but you only searched the first-class areas of the ship." He stood up. "He may inadvertently have strayed into one of the other areas and got lost."

"That can easily happen on a vessel this size," said Rutherford. "When I first joined the *Celtic* I was always getting confused. It takes time to work out her geography."

"If he got lost," she reasoned, wiping the last tears away, "David would have asked someone the way. He's very practical like that. He'd never have been away *this* long."

"Perhaps not," Dillman conceded. "On the other hand, he can't have just vanished into thin air. There are thousands of people on board. Someone must have seen him."

"I asked everyone I met, Mr. Dillman."

"Did you describe what your husband looks like?"

"Of course."

"We'll need the same description ourselves so that we can pass it on to the search team. Before we do that, however, I want you to retrace your steps for us. The last time you saw Mr. Lowbury was when he left you in the dining saloon. Is that right?"

"Yes, I told you."

"And what happened before you got there?"

She was bewildered. "Before?"

"What sort of a mood was your husband in?" asked Dillman gently. "Was he on edge? Did he seem worried in any way? Can you remember him doing anything uncharacteristic?"

"No, Mr. Dillman."

"Think back very carefully."

"I don't need to. He was exactly as he always is — completely at ease. David had no cause to be worried."

"So he had no problems of any kind?"

"None at all."

"Had he had any disagreements with anyone?"

"Not that I know of," she said. "David was very easygoing. He could get along with almost anybody. He made lots of friends on board. That was the sort of person he was. You can ask Mr. Spurrier."

"Who?" said the purser.

"Frank Spurrier," replied Dillman. "He's a gentleman who runs an auction house in London. I gather that he's returning from a buying expedition in America."

"You know him?" asked Jane.

"Only by repute."

"He's a very interesting man."

"How did you come to meet him, Mrs. Lowbury?"

"We sat at the same table," she explained. "David talked to him a lot. My husband is a financier, you see, and he's always looking for shrewd investments. He was fascinated to hear about the world of antiques. He and Mr. Spurrier seemed to have a lot in common."

"Did you dine with Mr. Spurrier this evening?"

"No, that was the odd thing."

"Odd?"

"He deserted us."

"Oh?"

"I'm not even sure if he came into the dining saloon. I certainly didn't see him. All I know is that he wasn't in his usual seat." Her face puckered. "I wonder why."

"I may need to ask him, Mrs. Lowbury." Dillman extracted a small notebook and pencil from his pocket. "Could you describe your husband for us, please?" he requested. "As soon as you've done that, I'll organize the search for him."

Genevieve Masefield entered the cabin with a mixture of curiosity and apprehension. Eager to find out what actually happened at a séance, she realized that she would be taking part in an exercise over which she had no control. That was unsettling. She needed to put complete trust in Thoda Burbridge, and although she had seen evidence of the woman's psychic powers, she was not convinced that anyone could make contact with the spirits of the dead. Did the medium possess such gifts or was she simply dabbling in the supernatural?

"Come on in, Miss Masefield," said Thoda, shaking her hand. "It's so nice of you to join us. I believe that you've met Mrs. Trouncer already?" she went on, indicating Sophie. "Allow me to introduce Sir Arthur and Lady Conan Doyle."

"It's an honor," said Genevieve, exchanging handshakes with each of them. She looked around. "But I understood that there would be six of us here this evening."

"Mr. Agnew decided to withdraw," said Thoda.

"That's no great loss," Conan Doyle opined. "Mr. Agnew was far too impatient. He expected instant results. He also appeared to believe that the séance was arranged solely for his benefit."

"Be that as it may, Sir Arthur, we have an able deputy in Miss Masefield. I have high hopes of a more successful outcome this time." She waved a hand. "Shall we take our seats?"

Since the furniture in most cabins was

secured to the floor as a precaution, Genevieve had wondered how they could all sit around a table. She now had her answer. Five free-standing chairs had been borrowed and set out around a folding table erected for the occasion. A series of strange markings were etched around the circumference of the table. Genevieve peered at them but was unable to decipher their meaning.

"I always travel with my own table," explained Thoda. "It's very cumbersome, but I could not conduct a séance without it. A Ouija board would be easier to carry but I'm not able to use one."

"The medium I visited in London had a Ouija board," said Sophie, tingling at the memory. "I'd never seen one before. It was uncanny. It spelled out my late husband's name."

"Each of us works in different ways, Mrs. Trouncer."

"Naturally."

"What is important is the end result."

"I was astonished by what the other lady was able to reveal."

Thoda smiled benignly. "I'm glad that it was so satisfactory."

Genevieve admired the way that Thoda Burbridge gave the impression of validating the séances Sophie Trouncer had attended even though she was convinced — on the basis of what she had heard about them — that the medium in question was a fraud. No hint of criticism came from her. It would have been too hurtful to suggest that Mrs. Trouncer had been the victim of a hoax.

"When I was in America," Thoda continued, "I had the privilege of meeting Mrs. Piper. I'm sure that name is known to you, Sir Arthur."

"Yes," he confirmed. "I've read a great deal about her and spoken to people who attended sittings with her when she came to England. A truly remarkable woman." He looked at Genevieve. "Are you familiar with the name of Leonora Piper, by any chance?"

"No," admitted Genevieve.

"She's mentioned in the book I've been reading," said Sophie.

"Quite rightly," said Conan Doyle. "Some of the things she's been able to communicate during her trances are quite astounding. Mrs. Piper has her detractors, but the eminent psychologists who have examined her, on both sides of the Atlantic, have all come to the conclusion that she has extraordinary powers."

"Professor James was one of them," Thoda observed, saying the name with exaggerated respect. "As a literary man, Sir Arthur, I daresay that you've met his brother, Henry."

"A number of times."

"That's another phenomenon that defies explanation. How can the human brain produce the sort of brilliant work for which you and Henry James are justly celebrated? Who taught you such intellectual dexterity? From where did you get such profound insights into human behavior? It's a form of magic."

"No," said Lady Conan Doyle. "My husband is no magician. His books are the product of hard work and innate genius."

"Some of them, anyway," he said modestly.

"Your stories have given untold pleasure to a huge audience," said Thoda, "and I'm sure that audience will continue to grow."

Genevieve could see what she was doing. Thoda Burbridge pretended to be engaging in casual conversation, but she was making sure that her guests were thoroughly relaxed. The longer they talked, the more control she seemed to exert. Without raising her voice or dominating openly, she nevertheless became the central figure in the room. It was almost as if she had grown in size. Like the others, Genevieve found herself submitting without resistance to her will.

Thoda Burbridge remained a comforting

presence. Offsetting her voluminous black gown of taffeta was a string of pearls that rested on her ample bosom. Pearl earrings matched the necklace. Sophie Trouncer had also chosen a black dress while Lady Conan Doyle wore a gown of dark green velvet. In her red silk evening dress, it was left to Genevieve to bring real color and style to the occasion. Thoda was at her most maternal. With her warm smile and affectionate manner she looked less like a medium than a proud mother presiding over her family during a meal. She beamed at Genevieve.

"You must be wondering what to expect, Miss Masefield."

"I am," confessed Genevieve.

"Then you are in the same boat as the rest of us, if you'll forgive a hideous pun. None of us really knows what is going to happen."

"It's a psychic adventure," said Conan Doyle.

"That's how I always view it. The procedure is quite simple, Miss Masefield," said the medium. "There are no apparitions and no ectoplasmic manifestations of any kind. There will be no levitation and no objects flying around the cabin. All that will happen — when I turn out the light — is that I will attempt to go into a trance. It may take time, so I ask you all to be patient with me."

Her tone sharpened a little. "Please put your hands on the table, palms downward. That's right," she said approvingly as they all obeyed. "Now move your hands outward so that your fingers are touching those of the people on either side of you."

Genevieve was sitting between Lady Conan Doyle and Sophie Trouncer. As she spread her hands, she made contact with their fingers. Thoda walked across to the light switch.

"Are we all ready?" she asked.

Then the cabin was plunged into darkness.

George Dillman acted swiftly. After escorting Jane Lowbury back to her cabin, he took charge of the search party that the purser had assembled for him. It consisted largely of stewards, trained men and women who knew every nook and cranny of the ship. Gathering them together, Dillman gave them a description of the missing man. He then deployed them throughout the various decks of the *Celtic.* Nelson Rutherford was impressed with the way the detective had supervised operations. They were standing outside the first-class dining saloon as the search party went about its business.

"You've done this before, Mr. Dillman," he commented.

"Once or twice."

"How is Mrs. Lowbury?"

"Still very upset. Ideally, I'd like my partner to be with her but she's attending a séance at the moment. When she comes back I'll ask her to visit Mrs. Lowbury."

"Did you see anything in the cabin?"

"There was nothing to see," said Dillman. "I thought there might be signs of a struggle or at least some small clue as to what might have occurred, but it was in exactly the state that Mrs. Lowbury left it."

"What about their steward?"

"I've spoken to him, Mr. Rutherford. He'd finished work by the time Mr. Lowbury went back to the cabin to get his wife's pills, so he was unable to help us. Since the pills are missing, we can assume that Mr. Lowbury took them."

"But that was almost two hours ago now," said Rutherford, checking his watch. "No wonder his poor wife is so alarmed."

"Yes," said Dillman. "I feel so sorry for her."

"Why did you ask about her husband's frame of mind?"

"Because I wondered if they'd had a row over something. It does happen — even on a honeymoon. I don't know Mr. Lowbury, so it would be wrong to speculate about him, but I can think of some husbands who might deliberately go missing."

"We had one like that on the *Baltic,*" said the purser. "He and his wife had a violent argument and he stalked out. After she'd failed to find him, she came running to me, certain that something dreadful had happened to him."

"And had it?"

"Not in my opinion. He was holed up in a cabin with three other men, drinking whiskey and playing cards. I seem to remember that he won a packet of money. That helped to placate his wife."

"We're dealing with a different situation here."

"Exactly. No man in his right mind is going to walk out on someone as gorgeous as Jane Lowbury."

"Especially on their honeymoon."

"So where does that leave us?"

"With two main possibilities," said Dillman, thinking it through. "It may be that Mrs. Lowbury is deceiving us and that her husband is *not* in his right mind. He may be disturbed in some way and therefore not responsible for his behavior."

"And the other possibility?"

"Someone stopped him from returning to his wife. The fact that he picked up those pills suggests that he intended to go back to her. Before he could do that, he might have been intercepted."

"By whom?" asked Rutherford, stroking his chin meditatively. "You heard his wife. He's gregarious and even-tempered. David Lowbury made friends easily."

"If he's engaged in high finance, he must have a ruthless streak as well. Business rivals may not look so kindly on him."

"We can't be certain that he has any of them on board."

"Not at the moment, Mr. Rutherford, but who knows what we'll find when we start to dig beneath the surface?"

"What's your next move?"

"I'd like to have a word with Frank Spurrier. If he deserted them at dinner, he must have had a good reason for doing so. In any case," said Dillman, thinking about Genevieve, "it's high time I met the man. I've heard a lot about him."

"If the search party finds Mr. Lowbury, I'll contact you at once."

"Thank you."

"One last question before you go," said the purser. "Why is Miss Masefield taking part in a séance?"

"By way of research."

"I see."

"Sir Arthur and Lady Conan Doyle will be there as well."

"I'll be interested to hear how she gets on."

"So will I," said Dillman. "Very interested."

Their eyes gradually became accustomed to the darkness. Still touching the hands on either side of her, Genevieve could make out the shape of Thoda Burbridge sitting bolt upright and lost in a trance. What she could not see was that the medium was holding a pencil and that it was poised over a sheet of paper in front of her. Minutes passed by, then Genevieve felt a vibration under her hands. At first she thought it was caused by one of the people sitting on either side of her, but when she experienced it again she realized that the table had moved slightly of its own accord. She was both disturbed and intrigued. Even if she had wanted it, there was no means of escape. The intense concentration of the group was an unbreakable bond. Because her fingers were touching those of Lady Conan Doyle and Sophie Trouncer, she was effectively manacled.

When the table moved for the third time, it trembled beneath their palms. It was an odd sensation that Genevieve could not begin to explain. Clear, arresting, almost playful, it did not induce any real fear. Then, when she least expected it, she heard Thoda break the prolonged silence, but it was not in the voice she had used before. Thoda spoke in a weird, high-pitched whine, her head thrust back as she addressed an unseen listener.

"Are you there?" she called. "Will you speak to me?"

Whatever the replies, only Thoda could hear them. Even though she was not even looking at the paper, she began to write.

"Yes, the lady is here," she said, scribbling away. "You have the correct name. Do you have a message for her?"

Genevieve's mouth went dry and her cheeks burned with embarrassment. The thought that Thoda Burbridge might be talking about her was very disquieting, and she began to wish that she had not come to the cabin that evening. She did not have the genuine interest that had impelled the others. Genevieve was very much the outsider in the gathering. Could it be that, by some bizarre trick of fate, she was the one who had been picked out?

By whom?

"What else do you wish to say to her?"

asked Thoda, the pencil moving ever more rapidly in her hand. "Yes, I'll pass that message on. Do you have something more to tell me?"

Genevieve was squirming in discomfort. Unseen forces were keeping her in her seat and the notion that she had been singled out only compounded her agony. The questions kept coming and the answers were duly noted down on the paper. Who was talking to the medium, and what was he or she saying? The dialogue seemed to be endless. Thoda had filled page after page. Genevieve prayed that the ordeal would come to an end.

"Good-bye!" said Thoda.

She breathed in deeply through her nose, then lapsed back into silence. Several minutes passed. Genevieve wondered if Thoda had fallen asleep. Conan Doyle offered some reassurance.

"We have to wait while she comes out of the trance," he said.

"Is it always like this?" asked Genevieve.

"A seance takes a lot out of her. Be patient."

They sat there for a few more minutes, their fingers still touching as if held there by some sort of spell. Genevieve was grateful that the table did not move again. With a grunt of surprise, Thoda suddenly jerked her head as if coming out of a dream. She took a moment to get her bearings, then she let out a quiet laugh.

"It happened," she said, reverting to her normal voice. "Oh, I'm so glad that it worked this time." She got to her feet. "You can let go of the table now." They withdrew their hands. "Be warned. I'm going to switch on the light again. It will seem quite fierce on your eyes at first. Here it comes."

She switched on the light and they all shaded their eyes against its glare. Resuming her seat, Thoda began to sort through the pages to put them in the correct order.

"I only have a message for one of you, I'm afraid," said Thoda. "He was very anxious to make contact."

"With whom?" asked Lady Conan Doyle.

Convinced that it would be her, Genevieve braced herself.

"With Mrs. Trouncer," replied the medium, turning to her. "This is a private message, Mrs. Trouncer, and you may not want anyone else to hear it. The decision is yours."

"No, no," said Sophie breathily. "Read it out. Share it."

"As you wish."

"May I ask how you could write in the

dark?" said Conan Doyle.

"A more pertinent question is how I can write in shorthand," said the medium, "for I never learned it. Yet I have pages of squiggles and can read them with ease."

"Who spoke to me?" said Sophie.

"Geoffrey Trouncer."

"My husband!"

"He asked you to take good care of the garden."

"Oh, I always do. It was his pride and joy. A gardener comes three times a week and keeps it exactly as Geoffrey would want it."

"Don't cut down any of the sycamores."

"I wouldn't dare."

"And plant some more roses by that new trellis."

"How did he know that I had that trellis put up?" she said in wonderment. "It has to be Geoffrey you spoke to. It was my husband."

More information about the garden followed, then the comments became more personal. Sophie was enjoined to continue her various activities in the village where she lived and to visit his grave often. Though they were only listening to domestic trivia, Genevieve and the others were enthralled. There could be no doubting the fact that Thoda Burbridge had made contact with the spirit world. She could not possibly have known the details that poured out.

Sophie Trouncer was elated. She hung on every word that was read out, making frequent comments or simply sighing with joy. Her face was radiant. Genevieve was happy on her behalf, though mystified as to how the medium had collected the messages. When the last page came into view, Sophie craned forward to see if she could make sense of the shorthand. Her excitement was building all the time.

"Geoffrey sends his love," said Thoda. "He misses you badly."

"I miss *him!*" cried Sophie.

"But he has one important piece of advice for you."

"Go on."

"He does not want you to pine for him any longer, Mrs. Trouncer. You have mourned enough."

"It's my duty."

"And you've done it very well. The time has now come to think about yourself for a change. That was his message."

"Myself?"

"He thinks that you should get married again."

Sophie Trouncer let out a gasp of surprise and leaped to her feet so quickly that she knocked over her chair. Her eyes widened, her mouth fell open and both hands came up to her throat. Then, without any warning, she collapsed in a heap on the floor.

The séance was over.

Saul Pinnick was a sociable man. Since they had sailed from New York he had made a number of friends and offered warm sympathy to anyone who, like himself, had been refused entry into America. He was also a willing guide to anyone visiting England for the first time, speaking about the country with such enthusiasm that people wondered why he had been ready to emigrate from it. Miriam Pinnick, however, was too caught up in her own distress to care overmuch about others. In her mind, England was simply the place where they would soon wither and die.

"I think I should go and speak to him," said her husband.

"Who?"

"Mr. Rush."

"Why do you worry so much about him?" she complained. "You should take more notice of your wife and less of complete strangers. What's so special about him?"

"You know very well, Mirry."

"He has nothing like the worries *I* have."

"You're not talking about suicide," he reminded her. "He is."

"What's this if it's not a kind of suicide?" she asked with a touch of belligerence. "We're going back to nothing — no house, no job, no money, no future. We're killing ourselves, Saul. The only difference is that it will take us a little longer than Mr. Rush."

"Don't you *care,* Mirry? Taking your own life is the most awful thing a man can do. Imagine how he must be feeling. And before you tell me about *your* despair," he went on with a flash of anger, "just remember that you have someone to share that with you. Mr. Rush doesn't. He's all alone."

They were huddled side by side in the lounge, two weary figures among the hundreds of steerage passengers who were still up. It was time to go to bed, but Pinnick was more concerned about Leonard Rush's sleeping arrangements.

"Would you stay out on deck all night?" he challenged.

"You know I wouldn't, Saul."

"Then have some concern for someone who does."

"He's not the only one," she argued. "There's others who'd rather sleep under the stars because their cabins are too crowded."

215

"Younger people, Mirry. Fitter people. You heard him cough. The man is ill. That's why they turned him back at Ellis Island."

"What can we do?"

"Show him that he has friends."

"We've already done that."

"We have to keep doing it — especially at night. That's the worst time for him. That's when the death of his wife preys on his mind."

She gave a tired smile. "You're a good man, Saul Pinnick."

"I hate to see someone suffer like that."

"You're not his keeper."

"I just want to make sure that he's all right." He got to his feet. "Or, to be honest — that he's still aboard. Will you come with me?"

"I think you'd rather go on your own, wouldn't you?"

"Yes, Mirry. I would."

"You know how to talk to him — I don't."

"Wait for me here, my love."

"Ha! Where else can I go?"

Picking his way between the seats, Pinnick made for the door. He went out onto the main deck and walked along it. Several people were about, enjoying a stroll before bedtime or standing at the rail and watching the reflection of the moon on the sea.

Pinnick saw three or four passengers, curled up under blankets in places where they had some protection from the wind, but there was no sign of Leonard Rush. The old man went twice around the deck, peering into the darkest corners in search of his friend. Rush had last been seen in the dining saloon where he had wolfed down his meal before leaving early. Pinnick could not believe that he would have bothered to eat if his mind had been set on suicide.

After a fruitless search he finished up in the stern of the ship. He could hear the engines pounding away and see the bubbling foam that the huge propellers were creating. Beyond, in the darkness, was complete oblivion. Somewhere in that vast expanse of water, Pinnick decided, was Leonard Rush. He offered up a silent prayer for the safety of the man's soul. Blaming himself for not having been able to save Rush, he turned on his heel to walk back to the lounge.

Someone stepped out of the shadows to block his way.

"I thought it was you," he said.

Pinnick was delighted. "You're still here!" he cried.

"Yes," said Leonard Rush. "For the time being."

■ ■ ■ ■

Joshua Cleves was relaxing with a cigar when his friend came into the smoking room. He beckoned Frank Spurrier across to him. Taking a seat beside him, Spurrier pulled out his cigarette case.

"You're slipping, Josh," he teased. "Miss Masefield enjoyed your company so much over dinner that she left early."

"She had a prior engagement."

"I think she was just anxious to get away from you."

"Genevieve went off to a meeting of some sort."

"Any excuse to get free of you."

Cleves chortled. "I can hear the envy in your voice, Frank," he said smugly. "We've been on the ship for days and you've got no nearer to Genevieve. She's all mine."

"The voyage is not over yet." After putting his case away, Spurrier lit his cigarette and inhaled. He blew out the smoke. "You're overlooking the one great advantage I have."

"What advantage?"

"I'm a bachelor with no blemishes on my private life."

"Then I'm sorry for you, Frank. Your life

must have been unbearably dull. Mine, however, has been continually exciting."

"Would you describe having two wrecked marriages as a form of excitement? You're like a driver who's been in two bad car accidents, Josh. No woman would trust you at the wheel."

"Actually," said Cleves with a triumphant grin, "I have a chauffeur, as you well know. I can afford to let someone else do the driving. If I take Genevieve to the Ritz, I'll pick her up in a taxi."

"She'll have discarded you long before then."

"It may be the other way round, Frank."

"I doubt it."

"When I've won my bet, I may have no further use for her. But never let it be said that I'm not generous," Cleves went on. "Because you've signally failed to make an impression on Genevieve, I decided to give you a helping hand."

"I need no assistance from you, Josh."

"Then you'll have to turn the invitation down."

"What invitation?"

"Drinks before dinner tomorrow in Rupert and Agnes's stateroom. I asked if I might bring a friend, so you are included in the party — along with Genevieve Masefield, of course."

Spurrier was pleased at the unexpected opportunity he had just been given but annoyed that it had come from his rival. Conscious that Cleves was taunting him, he nevertheless saw how perverse it would be to turn down the invitation. He was about to accept graciously when someone bore down on him. George Dillman was quietly purposeful.

"Mr. Spurrier?"

"Yes," replied the other.

"My name is George Dillman. Pardon this intrusion, but I wondered if I might have a word in private with you?"

"On what subject?"

"I'd rather discuss that when we're alone."

"If it can't be aired in public," said Spurrier, "then we'll not discuss it at all. Who the devil are you, Mr. Dillman?"

"I work for the White Star Line as a ship's detective."

"He's come to arrest you," said Cleves with a laugh. "What have you been up to, Frank?"

Spurrier was indignant. "Nothing at all."

"I'm sure that's true," said Dillman calmly. "I just wondered if I might ask you a few questions, sir."

"Such as?"

"Why didn't you sit in your usual place at dinner?"

"What's that got to do with you?"

"There must have been a reason, Mr. Spurrier."

"There is — I sit where I choose."

"And you chose not to sit opposite Mr. and Mrs. Lowbury. Why?"

"What right have you to ask that?" said Spurrier with barely contained anger. "Is it a crime to change seats in the dining saloon?"

"No, sir. Of course not."

"Put the handcuffs on him, Mr. Dillman," urged Cleves, enjoying the situation hugely. "Make him pay for his villainy at last."

"I'm sure that he's not guilty of any," said Dillman, trying to appease Spurrier with a smile. "It's just that it would help me if I had his assurance that he did dine in the saloon this evening."

"Why are you checking up on me?" demanded Spurrier.

"It's a routine inquiry, sir."

"Are you going to put the same question to Josh and to everyone else in the room? Or am I being singled out for some reason?"

"Mr. and Mrs. Lowbury expected you to join them."

"There's you answer, Frank," said Cleves,

relishing his friend's embarrassment. "David Lowbury is going to sue you for failing to sit opposite him. He's taken out a writ against you."

"He's in no position to do that," said Dillman seriously. "A search party is at present looking for him. He's disappeared. David Lowbury hasn't been seen for almost two hours."

Spurrier was outraged. "This is monstrous," he said. "Are you accusing me of having something to do with his disappearance?"

"Not at all, sir."

"Then why did you bother me in the first place?"

"Come on," said Cleves, baiting his friend. "Own up. Tell us where you've hidden him."

Dillman rounded on him. "This may amuse you, sir, but it's caused the greatest concern to his wife. I'm sorry that you find her torment so diverting."

Cleves was unrepentant. "The lady is worrying unnecessarily, Mr. Dillman," he said with confidence. "Her husband's disappearance is probably the result of a marital tiff. I should know. I'm an authority on the subject."

"We've considered that possibility and rejected it, so I'd be grateful if you stopped your inane interruptions."

"I endorse that, Josh," said Spurrier. "Please shut up. As for you, Mr. Dillman," he added, "I simply cannot see why you involve me in your inquiry."

"It was because Mrs. Lowbury found your behavior odd, sir."

"Odd or suspicious?"

"Since you had, apparently, developed a friendship with her and her husband, she wondered why you had deserted them this evening."

"Then I'll be happy to tell you. After what David Lowbury said to me earlier — and to Josh, as it happens — I'd no wish to endure his company for another meal. The man is boorish," said Spurrier. "I like his wife, but I've no time at all for Lowbury himself."

"The same goes for me," said Cleves.

"Is it odd to prefer the society of agreeable people?"

"No, Mr. Spurrier," said Dillman. "But, in fairness to the lady, it must be remembered that when she passed that remark about you she was unaware that her husband had antagonized you."

"We have no quarrel with Mrs. Lowbury," said Cleves.

"None at all," insisted Spurrier. "She's an attractive young woman who deserves better than David Lowbury. He deceived me at first. I freely admit that. Then he showed us another aspect of his character and I lost all respect for him."

"Frank answers for both of us on that."

"I resent the fact that you've spoken to me like this, Mr. Dillman, and I hope that you'll keep your distance in future. With regard to David Lowbury, I have only this to say." Spurrier's eyes glowed with hatred. "If he's disappeared — good riddance to him!"

Genevieve Masefield had no time to reflect on the séance and its dramatic effect on one of her companions. She waited until Sophie Trouncer had recovered and was relieved to see that she had sustained no real injury when she fell. After thanking Thoda Burbridge for inviting her, she excused herself. When she got back to her cabin she found a note from Dillman informing her of Lowbury's disappearance and asking her to go, as a matter of urgency, to offer succor to the man's wife. Genevieve obeyed at once and hurried off along the corridor.

The moment she knocked on the relevant cabin door, it was opened. Jane Lowbury had a look of mingled hope and fear in her eyes. When she saw a woman standing there, she was puzzled.

"Hello, Mrs. Lowbury," said Genevieve softly. "My name is Genevieve Masefield and I work as a detective on board the *Celtic*. My colleague, George Dillman, asked me to come and see you."

"Is there any news?"

"Not yet."

"Are you sure?" said Jane, anxiety corrugating her features. "I'd rather know the truth, Miss Masefield."

"You will, I assure you. As soon as there's any definite news it will be brought directly to you." She offered a consoling smile. "May I come in, please?"

"Yes, yes, of course."

Jane stood back to admit her, then closed the door behind her. After a glance around the cabin Genevieve suggested that they sit down, but the other woman was far too restless. She kept pacing up and down. It was clear from the moist rings under her eyes that she had been crying. Genevieve's guilt stirred. While she had been involved in the séance, a passenger had been in great distress. Genevieve should have been there to help her. She tried to make up for lost time.

"I understand that your husband left the table in the middle of dinner," she began.

"Yes," replied Jane, "and I haven't seen him since."

"Has he ever done this kind of thing before?"

"Never. David has always been so dependable. That's why I think that something frightful must have happened to him. He should have been back with my pills within minutes."

Dillman's note had not mentioned the reason that brought David Lowbury back to the cabin. Genevieve was interested to hear what it was and surprised that someone as young and self-evidently healthy as Jane required medication of any kind.

"Why did you need the pills?" she asked.

"I have palpitations sometimes. Nothing serious."

"But the doctor nevertheless prescribed the pills."

"Only as a safeguard, Miss Masefield." She put a hand to her head. "Oh, if only I'd remembered to take them with me, none of this would have happened."

"You don't know that, Mrs. Lowbury."

"I do — it's all my fault."

"That's simply not true," said Genevieve, guiding her to a chair. "Please sit down. I need to ask you some questions."

"Mr. Dillman did that."

"I just want to double-check a few things." Jane agreed to sit down and Genevieve sat close to her. "What sort of man is your husband, Mrs. Lowbury?"

"The very best sort. He's honest, loving and hardworking."

"Not given to playing tricks on you, then?"

"It would never cross his mind," said Jane. "He hates that kind of thing as much as I do. Besides, David would never deliberately inflict suffering on me. That would be cruel and he's the kindest man alive. We're on our honeymoon, Miss Masefield. He's been wonderful to me from the very start."

"Have you made many friends since you've been aboard?"

"Quite a number — though we prefer our own company most of the time. David likes to talk business, but I've never been terribly interested in that, so I just let him get on with it."

"So he may have made the acquaintance of one or two people that you don't know about?"

"Oh, he did. There's no question about that."

"Did he talk about them?"

"Of course. He tells me anything. David likes to have a cigarette after meals and I know he met various people in the smoking room."

"Did he mention any business deals in the offing?"

"No, Miss Masefield. We're on vacation."

"Some men find it hard to leave their work behind them."

"David is not like that. He gave me his word. This voyage was purely and simply about us. We're thinking of buying a house in England one day, you see."

"Were you going there to look at properties?"

"That was part of the reason."

"What was the other part?"

"David was going to take me to Paris." Jane smiled wistfully. "It's somewhere I've always wanted to go." Her face crumpled. "And now it will never happen."

"Don't even think that, Mrs. Lowbury."

"I can't go without my husband. There'd be no point."

"You're assuming the worst when there's no reason to do so," said Genevieve. "Try to be patient. They're searching for him at this very moment."

"Then why haven't they found him?"

"I don't know. I wish I did."

"Has this sort of thing ever happened before?"

"Very rarely."

"But this is not the first time?"

"No, Mrs. Lowbury."

"And on the previous occasions, was the missing person always found?" Genevieve was hesitant. "Well?"

"Not always."

Jane was aghast. "You mean that someone went overboard?"

"It was not a comparable situation," said Genevieve quickly. "Don't worry about what occurred in other cases. They're immaterial. All that need concern you is what happened to your husband."

"And what did happen? What *could* happen?"

"All sorts of things, Mrs. Lowbury."

"Such as?"

"I don't think we need go into that."

"He's been attacked, hasn't he?" said Jane, grabbing Genevieve's arm. "David was wearing a watch and carrying a lot of money in his billfold. He's been attacked and robbed."

"That's highly unlikely."

"Why?"

"Because we do not have thieves roaming the corridors of the ship, Mrs. Lowbury. When it comes to crime, the White Star Line has a good safety record. No unauthorized person is allowed in the first-class areas," said Genevieve. "And there's another important point."

"What's that?"

"How could anyone know that your husband would return here during the meal? Nobody was waiting to assault him. You can stop torturing yourself with that thought."

"I just can't get it out of my mind."

"I know it's difficult, but you mustn't let your imagination get the better of you. A thorough search is being made of the whole ship."

"Why is it taking so long?"

"Because they want to look in every conceivable corner," said Genevieve, trying to sound optimistic. "It's only a question of time before they find your husband."

Wilfred Carr was among the first to volunteer to join the search party. Having helped to comb the first-class areas, he joined the others in second class to continue the hunt there. When they failed to find any trace of David Lowbury, the steward insisted on adding another pair of eyes to the team in steerage. It was the most unpromising place because a man in white tie and tails would be so conspicuous there. Notwithstanding that, they conducted a painstaking search of the public rooms and the corridors, asking everybody they met if they had seen a man who answered to the description of David Lowbury.

It was all to no avail. Carr did not give up easily. Carrying a torch and accompanied by another steward, he began to search the main deck. The other man was skeptical.

"They've already been here, Wilf," he said.

"It won't hurt to take a second look," said Carr, shining his torch in dark corners as they walked along. "They were only looking for a human being. I'm after something else."

"And what's that?"

"Evidence."

Carr made his way slowly along the deck. He had begun life as a steward in steerage and was deeply grateful that he now breathed the more rarefied air of first class. But he had not forgotten that some passengers found sleeping accommodation on the main deck. There were all sorts of corners where they tucked themselves away. Carr and his companion searched every one, unwittingly waking people up in some cases and earning a few rebukes in the ripest of language. They pressed on until they came to a bulkhead.

"He ain't here, Wilf. We might as well give in."

"I never give in," said Carr defiantly. "Never. I got this feeling we'll find something."

"Not in the dark. Let's wait until dawn."

"Think of his wife, man. She must be in a dreadful state. Do you want to go and tell *her* to wait until dawn?"

The other man hung his head. "Maybe not."

"Then let's scour every inch of the deck."

Slowly and methodically, they moved on. Carr was indefatigable. He not only peered carefully at the deck itself, he even lifted the tarpaulins to look inside the lifeboats.

"He's not going to be in there, Wilf," said his friend.

"You never know."

"What's he doing — playing hide-and-seek?"

"I'll ask him when I find him."

"Not down here. He's a toff. He don't belong in steerage."

Carr ignored him. Walking along to the next lifeboat, he raised the tarpaulin and stood on tiptoe to look underneath. His torch illumined something rolled up under one of the seats. He reached in to retrieve it then shook it out so that he could see what he was holding.

It was a gentleman's frock coat.

NINE

Holding it up in one hand, George Dillman examined the coat with care. He was in the purser's office with Nelson Rutherford and Wilfred Carr, both of whom looked on with interest.

"Nothing in the pockets?" asked Rutherford.

"Nothing at all," replied Dillman.

"Then he was robbed before he was killed."

"Let's not jump to any conclusions. We can't be certain that this coat belonged to Mr. Lowbury, and even if it did, we've no proof that he was murdered. He may still be on the ship somewhere."

"I wish that was true, sir," said Carr gloomily, "but I doubt it. We've searched everywhere except under the bunk in the captain's cabin."

"But you did find the coat," Rutherford noted, "and that's to your credit. Well done,

Carr. It's the only real clue we have."

"Yes," said Dillman, examining a tear under one of the armpits of the coat, "and it's a very valuable one. Can you see where this is torn?" he asked, pointing. "Nobody would have worn it in that condition. I think the person who owned this coat may well have been involved in a struggle of some sort."

"One that he lost, by the look of it."

"Yes. Where exactly did you find this, Mr. Carr?"

"In one of the lifeboats," said the steward.

"I'll need you to show me the exact spot."

"Now, sir?"

"No," said Dillman. "We'll need to get the coat identified by Mrs. Lowbury first. That's the next step. In the meantime, I don't want you to spread news of what you found."

"You can count on me, Mr. Dillman."

"And on the others," said the purser. "Before they began their search I impressed upon them that they were to do nothing to raise alarm among the passengers. If people know that we have a possible murder on our hands, it will unsettle the whole ship."

Carr sniffed. "Then it's just as well we didn't take Roley."

"Who?"

"Roland Finn, sir — first-class bedroom

235

steward. The less he knows about this, the better. Roley has a wagging tongue. In fact, I've been meaning to talk to Mr. Dillman about him."

"Why?" asked the detective.

"Because he's sweet on Mrs. Burbridge's stewardess, Hannah Jympson, that's why. They're close friends."

"I don't want to hear any tittle-tattle about the private lives of the crew," said Rutherford irritably.

"But it's important, sir. Hannah told Roley, you see, and my guess is that Roley told every Tom, Dick and Harry on board."

"Told them what?"

"About that séance being held in Mrs. Burbridge's cabin. When she heard that Sir Arthur Conan Doyle was going to be there, Hannah couldn't wait to pass on the news."

"This could be relevant," said Dillman. "That book was stolen from Sir Arthur's cabin while he and Lady Conan Doyle were at that séance. I assumed that only a few people were aware it was taking place, but it now seems the news reached a wider audience."

"I'd forgotten about the stolen book," admitted Rutherford.

"It's something we have to keep in mind. Obviously, this latest development must take priority, but that doesn't mean we stop looking for that copy of *A Study in Scarlet.*"

"Quite."

"Unlike Mr. Lowbury, it's something that we can be confident is still on the *Celtic.* Well," he continued, folding the coat over his arm, "I'd better show this to his wife."

"Would you like me to go with you?" said the purser.

"No, thank you. If our worst fears are realized, what she will really need is some female company."

"That's one thing I can't provide."

"My partner will certainly be with her by now," said Dillman. "In situations like this, she comes into her own."

"What about me, sir?" asked Carr.

"I'll come for you in due course so that you can show me where you found the coat. You've got very sharp eyes. We're very grateful that you were in that search party tonight."

"I do my best, Mr. Dillman. Can I go now, sir?"

"Yes."

"You know where to find me."

Rutherford waited until the steward had left the room.

"This is all very disturbing," he said, running a hand through his hair. "A killer on board? It's unthinkable. The captain will have to be informed immediately."

"Wait until we have a positive identification," advised Dillman. "If this coat did belong to David Lowbury, we may well be involved in a murder investigation — unless, of course, the gentleman took his own life. In theory, that's not impossible."

"Is it likely?"

"No, Mr. Rutherford. Someone who's about to jump overboard would hardly take off his coat first and roll it up so that it can be hidden inside a lifeboat. And from what we know of David Lowbury, he was not a man of suicidal inclination."

"What's your honest feeling about this case?"

"Let me speak to Mrs. Lowbury first."

"And after that?"

"I'll start hunting for the killer," said Dillman.

Jane Lowbury was still very agitated. Though she was now sitting down, she could not relax. Her face was a mask of concern, her body kept twitching nervously and she twisted a handkerchief between her fingers. Genevieve Masefield did her best to comfort her but without any real success. She continued to probe for detail.

"Who else did your husband meet in the smoking room?"

"I've given you all the names I can remember, Miss Masefield."

"You say that he took a particular interest in Frank Spurrier."

"That's right."

"Why was that?" asked Genevieve, thinking about her own encounters with Spurrier. "Did your husband wish to buy antiques?"

"He thought that we might go to an auction in London."

"Did he get a direct invitation from Mr. Spurrier?"

"Yes," said Jane. "He gave David his card."

"And what was your opinion of him?"

"He's a most unusual person, Miss Masefield. When you first meet him his face looks rather unsightly. Yet after you've talked to him for a few minutes he doesn't seem so ugly at all. Mr. Spurrier has a most engaging manner."

"Yes, I know. I've met him."

"He's strangely attractive, isn't he?"

Genevieve did not commit herself, and in any case would not have had the time to do so. There was a tap on the door and Jane leaped from her seat to rush across to it. Genevieve also got up. When the door was opened they saw Dillman standing there.

"Have you found him?" asked Jane eagerly.

"Not exactly," said Dillman. "May I come in, please?"

"Yes, of course." She stood back to let him in, then noticed the coat that he carried over his arm. "What's that?"

"I hope that you'll be able to tell us." He closed the door behind him, then handed the coat to Jane. "Do you recognize it?"

She inspected it hurriedly. "I'm not sure," she said. "It could be David's coat, I suppose. Was there anything in the pockets?"

"Nothing at all."

"Where was it found?"

"On the main deck."

Jane noticed the torn armpit. "How did this happen?"

"I don't know, Mrs. Lowbury."

Having looked at the outside of the coat, she could not be certain that it belonged to her husband. When she turned her attention to the inside, however, it was a different matter.

"Oh my God!" she exclaimed, swaying slightly.

"Are you all right?" asked Genevieve, moving in to support her.

"It's his — this coat is David's."

"Are you sure of that?"

"Yes," said Jane, pointing to the maker's name. "This was my husband's tailor in New York. It has to be his." She burst into tears. "What's happened to him?"

"Come and sit down again," said Genevieve, helping her to the nearest chair and lowering her into it.

"I want to know where my husband is!"

"The truthful answer," Dillman confessed, "is that we don't know at this stage. But we'll find out, Mrs. Lowbury, I promise you that. If you're absolutely convinced that this coat belonged to your husband, then I'm afraid that we must suspect foul play."

"No!" shrieked Jane. "Who could want to harm David?"

"It could be someone you know," said Genevieve with an arm around her shoulder. "That's why I was asking you about the people you'd met on board."

"But he didn't have an enemy in the world."

"It appears that he did, Mrs. Lowbury," said Dillman quietly.

"Why?" demanded Jane, increasingly distraught. "Why would anyone want to kill him?"

"His billfold is missing. It could be murder for gain."

"What was he doing on the main deck in

the first place?"

"He may not have gone there of his own volition," said Dillman.

"Somebody *forced* him to go? Is that what you're saying?"

"It seems a possibility, Mrs. Lowbury."

"This is unbearable!" howled Jane, staring down at the coat. "They've stolen David from me. They've murdered my husband!"

With a cry of despair she buried her head in the coat.

Sir Arthur and Lady Conan Doyle had been the last to leave Thoda Burbridge. When they returned to their stateroom they were at last able to discuss what had happened during the séance.

"What a singular experience," he remarked. "I'm so glad that we were able to be present."

"It was extraordinary. It removed all my doubts about Mrs. Burbridge. She really can commune with spirits."

"I reserve my judgment on that."

"But you were there, Arthur. You saw what happened."

"I did, but I'm not entirely ready to take it at face value."

"Why not?"

"I suppose that there's always that nag-

242

ging suspicion at the back of my mind that collusion is involved. I *want* to believe, Jean. I'm ninety-nine percent certain that we witnessed a genuine example of psychic powers this evening. But," he added, stroking his mustache, "I wish that the messages had not been solely for Mrs. Trouncer."

"You don't begrudge her, do you?"

"Not at all. I shared in her delight."

"Yet you still think collusion is possible?"

"Unwitting collusion," said Conan Doyle. "Mrs. Trouncer is a nice lady, but she does rather let her tongue run away with her sometimes. The first time I met her she told me about her late husband's love of his garden. I daresay she confided similar information to Mrs. Burbridge without even realizing that she was doing so."

"Well, I have no qualms about what we saw in that cabin."

"Neither do I."

"Then what do you have?"

"A minuscule amount of distrust," he said. "I'll be interested to know what Miss Masefield made of it all."

"Yes — what an enchanting young lady! I'm so grateful that she came in place of that odious Mr. Agnew. He spoiled everything yesterday." She began to take off her jewelry. "Miss Masefield was a much more suitable member of the group. Don't you agree?"

Conan Doyle chuckled. "I never complain about sitting in the dark holding hands with attractive women."

"Arthur!"

"I'm just sorry that Genevieve Masefield wasn't one of them."

"We were there for a serious purpose."

"I know that, Jean," he said, mollifying her with a kiss on the cheek, "and I was thrilled at the way it turned out. I was also relieved that nobody leveled the usual charge against me."

"What do you mean?"

"The apparent contradiction between what I write and what I believe. Most people simply can't accept that I can create an apostle of cold logic like Sherlock Holmes while at the same time espousing the cause of spiritualism."

"I see no contradiction."

"That's because you know me, Jean."

"You're the most consistent person I've ever met."

"Tell that to my critics."

"I always do," she said loyally, putting her earrings on the table. "Just because you went to medical school doesn't mean that you have to agree with everything that science tells you."

"Science tells me that spiritualism is a futile pursuit."

"That hasn't put you off."

"Nor you, Jean."

"To a logical mind, it's ludicrous even to consider the notion that someone can make contact with those who've passed away. Yet that's exactly what Mrs. Burbridge did this evening," she affirmed. "I saw her do it. I heard her speak. I felt I was present at a significant event. How would a scientist have reacted?"

"With complete disbelief, I should imagine."

"Will spiritualism ever be accepted as having validity?"

"No, Jean."

"Why not?"

"Because it's something beyond the bounds of science," he said, "and therefore beyond its control. Science is always very skeptical. It sneered at Newton and his outlandish theories for twenty years. I remember pointing that out in a book of mine."

"I know — it was *The Mystery of Cloomber*."

"Do you recall what else I wrote?"

"Yes, Arthur," she said, turning to face

him. "You reminded your readers that science refused to believe at first that an iron ship could float, let alone steam its way across the Atlantic."

He laughed. "So why aren't we all at the bottom of the sea?"

Having shed his tails in favor of an overcoat, George Dillman climbed into the lifeboat, and using a lantern, subjected it to a thorough search. He found nothing. When he clambered out he helped Wilfred Carr to tie the tarpaulin back in place. The wind had stiffened and the swell had increased. The main deck was not a very hospitable place to be at that time of night.

"Is this where it happened, Mr. Dillman?" asked the steward.

"Possibly. It would be an ideal place. It's isolated and largely shielded from sight. I'll come back again in daylight," said Dillman. "If there was a struggle here, there may be more evidence of it."

"Mr. Lowbury must have been a very rich man."

"He was a financier."

"That coat of his cost more than I earn in a year."

"Does that make you envious?"

"No," said Carr levelly. "I'm alive to spend

my wages. He's never going to wear that coat again, is he?"

"I'm afraid not."

"His wife must have been stunned when you told her."

"She was," said the other. "Mrs. Lowbury is still in a state of shock. We sent for the doctor to see if he could prescribe something."

"Poor lady!"

"I don't know how she's going to cope with this situation. What makes it worse, of course, is that she doesn't know the truth of what actually happened."

"Perhaps it's better if she doesn't, Mr. Dillman."

"She deserves the full facts and somehow I don't think that she'll flinch from them. It will bring some sort of closure."

"What does that mean, sir?"

"Mrs. Lowbury will be able to lay her husband to rest — in her mind, anyway. It would be intolerable if she had to spend the rest of her life brooding on how he might or might not have died." He looked at the steward. "Has there ever been a murder on any of the ships you've sailed on before?"

"No, sir," declared Carr. "We've had deaths from natural causes, mind you, especially in winter. In fact, a woman in steerage died on the westbound voyage. She was buried at sea."

"So, I fear, was Mr. Lowbury."

"Yes."

"And without a proper burial service, by the look of it." Dillman turned to walk away and the steward fell in beside him. "Goodbye, Mr. Carr. I shan't need you again tonight. You've set this investigation in motion. I can't thank you enough for that."

"Find the bastard who did this, sir," said Carr with feeling, "and find him soon. That's all the thanks I want."

Joshua Cleves pored over the chessboard as he considered his next move. Sipping his brandy, Lord Bulstrode watched him with hawklike intensity. Cleves had more pieces intact but he had lost both knights, a bishop and, crucially, his queen. His opponent had sacrificed all his pawns and both castles while retaining what he thought of as his heavy artillery. After patient tactical play, he had Cleves in check.

"Come on," he encouraged.

"Don't rush me, Rupert. I need time."

"I thought we agreed to a maximum of five minutes before each move. You've already exceeded the limit, Joshua."

"Only because you've put me in a damnably awkward position."

"I think you did that yourself," said Lord Bulstrode with contentment. "You didn't anticipate my gambit."

"Call it by its proper name. It was a feat of low cunning."

"That, too, has its place in the game of chess."

Knowing that he could only gain temporary respite, Cleves finally moved his king to get out of check. Lord Bulstrode responded immediately. Two minutes later, it was all over. Checkmate.

"Nice to know we can still beat the Americans at something," said the old man, gathering up the pieces to put in the box. "Thank you, Joshua. It was a good game."

"You caught me on a bad night."

"I had to get my revenge. You won two games this afternoon."

"Then why was I so hopeless now?" asked Cleves, picking up his glass and staring into it. "Did you put something in my brandy?"

"No excuses. You lost fair and square."

"I admit that, Rupert. I was outthought and outgunned."

Cleves sipped his brandy. The two of them were among the small number of survivors in the first-class lounge. Most people had retired to their cabins, but they had stayed up to continue their rivalry on the chess-board.

"Our stateroom would have been more private," said Lord Bulstrode apologetically, "but Agnes wanted to play cards in there with her friends."

"For money?"

"I think that they only use matchsticks. My wife is not a true gambler. She only plays games for the pleasure of it." He gurgled down the last of his drink. "Agnes had hoped that Genevieve Masefield would join her at the card table but she had other plans."

"A meeting of some sort, I believe."

"I suppose you might call it that."

"Go on," said Cleves, intrigued by the mischievous twinkle in the other man's eye. "You know something, don't you?"

"I might do."

"Then share it with a friend."

Lord Bulstrode leaned forward "A little bird tells me that the meeting Miss Mase-field went to this evening was actually a séance."

"Can this be true?" said Cleves in aston-ishment.

"According to my wife, it is. Agnes heard it from our steward, who had, in turn, picked it up from another member of the staff. I first learned about it when I went to collect the chess set. We have a medium aboard, it transpires."

"A crook, more likely."

"Miss Masefield obviously trusts the lady."

"That's what amazes me," said Cleves. "How can someone as level-headed as her believe in all that nonsense about talking to people beyond the grave? It's lunacy."

"Not if you happen to be a lunatic."

"You're surely not defending spiritualism."

"No, but I'm not attacking it either."

"Show me a medium and I'll show you a complete charlatan. How can any intelligent person take an interest in such hogwash?"

"You'll have to ask Sir Arthur Conan Doyle."

"Why?"

"Because he was at the séance as well. I never touch detective fiction myself," said Lord Bulstrode grandly, "because I regard it as one of the lower forms of literature. But I did read what Sir Arthur had to say about the Boer War and I admired the fellow for it. His book was lucid, cogent and extremely well written. In short, we are talking about a highly intelligent man."

"Then how has he been tricked into attending a séance?"

"I should have thought you'd be more interested in how Miss Masefield came to be there."

"I am," said Cleves.

"We've both noticed that you've taken a liking to her."

"What sane man could fail to do that?"

"One sitting beside his wife," said the old man with a wicked smile. "I hope that this revelation about Miss Masefield hasn't made you think any the less of her."

"Nothing could do that, Rupert."

"Then why do you seem to be so disappointed?"

"I don't know," said Cleves, sitting back in his chair. "I suppose that I thought her above that sort of thing. Genevieve Masefield is so poised and sophisticated. How on earth could she be taken in by that nonsense?"

"You obviously misjudged her."

"So it appears. Thank you, Rupert. Thank you very much."

"For what?"

"Showing me that the young lady is not as well defended as I thought. If she believes in spiritualism, there's a definite chink in her armor." He rolled his brandy glass between his palms. "I can't tell you how much I'm looking forward to seeing her again."

"What did the doctor advise?" asked Dillman.

"He suggested a sedative but Mrs. Lowbury refused to take it."

"Why?"

"She doesn't *want* to sleep, George. She feels that she'd be betraying her husband if she does that. She'd rather stay awake and mourn." Genevieve heaved a sigh. "There was no persuading her."

"Is she on her own now?"

"Yes. I offered to stay with her but she insisted on being left alone. I told her that she could call on me at any time in the night."

"That was kind of you, Genevieve."

"I hate to see anyone in such anguish."

They were in Dillman's cabin. She had met him there to hear about his visit to the main deck and to report on Jane Lowbury's condition. Genevieve was worried about her.

"She wouldn't even ask for some pills from him, George."

"Pills?"

"Mrs. Lowbury has mild palpitations from time to time. That's why she asked her husband to fetch the pills from their cabin.

253

Everything that's happened in the past few hours must have made her heart pound, yet she wouldn't take anything from the doctor."

"Why not?"

"Because she feared he might slip her a sedative."

"Did he examine her?"

"She wouldn't allow it," said Genevieve. "When she stopped crying she walked up and down that cabin as if trying to wear out the carpet. She talked incessantly about her husband and how happy they'd been together. They hadn't known each other all that long."

"Perhaps that was the problem."

"In what way?"

"I fancy that Mrs. Lowbury is only aware of her husband's virtues," he said. "She hasn't found out if he had any vices yet or if there are things in his past that might have put him in jeopardy."

"She loved him, George."

"It blinded her to his faults."

"Not necessarily," she said, stroking his arm. "I love you but it hasn't blinded me to your faults."

"I don't have any, Genevieve."

"That's the first of them — complacence."

"Then I'm not going to ask what the others are," he said with a laugh, slipping his arms around her waist. "I've missed you."

"So I should hope."

"I really needed you when the alarm was first raised."

"Yes," said Genevieve, "I feel so bad about that. I should have been here to help, not sitting in Thoda Burbridge's cabin."

"What happened at the séance? We've been so busy since you got back that I haven't had time to ask. Was it a success?"

"I think so."

"What about the others?"

"Oh, they were equally impressed," said Genevieve. "In fact, Mrs. Trouncer was almost ecstatic."

"Why?"

"She received messages from her late husband."

Genevieve explained what had taken place at the séance and how her prejudices against spiritualism had been slowly eroded. The demonstration by Thoda Burbridge had won her over completely.

"Even you would have been convinced, George."

"I don't convince very easily."

"I know. It's another of those faults I mentioned."

"Stop teasing," he said, pulling her close

and kissing her. "And you've no need to feel guilty about going. You not only met Sir Arthur and Lady Conan Doyle, you gathered useful intelligence."

"Yes, I did. I'm able to alert you."

"To what?"

"Sophie Trouncer," she said. "The last thing her husband said to her was that it was time for her to start afresh with a second husband." She grinned. "You'll have to learn to dodge her."

"I will, have no fear." He hugged her. "I'm sorry, darling."

"For what?"

"I promised you this voyage would be free of any of the usual complications. Yet here we are with a murder on our hands."

"Not to mention a theft."

"Yes," he said, "we mustn't let one crime obscure the other. As it happens, I've been thinking about *A Study in Scarlet.*"

"Have you?"

"I'm wondering if we're looking in the right direction."

"I don't follow."

"Well, we've assumed that the thief is either an admirer of the book or someone who wants to exploit its commercial value."

"Who else could it be, George?"

"Someone who despises the book."

"I haven't read it," said Genevieve, "so I'm not really qualified to judge, but I thought that it was universally praised."

"So did I."

"Then why should anyone despise it?"

"Because of its unrelenting attack on their beliefs," he told her. "The first half of the book is about some murders that baffle Scotland Yard. By using deductive reasoning, Sherlock Holmes, who describes himself as a consulting detective, eventually solves the crimes."

"What about the second half of the book?"

"That's set very largely in America."

"America?"

"In Utah, to be exact," he told her. "Actually, it's the only part of the novel where Sir Arthur falters a little. He doesn't really have complete control of the American idiom. It leads to a few jarring moments. But that's a minor complaint," he went on. "What he gives us is a thrilling story that clearly explains why the murders were committed."

"And why were they?"

"Because of what happened in a Mormon community in Utah."

Genevieve was curious. "There are Mormons in the book?"

"The whole plot turns on their doctrine of polygamy. Sir Arthur pours scorn on it,

257

arguing that women are forced into marriages that have no right to bear the name. He portrays the Mormons as cruel, inflexible and intimidating. How true that is I can't say," admitted Dillman, "but I know that I'd be deeply offended by the novel if I was a devout Mormon. Perhaps we have one on board."

"We do, George."

"Really?"

"Philip Agnew was raised in the Mormon Church. At least, that's what Thoda Burbridge sensed about him. According to Mrs. Trouncer, he denied it hotly, but I wonder if he was lying."

"Running a menagerie is hardly a Mormon activity."

"No," she said, "but he might still have loyalties to the Church. *A Study in Scarlet* could still cause him offense."

"How could it when he's never even read it?"

"He doesn't have to read it to be aware of its harsh criticism of Mormon doctrines. Most churches have a list of banned books."

"Mine certainly did," he said reflectively. "Our preacher was always condemning certain writers from the pulpit because he felt they were unchristian. I used to sneak off to the library to find out why those books had upset him so much."

"And did you?"

"No, I always enjoyed the books immensely."

"So you disobeyed your preacher."

He smiled. "You'll have to add that to my list of faults."

"Coming back to the theft, do you take my point, George?"

"I can see that a Mormon might be outraged by *A Study in Scarlet,* but how could Mr. Agnew possibly know that Sir Arthur had a copy with him?"

"Perhaps he didn't," she argued. "By way of revenge, he went to steal anything written by Sir Arthur Conan Doyle and happened on that particular novel."

"But he was taking part in the séance."

"Not for the whole time. Mr. Agnew was so disappointed with what happened that he stalked out early on."

"Knowing that Sir Arthur and his wife were still absent from their stateroom." Dillman pursed his lips in thought. "This may have nothing to do with him being a Mormon," he continued. "Philip Agnew had another reason to detest Sir Arthur — he's killed animals. If he did steal that book, he might have done it out of sheer spite."

"Would you describe Mr. Agnew as a

spiteful man?"

"Oh, yes. Extremely spiteful."

Nobby Ruggles waited until his first customer had settled into the chair before putting a cape of crisp white linen around him. Tying it at the back of the man's neck, he glanced in the mirror so that he could see Philip Agnew's face.

"A trim, sir?"

"Yes, but don't take too much off. I've got little enough hair as it is. Just tidy it up, please."

"Of course, sir."

Ruggles swiveled the chair slightly so that he could look at his customer from the front, then he used his comb to train a few wayward strands back into place. Most of the surviving hair had retreated to the fringes, but there was still a narrow band stretching across the top of his head like a hirsute bridge across a dome of baldness. Having sized up his task, Ruggles reached for his scissors and began work.

"Did you go to the concert yesterday, sir?" he asked.

"No," said Agnew bluntly.

"Then you missed some wonderful entertainment. The purser always takes part. Mr. Rutherford plays the clarinet."

"I've got no time for music."

"Then you would have enjoyed the conjurer."

"I doubt it."

"The act that everyone really enjoyed was the lady with the performing dog. It was a poodle and she's taught it lots of tricks."

"Then I'm glad I wasn't there," said Agnew brusquely. "I hate performing animals of any kind. I own a menagerie where I give my animals as much dignity as I can. Circuses are the worst. They make lions, tigers, elephants and seals do things that the creatures would never do in the wild. I think it's shameful. I love animals. I'd never humiliate them."

"But the dog seemed to enjoy doing the tricks."

"Why couldn't the owner just let it be a dog?"

During his years as a barber Nobby Ruggles had learned never to upset a customer. To that end he never talked about politics, religion or marriage, three subjects that could easily become too controversial. If any of his customers broached them, Ruggles took the line of least resistance and agreed with everything they said. Agnew was evidently not a man with whom to pick an argument. Instead, Ruggles asked politely about the menagerie and heard how it had been set up and developed.

When the topic had been exhausted, Ruggles brought the conversation back to the concert. He beamed proudly.

"There'll be another concert this afternoon, sir."

"Thanks for the warning."

"I only mention it because I'll be one of the artistes."

"What do you do?" asked Agnew. "Cut someone's hair on stage?"

"No, sir. I recite poems."

"That's worse than watching a poodle stand on its hind legs."

"My work has been well received," said Ruggles defensively. "At yesterday's concert I gave a performance of 'Corporal Dick's Promotion' and got a big round of applause. The man who wrote the poem also congratulated me and you can't have higher praise than that. Sir Arthur thought I had a real talent."

Agnew grimaced. "Would that be Sir Arthur Conan Doyle?"

"Yes, sir."

"I dislike the man."

"He's one of my idols."

"I don't approve of any man who slaughters animals."

"You should have seen what he did for us during the Boer War."

"Who cares about that?"

"I do, sir. I was there, in the British army."

"Then show your medals to someone else," said Agnew sourly. "All I know about the Boer War is that the British army went to South Africa and killed thousands of wild animals."

"We had to eat, sir."

"Live off fruit and vegetables as I do. It's healthier for you."

"Shall I tell you why I respect Sir Arthur so much?"

"Not unless you want me to call for another barber. What's your name, by the way?"

"Ruggles, sir. Nobby Ruggles."

"Are you allowed to take tips?"

Ruggles's face brightened. "Yes, sir."

"Well, you won't get one if you mention that man's name again."

"Sir Arthur?"

"I told you not to mention it!" bellowed Agnew.

"I'm sorry, sir."

"How much longer are you going to be, Ruggles?"

"I'm almost finished."

"Then hurry up and let me out of this

chair," said Agnew, glaring angrily into the mirror. "Hearing about the lady and her poodle was bad enough. But I'm not going to sit here and listen to you talking about Sir Arthur Conan Doyle. I loathe the man."

George Dillman went back to the main deck that morning to take a closer look at the lifeboat in which the frock coat had been found, and to search in its vicinity. The light rain did not deter him. Having peeped into the boat again, he secured the tarpaulin.

"You won't find him in there," said a voice behind him.

Dillman turned to face Saul Pinnick. "Who?"

"Mr. Rush."

"I wasn't looking for anyone of that name."

"He did think about it," said Pinnick. "Sleeping in one of the lifeboats, that is. But he found it too uncomfortable. Sorry," he went on. "We haven't met, have we? I'm Saul Pinnick."

"Pleased to meet you. My name is George Dillman."

"What brought you out here in the rain?"

"I wanted some exercise," said Dillman, careful not to disclose his reason for being there. "You mentioned a Mr. Rush."

"Yes," said Pinnick, "he's like us. He was turned back at Ellis Island because of his bad chest. Mr. Rush was a miner, you see. It's a job that plays havoc with your lungs. He took it hard, being refused entry to America. I'm sorry for him. He'd suffered enough already."

"Had he, Mr. Pinnick?"

"Yes, his wife died on the way to America. Cruel. Mr. Rush was supposed to be the invalid in the family, but she was the one who passed away. It was a real tragedy. She was buried at sea."

"I think I heard about that," said Dillman, recalling what Carr had told him. "Is this gentleman a friend of yours?"

"Not really, but I like to keep an eye on him."

"Why?"

"He worries me, Mr. Dillman," said the old man, pulling up the collar of his overcoat and adjusting his hat. "To lose his wife was a savage blow, but he felt that she'd have wanted him to go on to be an American citizen."

"But he was rejected on health grounds."

"That happened to Mirry and me as well, so I know how it feels. For Mr. Rush, it was like a death sentence. It took away his will to live. He talked about joining his wife in a watery grave."

"He threatened to commit suicide?" said Dillman in dismay.

"In so many words."

"You should have reported this, Mr. Pinnick. The chaplain could have spoken to him and tried to give him some peace of mind."

"It would have been a waste of time."

"Is he still on board?"

"Oh, yes. I saw him at breakfast earlier on. He was as pale as a ghost," said Pinnick sorrowfully, "but who wouldn't be after spending the night on deck?"

"So he really did sleep out here?"

"He did, Mr. Dillman, and he wasn't the only one."

It was a useful reminder. Every time Dillman had crossed the Atlantic, some steerage passengers had chosen to remain on deck at night unless a gale was blowing. Instead of sharing a small cabin with three, or even five, other people, they elected to brave the elements to get a measure of privacy. Dillman was bound to wonder if any of those curled up on deck had witnessed anything suspicious the previous night.

"Where would I find this Mr. Rush?" he asked.

"I couldn't say. He comes and goes."

"But he turns up for his meals?"

"Yes, Mr. Dillman. That's the one hopeful sign I've had from him. It's like I told Mirry — she's my wife. A condemned man is always given a hearty breakfast before execution, but Mr. Rush has decided that he likes lunch and dinner as well." He wiped his face as rain was blown in under the brim of his hat. "It's getting much worse. I'm going back indoors. What about you?"

"I'll continue my stroll, Mr. Pinnick."

"Good-bye."

Dillman waved him off. Pinnick scurried away and disappeared through a door. After pulling his hat down, Dillman carried on with his search, bending down to look under the lifeboat and along the bottom of the bulwark. At first he could see nothing, so he moved a few yards to the left, still without success. He was about to move to the other side of the boat when he saw something out of the corner of his eye. It was a tiny white object floating in a little puddle that had formed against the bulwark. Dillman picked it up and realized what he was holding. Sodden and misshapen, it was a business card.

He could just make out the name on it — Frank Spurrier.

■ ■ ■ ■

When she knocked on the cabin door, Genevieve Masefield had to wait some while before it opened. Jane Lowbury looked tired and forlorn. Having shed her evening dress, she was wearing a dressing gown and slippers. She seemed smaller and frailer than Genevieve recalled.

"How do you feel today, Mrs. Lowbury?"

"Not very well."

"I spoke to your steward," said Genevieve. "He told me that you refused to eat any breakfast this morning."

"I'm not hungry, Miss Masefield."

"You must have something."

"Later, perhaps."

"Do you want some company?"

"No, thank you," said Jane. "I just want to be on my own." She rallied slightly. "Have you found out anything else?"

"Mr. Dillman is conducting a search at this moment."

"Does he think there's any chance that David is still alive?"

"We must never give up hope, Mrs. Lowbury," said Genevieve, trying to sound optimistic. "I know that this is not the best time for you, but we would like to talk to you again in due course."

"Why? What can I tell you?"

"More than you may realize," said Genevieve. "You may have information that can help us to solve this crime. We'd like you to reconstruct, in your own mind, everything that happened to you and your husband since you boarded the ship — every last detail. Write it down, if need be. Could you do that for us, please?"

"I can try, Miss Masefield."

"Thank you. And if you need me, don't hesitate to call. Your steward will soon find me."

"You're very kind."

"Did you get any sleep last night?"

"Not really," said Jane. "I dozed off for an hour or so, but that was all. I keep thinking about what happened to David." She bit her lip. "Excuse me. I'll have to go."

"Of course."

Holding back tears, Jane closed the door. Genevieve wished that she could have offered more comfort to the woman. It made her think of her own situation. Married by the captain on board a P&O cruiser on which they were working at the time, she and Dillman had spent the first weeks of their marriage sailing first-class to Australia. Even though they had duties to discharge, it had been an idyllic time. Genevieve could imagine how she would have felt if her husband had been snatched away from her while they were on their honeymoon.

She turned away from the cabin and walked down the corridor. Someone came around a corner ahead of her and seeing Genevieve, greeted her with a cheerful wave. Thoda Burbridge hurried forward, her ample frame and double chin wobbling in unison.

"Good morning!" she called.

"Good morning, Mrs. Burbridge."

"I hoped to see you over breakfast."

"I ate it in my cabin today," said Genevieve. "But I must thank you again for letting me join you at the séance. It was captivating."

"Sir Arthur called it mesmerizing, and he chose the word with care. As a doctor he had a particular fascination with Mesmer, a physician who achieved miracle cures with the aid of hypnotism."

"You achieved a small miracle yourself last night. To be honest, I came into your cabin as a skeptic, but I left as a believer."

"I'm so glad that everything worked," said Thoda. "I'd have felt such a fool lugging that table of mine aboard without using it in a successful séance. All the vibrations were right, you see."

"Unlike the first attempt."

"I'd rather forget that, Miss Masefield. I made the mistake of inviting that American gentleman, Mr. Agnew. He was not in sympathy with what the rest of us were trying to do."

"I believe that you sensed something about him."

"I did — he challenged me to do so. When I proved that I could unearth something about him, he became rather truculent. I knew that he had once been a Mormon and that provoked him."

"Why? Is he ashamed of his past?"

"Who knows?" She stifled a laugh. "There is one explanation, I suppose, but it's too unkind on him, so perhaps I shouldn't voice it."

"No, no. Do go ahead."

"Well, he came to me in the hope that I could put him in touch with his late wife. Since I revealed that he'd been a Mormon, he was afraid I'd ask, '*Which* wife?' He may have been married to several." She raised an eloquent eyebrow. "I'm relieved I wasn't one of them."

"I'm told there was some friction between him and Sir Arthur."

"That was entirely Mr. Agnew's fault.

Everything was going well until Sir Arthur mentioned that he had once been a surgeon on a whaling boat. The way that Mr. Agnew turned on him you'd have thought he'd committed a heinous crime."

"Did he strike you as a man who bears grudges?"

"Mr. Agnew? Oh, yes," said Thoda darkly. "He never forgives."

"Will you be holding any more séances?"

"I don't think so. They always exhaust me."

"Then you're entitled to rest on the remainder of the voyage."

"I'm not allowed to, unfortunately, Miss Masefield."

"Why not?"

"Having psychic powers can be a burden sometimes. My mind keeps picking up things when my body would rather just relax. What you saw last night was an example of automatic writing," she went on. "The words just come to me in a steady flow."

"You made Mrs. Trouncer very happy."

"If only I could do the same for you!"

"Oh, I was more than content to be an observer last night."

"I'm not talking about the séance, Miss Masefield. When I woke up this morning I had a presentiment and it alarmed me somewhat."

"What kind of presentiment?"

"It concerns your husband."

"But you've never even met him, Mrs. Burbridge."

"Yes, I have — through you, Miss Masefield. You and he are very close, so I sense things that affect both of you."

"And what did you learn this morning?"

"Something very disturbing," said Thoda, taking her gently by the wrist. "You must warn him before it's too late."

"Warn him about what?" asked Genevieve.

"The fact that his life is in grave danger."

TEN

Since his wife had an appointment there that morning, Conan Doyle accompanied her to the hair salon, intending to go on to the library. To do so, he had to walk straight past Nobby Ruggles in the men's salon, and the barber caught sight of him through the window. Excusing himself from his customer, Ruggles brushed some hair from his sleeve and hurried out to waylay the author.

"Good morning, Sir Arthur," he said.

"Ah — hello there, Ruggles."

"Have you come for that free haircut?"

"Not just yet, I'm afraid."

"Any time, sir. I'm always here."

"I daresay you're kept very busy in there."

"Not as busy as the ladies' hairdressers," said Ruggles. "An average haircut for a man will take twenty minutes — half an hour, if it includes a shave as well. In the ladies' salon, customers can be there for hours. It's difficult to keep up a conversation for that long."

"Yes," said Conan Doyle, "I suppose that's part of your stock-in-trade, isn't it? Being able to chat to your clients."

"I listen more than I talk, sir. This job is an education. I've learned so much from various customers."

"And it's a lot safer than being in the army."

"Safer but not so exciting," said Ruggles. "I often think of my days in uniform. They gave me so many memories."

"Not all of them happy ones, alas," observed Conan Doyle.

"No, Sir Arthur." He stepped in closer. "But while you're here, I'd like to take this chance of passing on some information."

"Information?"

"It's about an America gentleman who came for a haircut earlier on. If I were you, sir, I'd keep well out of his way."

"Why?"

"He was a most unpleasant man. He said that he knew you."

"Are you talking about Philip Agnew, by any chance?"

"The very same."

"Then you've no need to tell me any more," said Conan Doyle with distaste.

"Mr. Agnew and I crossed swords on sight. Because I happened to have killed a few seals in younger days, he thinks I'm the most wicked man since Herod the Great."

Ruggles thrust out his chest. "I did speak up for you."

"Thank you. I appreciate that."

"It only seemed to annoy him even more."

"Mr. Agnew is rather too easily annoyed. But," he added with a sigh, "one must be charitable, I suppose. The fellow is still suffering from the death of his wife. I know, from personal experience, how distressing that can be."

"He was downright rude," said Ruggles, "and there's no excuse for that. I'll not let anyone run you down."

"Good man, Ruggles."

"I just thought I ought to mention it to you." He glanced over his shoulder and made to leave. "I've got a customer waiting, so I must go."

"Good-bye."

He paused. "Oh, I forgot to mention the main thing, Sir Arthur."

"What's that?"

"This afternoon's concert. I'll be taking part again."

"Good for you," said Conan Doyle, dreading what was to come.

"I thought I'd give them another gem from the master," said Ruggles with a grin, "so I chose your poem 'the Groom's Story.' "

"Why not recite something from Kipling?"

"Because there's nothing to compare with this."

Adopting a stance, Ruggles declaimed the first verse at speed.

"Ten mile in twenty minutes! 'E done it, sir.
    That's true.
The big bay 'orse in the further stall — the
    one wot's next to you.
I've seen some better 'orses; I've seldom
    seen a wuss,
But 'e 'olds the bloomin' record, an' that's
    good enough for us."

Conan Doyle quailed inwardly. He did not want a repetition of the previous day, when he was dragged reluctantly into the public gaze. Nobby Ruggles hovered as if expecting applause.

"You won't be able to miss the concert now, sir."

"That depends on my wife," said Conan Doyle, groping for an excuse. "It's possible that she may have other plans."

"Lady Conan Doyle can't miss one of

your poems."

"She's read them all many times, Ruggles."

"But it's not the same as seeing them brought to life."

"Indeed not. You certainly fill them with drama."

Ruggles clapped his hands. "I've just had an idea."

"What is it?"

"If you can't get to the concert this afternoon," said the barber helpfully, "I can give you a private performance in your cabin. How does that sound, Sir Arthur?"

Choking back a reply, Conan Doyle pointed at the salon.

"Your customer is getting impatient, Ruggles. Go to him."

Dillman received the warning with complete equanimity. Genevieve could not believe he was so calm when she herself was so worried.

"You have to take it seriously, George," she said.

"I do," he replied, "but I didn't need Mrs. Burbridge to tell me that I was in danger. Whenever we hunt a murderer we put ourselves at risk. If someone has killed once, they'll have no compunction about killing again. That's why we have to be on guard all the time."

"Perhaps you should go armed."

"That's a last resort, Genevieve. I'll only be courting peril when I start to get close to the man, and I'm some way off from doing that. I'm still not certain of his motive."

"The one you suggested to Mrs. Lowbury."

"Murder for gain?"

"Yes, George. His billfold was stolen."

"You don't have to kill a man in order to steal from him. You could knock him unconscious or simply pick his pocket. No, I think that David Lowbury was singled out for another reason. It's our job to find out what it was." He took the business card from his pocket. "We can start with this gentleman."

She read the card. "Frank Spurrier?"

"I found it on the main deck near that lifeboat."

"There's no mystery there. Mrs. Lowbury told me that her husband had Mr. Spurrier's business card. It must have dropped out of the pocket when his coat was removed."

"That's one explanation."

"What's the other?"

"David Lowbury was sending a final message."

"You mean that he deliberately left the card there?"

"It's a possibility we have to consider," said Dillman. "What puzzled me was how Mr. Lowbury got to the main deck in the first place. If he'd been killed or overpowered near his cabin, it would have taken a strong man to carry him there. But," he continued, taking the card from her, "if he'd been held at gunpoint, he could have been forced to walk there."

"Knowing that he was about to die," said Genevieve, following his train of thought, "he wanted to identify his killer, so he dropped the card." She shook her head. "No, George. I don't believe that Frank Spurrier is implicated. He's a respectable businessman."

"We've arrested quite a few of those over the years."

"He'd befriended David Lowbury. Why kill him?"

"I don't know, Genevieve."

"In any case, the murder took place while Mr. Spurrier was having dinner. He couldn't be in two places at once."

"Granted," said Dillman. "Though I've yet to confirm that he was actually in the dining saloon last night. He certainly didn't take up his usual seat opposite David and

Jane Lowbury."

"Do you know why that was?"

"Yes, I asked him."

"What did he say?"

"That he had no wish to eat with Mr. Lowbury. They may have been friends at one point but they seem to have had an argument, and it left a bitter taste in Spurrier's mouth."

"Did he tell you what the argument was over?"

"No, Genevieve, but the gentleman with whom you've been dining was there at the time."

"Joshua Cleves?"

"He, too, spoke harshly of Mr. Lowbury."

"Then the argument must have been quite serious. It takes a lot to upset Mr. Cleves. He's the most tolerant and carefree man I've ever met. Nothing seems to trouble him."

"David Lowbury did."

"Why did you speak to them?"

"I only intended to talk to Spurrier," said Dillman, "but he refused a private discussion. Since Cleves was in the lounge with him, he heard everything I had to say. Mrs. Lowbury was puzzled by the fact that Spurrier had not sat at their table. When I asked him if he'd been in the dining saloon earlier, he more or less exploded."

"Frank Spurrier?"

"You'd have thought I'd accused him of high treason."

"That's most unlike him," said Genevieve. "He's always so calm and collected. In fact, it's that icy control of his that unnerved me when I first met him. I can't imagine him losing his temper."

"I was on the receiving end of it."

"Did you tell him that David Lowbury had disappeared?"

"Of course."

"And what was his response to that?"

"Good riddance!"

Genevieve was puzzled. Everything she had heard was completely at variance with what she knew of Frank Spurrier and, indeed, of Joshua Cleves. She wondered what could possibly have upset them so much. It could not have been the way that Dillman had approached them. He was always tactful and discreet. The argument with David Lowbury had clearly cut deep.

"I daresay you want *me* to speak to Mr. Spurrier," she said.

"No, Genevieve, we'll hold off for a while."

"But that card might be the clue we need."

"We can't even be certain that it is a clue," he said realistically. "Speculation is one thing — proof is quite another. It's important that Spurrier doesn't know that you're a detective or he'll clam up on you as well. I think you should creep up on him from another direction."

"You want me to talk to Joshua Cleves instead, is that it?"

"Yes. He and Spurrier are obviously friends. They'll be aware of each other's movements. As you and Cleves are dining companions, you can speak to him without arousing suspicion."

"What am I to find out, George?"

"Why he and Spurrier fell out with David Lowbury. That could be crucial. Also, of course, I'd like to know if Spurrier was in the dining saloon last night, and if so, did he leave at any point during the meal?" Genevieve let out a gasp of surprise. "What's wrong?"

"I've just remembered something."

"You saw him there?"

"No," she said, "but I know someone who did slip away from the table at one point — Joshua Cleves."

It was the second report that morning and it worried the purser. The *Celtic* had sailed over halfway across the Atlantic and the only crime that had occurred had been the theft of a book written by Sir Arthur Conan Doyle. Within the space of the past twelve hours, Nelson Rutherford also had to contend with a possible murder and two burglaries. The woman sitting opposite him in his office was May Hoyland and she was quivering with concern.

"When did you first become aware of the theft?" he asked.

"Not until after breakfast, Mr. Rutherford."

"Where was the necklace kept?"

"In a box. I know that I should have had it locked away in a safe," she went on hurriedly, "but it's very dear to me and I like to have it to hand. We had no trouble at all when we sailed to America. Nothing was taken from our cabin."

"But the only thing that went astray this time was a diamond necklace?"

"That's right. Sophie — my daughter, that is — was wearing her jewelry. I was foolish enough to take the necklace off and leave it unguarded in the cabin."

"How did you discover that it had gone?"

"I lifted the box this morning and felt how light it was."

"I see," said the purser. "I suppose there's no possibility that you could have put the necklace down somewhere else in the cabin?"

May smiled wryly. "I may be getting old, Mr. Rutherford, but I'm not senile yet. When I take it off, that necklace always goes straight into its box. It was a wedding present from my second husband. I cherish it. I'm extremely careful how I handle it."

He jotted down the details on a notepad. He was tempted to point out that if Mrs. Hoyland valued the necklace that much, she should never have left it alone in her cabin, but that would only have been adding further pain. She freely accepted that she was to blame. His task was to console her.

"What are the chances of getting it back?" she said hopefully.

"Very strong, Mrs. Hoyland," he replied. "We have some excellent detectives on board. They're very experienced in this sort of thing."

She was disturbed. "Are you saying that the White Star Line is plagued by thieves?"

"Far from it. What's happened is the exception to the rule."

"Yet you told me earlier that I was the second victim."

"Let's just concentrate on your necklace, shall we?" he said, trying to still her anxiety. "You returned to your cabin shortly after dinner. Is that correct?"

"Yes, Mr. Rutherford. I took off the necklace there and then."

"Intending to undress for bed."

"That's right," she said.

"Where was your daughter at the time?"

"Attending a séance. I knew that she might be late coming back, so I thought I'd read while I was waiting for her. I'd already finished one book, so I decided to pop along to the library to borrow another."

"How long were you away?"

"No more than fifteen or twenty minutes."

"That's when the theft must have occurred because it was the only time the cabin was unoccupied."

"We had breakfast served there instead of going to the dining saloon. I take a long time to wake up in the mornings," she told him. "And I'm not ready to face the world until I've had breakfast. When I discovered that my necklace had gone, of course, I wished that I hadn't touched a thing. I felt sick, Mr. Rutherford. I was shocked."

"That's a natural reaction. Most of us would feel the same." His sympathy was tempered with quiet resolve. "I'm terribly sorry this has happened, Mrs. Hoyland, and I can assure you that we'll get on the trail of the thief at once. The one thing I need from you, however, is a description of the stolen item."

"Oh, I can do better than that." She opened her purse to take something out. "I have a photograph. We had it taken for the purpose of insurance."

"Very wise." When she passed it to him, he looked at the sepia photograph and saw the impressive array of diamonds. "May I ask for how much the necklace is insured?"

"Fifteen hundred guineas," she said with a nostalgic smile. "My second husband worshipped me."

Genevieve did not have to search for him. As soon as she entered the lounge, Joshua Cleves got up from his seat and came across to her.

"Good morning," he said. "I missed you at breakfast."

"I had it in my cabin."

"It would have been even more delightful to share it with you there." He flashed a smile at her. "Will you at least join me for coffee?"

"That would be very nice, Mr. Cleves."

"You simply must stop calling me that. It's so formal."

"I'm sorry," she said, wanting to win his

confidence. "From now on, Joshua it shall be."

"Thank you, Genevieve."

When they had sat down, he summoned a waiter with a flick of his fingers and ordered coffee. Then he appraised her with a mingled curiosity and doubt.

"Is something the matter?" she asked.

"I'm not sure," he said. "I feel as if I'm looking at a magnificent portrait and wondering if there's a tiny flaw in it."

"Why should you wonder that?"

"Because of that meeting you went to last night."

"Ah, I see. You found out."

"Rupert told me. Apparently, his wife heard about it from their steward. I have to admit that I was rather shocked by the news. What on earth persuaded you to go to a séance, Genevieve?"

"I was invited and thought it might be fun."

"Fun? You must know the whole thing was an elaborate hoax."

"But it wasn't, Joshua."

"What did the lady do?" he teased. "Conjure up the devil? Or make a ring of fairies dance on a pinhead?"

"Mrs. Burbridge simply acted as a conduit for messages."

"Messages from the dead, I presume?"

"Yes."

"And who made contact with you — the spirit of Queen Victoria?"

"If you're going to sneer," she said tartly, "then we'd better not discuss the subject."

"No, no, I'm not sneering," he claimed. "I'm quite sincere. I want to know why someone as sensible and well educated as you could be drawn into such a dubious gathering."

"You're quite right. It was dubious. I went into the cabin with the greatest reservations. I *expected* to be tricked in some way. Yet I wasn't, Joshua. I witnessed something I'd not have believed possible."

"How much did the medium charge you?"

"Nothing at all."

"What about the others?"

"The only clients who pay her are those who are put in touch with someone from their past, and they decide for themselves what the fee is. I paid nothing, and neither did Sir Arthur and Lady Conan Doyle. Mrs. Trouncer was the only person who felt obliged to offer some money."

"Why was that?"

"Because the messages came from her husband."

"Did you honestly believe that?"

Genevieve chose her words with care. "I did so at the time."

"But, on reflection, you realize you were all bamboozled."

"That's not what I said."

"Then you've discovered that this Mrs. Trouncer and the medium are actually confederates who work together to exploit impressionable people. That's why these so-called messages rang true."

"Sophie Trouncer is traveling with her mother. She'd never met Mrs. Burbridge until this voyage. If they're in partnership together," said Genevieve crisply, "they didn't do very well last night. The only money seen was the amount exchanged between them."

"That was a clever ruse to draw the rest of you in. At the next séance, these fake messages will be for you and the others."

"There's no chance of that, Joshua."

"Oh?"

"According to Mrs. Burbridge, there'll be no more sittings."

"What a pity!" he said. "I'd have been sorely tempted to come along myself and expose the medium as the fraud she is. But I'm relieved to hear that you won't be duped for a second time."

"Perhaps I was," she conceded, wanting

to move away from the subject, "but it was nevertheless a fascinating occasion." She looked around. "But I expected you to be in here with Lord Bulstrode. He seems to have adopted you."

"There's a limit to how many games of chess even I can play."

She looked him in the eye. "I thought you were playing one at this very moment, Joshua."

"Can you blame me?" he said with an appreciative laugh.

"That depends on what the rules are. For instance, how many of us are actually involved in the game?"

"Just the two of us, Genevieve. Who needs anyone else?"

"Mr. Spurrier appears to think that I do."

He chuckled. "What's Frank been up to now?"

"You can answer that," she said, watching him. "When I'm not talking to you, I keep finding him at my elbow. It's almost as if you take it in turns and I have to say that it's very annoying. Perhaps you'd be kind enough to tell him that."

"Tell him yourself," he advised. "Frank and I are only business acquaintances. If he's bothering you, speak to him about it. My guess is that he's jealous because I've had more attention from you." Seeing the expression on her face, he corrected himself. "Or, to be more precise, it's because of attention you've been receiving from *me*."

"How well do you know him?"

"Moderately well."

"So you don't know much about his private life?"

"He keeps that very secret."

"Does he have something to hide?"

"We all do, Genevieve — even you, I suspect."

His gaze was searching but she met it. A tension was suddenly hanging in the air. She was grateful when the waiter arrived with a tray of coffee to dispel the uncomfortable sensation she experienced. He stayed long enough to serve the coffee, then backed away.

"Frank Spurrier is like a chameleon," Cleves volunteered. "He can change color to suit any occasion." He raised a hand. "I'm not decrying him in any way. It's an art I wish that I could master."

"He always seems so devious to me. And there's something about him that's quite chilling."

"Yet he regards himself as essentially a ladies' man."

"There's no real warmth there," said

Genevieve, working her way around to the question she wanted to ask. "Mr. Spurrier is cold and unemotional. He looks like the sort of man who never gets really angry or loses his temper."

"Oh, he does get angry."

"Not in public."

"You're quite wrong there."

"Am I?"

"Yes," he said. "I was in the lounge with Frank only yesterday when he took exception to a remark made by Mr. Lowbury. He was very angry — and so, I admit, was I."

"Whatever were you talking about?"

There was a long pause. He tried to cover it with a bland smile but Genevieve had her answer. They had been discussing her.

With his back against the rail, Leonard Rush tried to roll a cigarette. The rain had stopped and the wind had eased, but the roll of the ship made the exercise tricky. George Dillman waited until the man had finally put the cigarette between his lips and lighted it.

"Mr. Rush?" he asked, coming forward.

"Yes," said the other, "that's me."

"My name is George Dillman, and though I may not look it, I'm part of the crew. I understand that you sleep on deck."

"Nothing wrong in that, is there?"

"A great deal, in these temperatures."

"I bring blankets with me."

It was encouraging news. Dillman felt that if the man were bent on suicide, he would hardly take such precautions to keep himself warm. Pulling on his cigarette, Rush looked as desperate and haunted as ever. He became suspicious.

"That old man put you on to me, didn't he? Saul Pinnick."

"I did speak to Mr. Pinnick, as it happens."

"You've come to talk me out of it."

"Out of what?"

"Are you the ship's chaplain?"

"No, Mr. Rush," said Dillman. "I'm not. And I haven't come to talk you out of anything. I just wanted to ask you a few questions."

"About what?"

"Sleeping on deck."

"The only way I get privacy."

"You pay a high price for it. For most of the night, it rained."

"Why should you care?"

"Because I'm interested in what happens down here on the main deck. You're not alone, I gather. Other passengers do the same thing."

"We keep out of each other's way."

"And do you actually get to sleep?"

"Now and again," said Rush, regarding him with displeasure. "At least, I'm not trapped in a cabin with three other men."

"You should be used to that, surely. You were a miner."

Rush was angry. "What else has Pinnick been telling you about me? I told him to mind his own business."

"He cares about you, Mr. Rush," said Dillman. "Much more than you care about yourself, by the look of it."

"You tell him to stay away from me."

"Kindness is in short supply. You should never spurn it." Rush gave a reluctant nod of agreement. "Did you see anyone else on the main deck last night? I don't mean fellow passengers who sleep out here. These would probably have been two well-dressed men."

"It was dark, Mr. Dillman. And I only have one good eye."

"There might have been the noise of a scuffle."

"I didn't hear it."

"Would you tell me, if you had?"

"No," said Rush flatly.

"Why not?"

"Because I don't poke my nose in where

295

it's not wanted, that's why. I'm not like Pinnick. I mind my own business."

"That means you *did* see something."

"Good-bye, Mr. Dillman," said the other pointedly.

"What was it?"

"Leave me alone."

"Just answer my question."

"Leave me, I said. That's not too much to ask, is it?"

"But this could be important."

"Not to me."

"I need your help, Mr. Rush."

"Ask someone else. I'm busy."

"You could be holding back vital information."

"That's better than badgering the life out of someone, the way you're doing." He glared at Dillman. "I saw nothing, heard nothing and smelled nothing. Satisfied now?"

When she received the summons, Genevieve Masefield went straight to the purser's office where she was told about the thefts that had occurred. Jewelry had been stolen from two different women. Unaware of the fact that she was Sophie Trouncer's mother, the first person she called on was May Hoyland. After introducing herself, Genevieve was invited into the cabin. Sophie goggled at her.

"You're a *detective?*" she said incredulously.

"Yes, Mrs. Trouncer."

"Why didn't you say so?"

"Because I work more effectively if I do so undercover," said Genevieve. "I'm sorry if you feel that I deceived you, but it's in the nature of my work."

"Is that why you went to the séance last night?" asked Sophie, glowering at her. "Was it to spy on Thoda Burbridge in case you had to arrest her for fraud?"

"No, Mrs. Trouncer. I was there out of sheer curiosity."

"What does it matter?" asked May Hoyland. "Miss Masefield is here to talk to me now. That's all that worries me."

"The purser has given me the details," said Genevieve, turning to the older woman. "I just have a few additional questions."

"Ask anything you want."

"Was last night the first time you wore the diamond necklace?"

"No." Sophie answered first. "Mother has worn it every night we've been on board."

"The question was put to me," said May reproachfully.

"I can't see why it was asked in the first place."

"It's quite simple," Genevieve explained. "If it had been on display already, the thief would have had time to take note of it and find out which cabin you occupied. Then he waited."

May was uneasy. "The very thought makes me shiver," she said nervously. "Do you think this man stalked me?"

"Let's just say that he seized his opportunity when it came."

"How did he get into the cabin?"

"He was a professional thief. He picked the lock."

"That's frightening! I thought we were safe in our cabins."

"You are, Mrs. Hoyland, I assure you. He only struck when you weren't here. It was the same with the other lady," Genevieve went on, "though, in her case, the theft took place while she was at dinner. She came back to find the contents of her jewelry box missing."

"Good gracious!"

"It makes you afraid to wear any jewelry at all," said Sophie, putting an instinctive hand to the emerald brooch on her dress. "We've been too trusting, Mother."

"I won't make that mistake again."

"The main reason your diamond necklace was taken," Genevieve resumed, "was that it has a high commercial value. A jewel thief will only pick out the best, but to do that he must have a close look at it. Now, Mrs. Hoyland, can you think of anyone who took an unusual interest in your necklace, someone who complimented you on it?"

"Lots of people did that — ladies, mostly."

"What about men?"

"That adorable Mr. Dillman noticed it because he sits opposite us at meals, but I'd never suspect him for a moment."

"Nor would I," said Sophie fervently. "He's above suspicion."

"There was that man you didn't like, Sophie."

"Which one was that?"

"He stood next to us as we queued to go into the dining saloon last night," said May. "That big, uncouth American gentleman. Now I think of it, he kept staring at the necklace."

"Can you recall his name?" asked Genevieve.

Sophie was rancorous. "I'd never forget it, Miss Masefield."

"Well?"

"Agnew — Mr. Philip Agnew."

■ ■ ■ ■

"Ah, there you are, Mr. Dillman! This is a fortuitous meeting."

"Good to see you again, Sir Arthur."

"Do you have any news for me yet?"

"Only that we remain confident of catching the thief."

"And retrieving my book in good condition, I hope."

"That goes without saying."

George Dillman had been walking past the library as Sir Arthur Conan Doyle was about to leave it. The author fell on him with enthusiasm. Dillman took him into a quiet corner.

"We continue to make inquiries, Sir Arthur," he said.

"I don't expect you to solve the crime in five minutes. Even dear old Sherlock Holmes never perfected that trick."

"Detection takes time. It can't be rushed."

"Oh, I'll put no pressure at all on you, Mr. Dillman," said Conan Doyle, patting him on the shoulder. "I know your pedigree from having talked to the purser, so I don't question your methods in any way."

"Thank you, sir. Would that every victim of crime had such a helpful attitude! But turning to *A Study in Scarlet,*" said Dillman, "my memory is that Sherlock Holmes dominates the book, yet is absent from most of the second half of it."

"I needed to portray the background to the murders in depth."

"That's exactly what you did."

"I made a few mistakes about American geography," admitted the other candidly, "but most readers seemed ready to forgive me for that and treat it as a minor solecism."

"It was the sequence of events in Utah that intrigued me."

"Then you'll know I'm not a great admirer of the Mormon religion. In some respects, I don't consider it to be a religion at all."

"You object to its doctrine of polygamy."

"Of course," said Conan Doyle. "What decent man wouldn't? It's against all civilized precepts. I tried to emphasize that in the novel. Because of that unholy doctrine, John Ferrier loses his life and poor Lucy is forced to marry the Elder's son and become what was, in effect, part of his harem. No wonder she pined away after only a month of such slavery."

"Was the book condemned by the Mormon Church?"

"I doubt if any member of it bothered to read the novel. They'd have no time for what they considered to be literary fripperies."

"It was much more than that, Sir Arthur. In retrospect, it was a historic piece of writing. Detective fiction will never be quite the same again. I'm just surprised that you had no indignant protests from Mormons."

"Ignoring me completely is a form of protest."

"There could be a more direct means," Dillman suggested.

"Such as?"

"Stealing that copy of the novel from you."

Conan Doyle was worried. "You think that's what happened?"

"It's a faint possibility."

"How would anyone know that I had the book with me?"

"That's what puzzled me at first, Sir Arthur. Then I remembered seeing a photograph of you in *The New York Times.* You were giving a lecture somewhere and holding your copy of *A Study in Scarlet* in your hands. I could see the title quite clearly," recalled Dillman. "It was obviously something you'd brought with you."

"You've made me anxious now, Mr. Dillman," confessed the other. "The one thing I had counted on was that the novel wouldn't be damaged in any way. But if it was taken by some vengeful Mormon, heaven knows what may have happened to it."

"As I said, it's only a faint possibility. A very faint one."

"Do we have any Mormons aboard?"

"I'm given to understand that we might have."

Conan Doyle's eyebrows formed a chevron of consternation. He was shaken by the notion that his copy of the novel might have been maliciously destroyed, along with the lecture notes he kept in it. He was still trying to come to terms with the idea when they were suddenly interrupted. Nobby Ruggles strutted along the corridor.

"Ah, this is lucky," he said, grinning broadly. "You've saved me the trouble of going to your stateroom, Sir Arthur. I was going to slip this under your door."

"What is it?" asked Conan Doyle.

"See for yourself." He handed over a sheet of paper. "It's the list of artistes in this afternoon's concert. As you see, I'm near the top." He looked at Dillman. "I'm going to recite one of Sir Arthur's poems."

"That's a fine tribute," observed Dillman.

"Yes," said Conan Doyle. "Thank you, Ruggles."

"Will we see you there?" asked the barber.

"Possibly."

"If you are, you can take another bow. Still," he went on with a gesture of apology, "excuse me for butting in, gentlemen. I didn't mean to interrupt." He remembered something. "But there was a favor I wanted to ask you, Sir Arthur."

"What is it?"

"Would you be kind enough to autograph my collection of your poems? It would mean so much to me."

"Yes, of course," said Conan Doyle, forcing a smile.

"Thank you. I'll bring it this afternoon."

After giving him a salute, Ruggles marched swiftly away.

"Who was that?" said Dillman.

"One of the barbers, Nobby Ruggles. It turns out that he served in the Boer War. We were both involved in the same military operation in Bloemfontein." He pulled a face. "He's a good man, but his enthusiasm for my work is a trifle overwhelming. He caught me unawares yesterday. When he recited one of my poems at the concert I was thrust into the public glare against my will."

"He must be one of your greatest fans."

"He is, Mr. Dillman. That's why the fellow troubles me."

"Will you be attending the concert?"

"I don't think so," said Conan Doyle. "I don't wish to go through that ordeal again. Ruggles has offered to give us a private rendition but I'll fend him off somehow. He reckons that he knows all of my poems by heart."

Dillman was pensive. "And he asked for your autograph," he recalled. He indicated the sheet of paper. "Didn't he say that he was about to slip that under the door of your stateroom?"

"Yes, Mr. Dillman."

"As a barber, he's restricted to certain areas of the ship."

"I never thought of that."

"Something else may not have crossed your mind, Sir Arthur," said Dillman. "How did he know where your stateroom is?"

As the first few passengers began to trickle into the dining saloon for luncheon, Frank Spurrier took up his stance behind a pillar near the entrance so that he could watch. It was not long before Joshua Cleves walked over to join him.

"I thought I'd catch you lurking here," said Cleves.

"I'm waiting for a friend."

"And we both know her name. My advice

is to give her a rest. You've already over-stepped the mark."

"What do you mean?" asked Spurrier.

"Genevieve is an intelligent woman. Because you kept pouncing on her at every opportunity, she realized that we're engaged in some sort of tussle over her."

"Then the blame lies with you, Josh. You were the one who aroused her suspicions by ingratiating yourself with Lord and Lady Bulstrode. You gave the game away."

"It doesn't mean that it's over."

"Then what does it mean?" said Spurrier.

"That we both give her some breathing space. Genevieve is on guard against us now. We need to step back."

"You can, if you wish."

"We both must," said Cleves.

"No, Josh. This is another one of your ruses. It's quite clear to me that you haven't won her over yet, whereas I've been making steady progress with Genevieve. Every time we speak I gain some of those small concessions that pave the way to ultimate success."

"Then why did she choose to have coffee with me, not with you?"

Spurrer was irked. "When was this?"

"Around mid-morning. Genevieve came looking for me."

"I don't believe you."

"Strictly speaking," said Cleves, "she came into the lounge on her own. But when I invited her to coffee she accepted gratefully. We had a long and interesting chat."

"About what?"

"About you, among other things. Genevieve said how irritated she was by the way that you kept popping up when she least expected it. In fact, she was more than irritated."

"You're making this up," Spurrier accused.

"You ambushed her once too often, Frank. That's why we must pull back for a while. She's worked out that we're in competition."

"We're not the only ones, Josh. I've seen other men paying court to her as well. If a beautiful woman travels alone on a transatlantic liner she's bound to attract male attention, especially if she dresses the way that Genevieve does. She can't suddenly turn into a vestal virgin," said Spurrier tetchily. "By the way she behaves she positively encourages interest."

"Genevieve enjoys interest but resents being pestered."

"Then why does she share a table with you?"

"She won't be doing that now," said

Cleves. "I told Rupert that I'd agreed to have luncheon with some business friends. That should prove to Genevieve that I've no wish to harass her. I'd recommend that you keep out of her way as well, Frank."

Spurrier became rueful. "What else did she say over coffee?"

"She spent most of the time on the defense."

"Why?"

"Because I teased her about her little weakness."

"What little weakness?"

"Genevieve Masefield is not the paragon of virtues that we thought. She has a guilty secret, Frank. She believes in spiritualism."

Spurrier blinked in surprise. "How do you know?"

"Because she attended a séance last night," said Cleves with derision. "There's a medium aboard, it seems, some woman looking to exploit anyone crazy enough to think that she can summon up the spirits of the dead."

"I wouldn't have thought Genevieve Masefield would be that gullible. What got her involved in spiritualism?"

"She claimed that she only went along out of curiosity."

"Perhaps she did."

"Then why was she so sensitive about it?" asked Cleves. "I think she protested far too much. Anyway," he said conspiratorially, looking over his shoulder as a steady flow of people went past, "I think we should both agree to ease off for a while."

"But we'll be seeing her at that drinks party this evening."

"A perfect opportunity to put the new code into practice. We don't ignore Genevieve but we don't crowd her either. Is it agreed?"

Spurrier hesitated. "How do I know this is not a trick?"

"Because the simplest thing for me to do was to let you carry on as you were doing and ruin your chances completely. Out of the kindness of my heart I'm trying to help you. If we give Genevieve a lot more freedom, we both stand to gain in the end."

"You're such an appalling liar sometimes. Josh."

"Trust me. It's for your own good, Frank."

"Is it?"

"Yes. Genevieve told me that she always found you so cold and undemonstrative. She couldn't imagine you losing control."

"What did you say to that?"

"Only that I'd seen you roused to a pitch of anger. I mentioned that we'd had that argument yesterday with David Lowbury."

Spurrier's eyes darted. "Why on earth did you do that?"

"I was trying to prove a point."

"Genevieve *knows* that we fell out with Lowbury?"

"Calm down," said Cleves with a hand on his arm. "There's no call to get so riled about it."

"I'm not riled," said Spurrier, pushing the hand away. "I'm just furious with you, Josh. I hope you weren't rash enough to tell her what the argument was about."

"I didn't need to, Frank. I think she guessed."

Spurrier swore under his breath.

Sophie Trouncer did not let the loss of her mother's necklace subdue her in any way. She was as buoyant as usual over luncheon and spent the whole meal trying to capture Dillman's attention. Her mother was an able assistant to her. Since she had been warned by Genevieve to say nothing public about the theft from their cabin, May Hoyland instead concentrated on singing the praises of her daughter.

"Sophie has always kept very active," she said. "She takes after me in that way. She swims, plays tennis and goes for long walks."

"Do you like walking, Mr. Dillman?" asked Sophie.

"When I have the time," he replied.

"We have the most glorious countryside around us, don't we, Mother?"

"Yes," said May, seizing her cue. "It's a rambler's delight. I may be prejudiced but I don't think there's a finer sight than the English countryside in spring."

"It's quite inspiring," said Sophie. "I walk for miles." She paused to finish the rest of her dessert. "How long are you going to be in England, Mr. Dillman?"

"A couple of weeks at most," he answered.

"And then where will you go?"

"I'll be sailing back to New York."

"You must find time to visit us before you leave," said May. "We've enjoyed your company so much. Sophie was saying only yesterday that meeting you has been an absolute delight."

"The feeling is mutual, Mrs. Hoyland."

Sophie laughed gaily. "You're so kind, Mr. Dillman. It would be lovely if you could spare a moment to call on us. The house is well worth seeing because it's over three hundred years old and it has a garden at the front and rear."

"The gardens are magnificent," said May. "Photographs of them appeared in a maga-

311

zine last year. Sophie has green fingers."

"I learned everything from my husband. He was the expert."

"Is there any chance you could visit us?"

"To be honest," said Dillman, "I won't know until I get to London and decide what my schedule is going to be. But it's an offer I'll certainly bear in mind. Thank you."

Though he could not even consider such a visit, he spoke as if it would be one of his priorities. Mother and daughter were thrilled. They exchanged glances before offering him more blandishments. Dillman decided that it was time to contrive a polite excuse to leave. In the event, he did not have to do so. A waiter approached and handed him a note. It was an urgent summons from the purser. Sensing trouble, Dillman got to his feet immediately.

"Do excuse me, ladies," he said, looking from one to the other. "As always, it's been a pleasure to spend time with you. I'm sorry that I've been called away."

The two women bade him farewell, then watched him fondly until he disappeared through the door. Dillman did not look back. He lengthened his stride until he got to the purser's office. After knocking on the door he went straight in. Nelson Rutherford was relieved to see him. He stood up from his seat.

"Thank goodness you've come!" he said.

"What's the problem?"

"There's more than one, unfortunately. I assume you've spoken to Miss Masefield today."

"Yes," said Dillman. "I heard about the thefts that took place last night. The diamond necklace was stolen from Mrs. Hoyland. When I had luncheon with her just now I was glad that she followed advice and said nothing about the incident."

"If only other passengers had the sense to follow advice!" said Rutherford with feeling. "But they don't."

"More thefts?"

"Three, Mr. Dillman."

"When were they reported?"

"In the last hour. They all seem to have occurred last night but they were not discovered until later this morning. That means the thief has had plenty of time to go to ground. The trail has gone cold."

"Not necessarily."

"The first victim was a Frenchman," said the purser, referring to some notes he had made on his pad. "Jean-Paul Fourier. The strange thing is that his cabin is directly opposite the one occupied by Mr. and Mrs. Lowbury."

"That may not be a coincidence. What did the man say?"

"His grasp of English was uncertain, so I may have got a few details wrong. The essence of it is this. His hobby is collecting clocks of all kinds. When he saw a French Empire carriage clock being advertised for sale while he was in New York, he felt obliged to buy it. He said something about it being his patriotic duty to return it to France. What amazed me," he continued, "was how much he was prepared to pay for it."

"Where was it kept?"

"In a valise in his cabin. When he opened it to take out some papers this morning, he realized that it had gone."

"What else was taken?"

"Not a thing, Mr. Dillman."

"Then the thief knew exactly what he wanted. I'll speak to M. Fourier as soon as I can," said Dillman. "The first thing I'll want to know is who his dining companions are. If he's so fanatical about clocks that he'll pay large sums for them, the chances are that he talked about his latest purchase."

"Then the same goes for Tom McCabe."

"What did he lose?"

"The gold cup he won in a golf tournament," said the purser. "He was inordinately proud of it. He insisted on telling me how he'd fought off every challenge to win. McCabe is a garrulous Irishman. My guess is that he's told everyone on board how he secured his victory, and how he kept the cup in his cabin so that he could gloat over it."

"Was anything else stolen?"

"Around five hundred dollars in cash."

"Five hundred?" Dillman was impressed. "I must take up golf."

"Just find that gold cup for him."

"What was the third case?"

"That's the most difficult of all," said Rutherford. "You might wish to hand it over to Miss Masefield."

"Why?"

"Because it concerns a fearsome lady named Griselda Nettlefold. The Frenchman is a pleasant character and McCabe is even more affable — but not Mrs. Nettlefold. She was frightening."

"What was stolen?"

"Her diamond tiara," explained the purser. "A family heirloom. She demanded it back instantly. I was threatened with everything short of being hanged, drawn and quartered. Mark you," he went on, "she did have good cause to be distressed."

"I can guess why," said Dillman. "It was

stolen when she and her husband were asleep in the cabin."

Rutherford gaped. "How on earth do you know that?"

"Because I think I've seen the lady. I've certainly seen someone wearing a diamond tiara that looks like part of the crown jewels. Is Griselda Nettlefold a tall, stately, white-haired lady in her sixties?"

"That's her, Mr. Dillman!"

"Her husband looks much older than she is."

"He is, indeed," said Rutherford, "and he also suffers from a heart condition. It wasn't helped by a nocturnal visit from a thief. Not that he was awake at the time, however, nor was she. According to Mrs. Nettlefold she has to take sleeping pills, so she didn't hear a thing when someone let himself into their cabin."

"The thief was counting on that."

"How could he possibly know they'd both be fast asleep?"

"At that age," Dillman reasoned, "people rarely stay awake for long at night. Besides, she may have mentioned in public that she took sleeping pills. Someone with his eye on her tiara might have sat near her in the lounge to catch that sort of useful detail."

"I don't envy Miss Masefield having to

deal with the lady."

"She may calm down a little in time."

"Only when she gets her tiara back, Mr. Dillman." The purser took a deep breath and flopped into his chair. "This is starting to look like an epidemic. If you count Sir Arthur Conan Doyle, it means we've had six people robbed aboard the ship."

"Then there's the small matter of a murder."

"That's my biggest worry. The captain was shocked to learn about that. We're now looking for a killer as well as a thief."

"Are we?"

Dillman was lost in thought for a full minute, turning over in his mind the sequence of events. What struck him as significant was the timing of the various crimes. Seeing the detective's furrowed brow, Rutherford did not interrupt him. He sat there patiently. Eventually, Dillman jerked himself out of his reverie.

"I'm sorry that I drifted off like that," he said.

The purser grinned. "I knew that you'd come back to me."

"An idea occurred to me, Mr. Rutherford."

"Go on."

"I'm wondering if the crimes are related."

"All of them?"

"All but the theft of Sir Arthur's book," said Dillman. "That just doesn't fit into the scheme of things. Also, it happened too early in the voyage. That sets it completely apart. Everything else could be the work of the same man."

Rutherford blanched. "The thief also committed murder?"

"I'm beginning to think so."

"But why?"

"Look at the facts," Dillman suggested. "Mr. Lowbury returned unexpectedly to his cabin in the middle of dinner. It could well be that he disturbed the thief."

"But nothing was stolen from his cabin."

"Think of the cabin opposite. That's where M. Fourier kept his carriage clock. Supposing that Mr. Lowbury was leaving his cabin when he caught someone trying to break into the one opposite?"

"The thief would have run away, surely?"

"Not if Lowbury was able to recognize him again. Where could he go, Mr. Rutherford? He's stuck on the ship like the rest of us. It would only have been a matter of time before he was caught."

"So he'd want to shut Lowbury up somehow."

"That means he was armed," said

Dillman, picturing the scene. "He pulled a gun on Lowbury and forced him down to the main deck. At some point, Lowbury tried to break free and that's how his coat was torn. But he was soon overpowered. It was too dangerous to shoot him, so his captor knocked him out with the gun."

"Then stripped off his coat and pushed him over the side," said the purser, continuing with the reconstruction. "I think you may be right, Mr. Dillman. It all fits."

"Let's not get too carried away."

"But you may have stumbled onto the explanation."

"All that I've done is establish the size of our problem," said Dillman. "Five thefts in one night, all carried out by someone who identifies specific targets and gets into their cabins at will."

"He must be a professional thief."

"He is, clever enough to wait for days before he strikes, thereby cutting down the amount of time we have to catch him. As for the murder, it's not the first time he's killed a man."

Rutherford shuddered. "I think I know what you're going to tell me," he said. "This looks like the work of a certain person."

"Edward Hammond."

"We've got a wanted man on board, after all."

Eleven

Genevieve Masefield had been pleasantly surprised over luncheon. Frank Spurrier had not intercepted her on her way there and Joshua Cleves had not taunted her about her brush with spiritualism. In fact, he had not even turned up at her table. She had been able to talk at leisure to Lady Bulstrode about the differences between England and America, and listen to Lord Bulstrode's confident predictions about the forthcoming Derby. It was the first meal during which she felt she did not have to be on guard. For that reason it was both refreshing and restoring. She was even allowed to leave the room without being accosted by either of her unwanted admirers.

Her first task was to call on Jane Lowbury to see if she had recovered from the initial shock of her husband's disappearance. As she approached the cabin she was heartened to see a steward coming out of the door with a tray. On it were two plates that were largely empty. Jane had at least started to eat again. Genevieve knocked on the door and was soon admitted.

"How are you?" she asked.

"Still very low," replied Jane. "I keep thinking about David."

"That's understandable, Mrs. Lowbury."

"I know it's ridiculous but I find it better to believe that he may still be alive. He could be tied up somewhere, held prisoner in someone's cabin. Or he's locked away in a storeroom."

"For what purpose?"

"That's what I can't work out."

"Every cabin is cleaned by a steward, so it would be impossible to hold someone prisoner in one of them. As for the store-rooms," she said, "each one of them was searched last night. If your husband is still on the ship — and I sincerely hope that he is — then he's being kept somewhere else."

"There must be lots of hiding places on a vessel this big."

"True."

"And if he was moved from time to time, he'd be missed by anyone in search of him." Jane flailed around as she tried to find a motive. "Someone may be playing a cruel trick on David. Or perhaps he's been kidnapped and held for ransom. It may even be that he upset someone accidentally and they wanted to get their own back on him." She paced the cabin. "There *has* to be a reason, Miss Masefield."

"We'll find it."

Genevieve was gratified that there were some signs of a return to normality. Jane had dressed and groomed herself. She had had her first meal since dinner the previous evening. She no longer looked quite so fatigued and drawn. But she remained on edge, horrified by what had happened and unable to think of anything else. She went to the table and snatched up a sheet of paper.

"Here you are," she said.

Genevieve took it from her. "Thank you."

"It's that list you asked me to draw up. Those are the names of the people we've met on the ship, the ones we've actually talked to."

"There must be forty or fifty here."

"I told you. David had a gift for making friends."

"You've put a tick by some names," noted Genevieve.

"Those are the people we knew best."

"This could be very useful to us."

"I'd hate to think that someone there

knows what happened to David. They were all so friendly toward us — for the most part."

"Who were the odd ones out, Mrs. Lowbury?"

"Philip Agnew was the main one," said Jane. "He wasn't exactly rude but he wasn't well mannered either. David didn't mind him so much because he's so tolerant."

"What about you?"

"I didn't like the way that he looked at me, Miss Masefield."

"Was he a nuisance?"

"No, there was just something about him."

"Did you mention it to your husband?"

"There was no point," said Jane. "David is very protective. He'd have felt the need to confront Mr. Agnew and I didn't want him to do that. So I tried to forget about it." Her face clouded. "You don't think that *he* could be involved, do you?"

"I don't know, Mrs. Lowbury." She folded the list up and slipped it into her purse. "Your husband was a financier, wasn't he?"

"That's right. He started out as a stockbroker."

"He must have had a shrewd business brain."

"Oh, he did, Miss Masefield," replied Jane with a surge of pride. "David always seemed to know when and where to invest. He used to say how important it is to make money work for you."

"He's probably right," said Genevieve, "though I've never had enough of it to test that theory. I can see why he was so at home on the *Celtic*. We have lots of bankers, financiers and wealthy people on board. In that sense we're surrounded by money."

Jane was dejected. "Until yesterday," she said, "I thought that we were rich, but you realize how little money matters when something like this happens. I'd give every penny we have to get my husband back again." Tears threatened but she bit them back. "Forgive me, Miss Masefield. Every so often it just overwhelms me."

"I'll leave you to rest."

"But you'll bring any news, won't you?"

"As soon as there's any news to bring, Mrs. Lowbury."

"Good or bad — don't hide anything from me."

"I promise."

"Thank you."

Jane embraced her impulsively, then drew back. She pulled out a handkerchief from her sleeve and Genevieve suspected that it would be used as soon as she left. Her compassion was roused but so was her determination to hunt down the man who had killed David Lowbury. After an exchange of farewells she opened the door and stepped out into the corridor. She had gone no more than a dozen steps when she saw Dillman coming toward her.

"There's no point in disturbing Mrs. Lowbury again," she said, raising a hand. "I've just seen her."

"How is she bearing up?"

"She had some food at last."

"Good."

"And she was able to give me a list of all the people whom they got to know on the voyage. There are some very familiar names on it."

"I'll look forward to going through it with you," said Dillman. "Meanwhile, I have to talk to Jean-Paul Fourier."

"Who is he?"

"Another victim of our thief. It seems that he was ubiquitous last night, Genevieve. Three more thefts have been reported. Of the three, M. Fourier's is the most interesting."

"Why?"

"He has the cabin directly opposite Mr. and Mrs. Lowbury."

"Who are the others?"

"One is an Irish golfer and the other is a

lady whom you will have to interview. Mr. Rutherford will give you the details. I don't envy you. She sounds like a battle-ax."

"Why do I always get the difficult people?" she complained.

He smiled impishly. "Because you handle them so well."

"I'm not sure that I handled Mrs. Lowbury all that well, George. I can't seem to say the right thing to cheer her up."

"There is no right thing, I'm afraid."

"She's in despair and I can't reach her."

"You've done your best, Genevieve," he said, "and nobody can ask more of you than that. Mrs. Lowbury is bound to be dejected. She's missing her husband dreadfully."

It was her turn to smile. "I know the feeling."

Sophie Trouncer arrived early for the concert so that she and her mother could get a seat near the front. Both women felt that they had made a good impression on George Dillman.

"He's so tall and manly," said May Hoyland.

"But he's quite a bit younger than me, Mother."

"That doesn't matter. Your father was younger than me. Besides, there's no reason why he should learn your true age."

"I couldn't be dishonest with him," said Sophie.

"The question may not come up. The crucial thing is that you look years younger than you really are and you have so much vitality. I'm sure that Mr. Dillman appreciates that."

"Do you think that he'll come to tea, Mother?"

"By the time I've finished working on him," said May with a muted cackle, "he'll be staying the night with us."

The idea coursed through Sophie Trouncer like a charge of electricity. She sat up, tingled all over and glowed. It was a fleeting happiness. Thoda Burbridge suddenly waddled into view and hailed her with a wave. Sophie cringed inwardly.

"Do you mind if I join you?" asked Thoda.

"Please do," said Sophie uneasily.

"Thank you."

"You've not met my mother properly, have you?"

"No," said Thoda, taking her seat and reaching across Sophie to shake hands with May, "but I've heard a lot about you, Mrs. Hoyland."

"I've heard about *you*," said May with forced politeness. "I don't know what hap-

pened at the séance last night, Mrs. Burbridge, but my daughter came back in a
state of high excitement."

"I was pleased about that."

"What exactly happened?"

"You'll have to ask Mrs. Trouncer. I never
divulge information about what happens in
the privacy of a séance."

Sophie writhed in embarrassment. She
was seated between a mother she loved and
a medium she respected, but the two women
had no common ground. Knowing her
mother's antipathy to the whole concept of
spiritualism, she had not confided details of
the contact she believed she had made with
her late husband, or disclosed the advice
that he had given her about searching for
his successor. May Hoyland had been offering her the identical counsel for months.
Given the medium's heightened awareness,
Sophie knew that Thoda Burbridge was
certain to sense her mother's hostility. It
took only a matter of seconds.

"I'm sorry that you disapprove of me,
Mrs. Hoyland," said Thoda graciously.
"Perhaps you'd prefer it if I sat elsewhere?"

"Not at all," replied May sweetly. "And I
don't disapprove of you at all. What I object
to is this absurd subject you've taken up."

"It was the other way round — spiritual-

329

ism took me up."

"Either way, you have my sympathy."

"Mother!" said Sophie, jabbing her with an elbow. "Please forgive her, Mrs. Burbridge. She doesn't understand."

"I understand perfectly well," said May defiantly.

"I beg leave to doubt that," countered Thoda.

"Fraud is fraud."

"And a closed mind is a closed mind. It's a terrible handicap to carry with you through life, Mrs. Hoyland. It means that you'll forever be mired in your own prejudices."

"They're not prejudices. They're decent Christian principles."

"This is not the time for an argument, Mother," said Sophie.

"I quite agree," said Thoda benevolently, "and I'll make allowances for Mrs. Hoyland's bad temper. I know how upset she must be after the theft of her necklace."

May was bewildered. "That's a secret," she said hotly. "How in God's name do you know about that?"

"Mrs. Burbridge has a sixth sense," Sophie told her.

"I call it witchcraft."

"Mother!"

"Somebody must have told her."

"*You* did," explained Thoda. "As soon as I sat down."

"There's something very strange going on here," said May.

"The world is full of strange and inexplicable things."

Sophie grabbed her mother's arm before May could respond with another gibe. It was going to be a long and uncomfortable afternoon. Sophie felt as if she were sitting on eggshells. When the chairman finally appeared to introduce the first artiste, she let out a huge sigh of relief.

He was the third to perform. When his moment came, Nobby Ruggles seized it gratefully. He was not dressed as a soldier this time. Carrying a broom, he was wearing a pair of old trousers, a shirt and a flat cap. He removed the cap to wipe imaginary sweat from his brow in order to give the impression that he had been cleaning out the stables. Then he launched himself into "The Groom's Story," scanning the room as he did so to see if the poem's author was there. Realizing that Conan Doyle and his wife were absent from the great occasion, he nevertheless gave a committed performance, rounding off the last verse with a chuckle in his voice.

"And master? Well, it cured 'im. 'E altered
from that day.
And come back to 'is 'orses in the good
old-fashioned way.
And if you wants to git the sack, the quick-
est way by far
Is to 'int as 'ow you think he ought to keep
a motor car."

The applause was mingled with a torrent
of laughter at the comic recital and Ruggles
feasted on it until it began to die away. He
did not linger. By the time the next per-
former was in action, the barber had collected a book and was on his way along a
corridor that led to some of the first-class
staterooms. Since he was not allowed in that
area, he moved furtively until he reached
his destination. Looking down at his book,
he flipped open the cover and read the title
page as if staring at Holy Writ. Then he
tapped respectfully on the door.

"Sir Arthur?" he called. "It's Nobby
Ruggles. Are you there?"

Nelson Rutherford had refused the invitation to take part in another concert so that
someone else could have the opportunity to

show off his talents. In any case, he could not spare the time. The purser had never had to cope with such a spate of crimes before and it put him under severe pressure. In one way the concert was a blessing. Since it attracted the majority of passengers in first class, it meant that he was liberated from the endless stream of people who knocked on his door to make requests or to register complaints. He took advantage of his temporary freedom to meet with the two detectives in George Dillman's cabin. When the purser arrived, only Dillman was there.

"How did you get on?" asked the purser.

"Jean-Paul Fourier was heartbroken at the loss of his clock and accepts that he was foolish to keep it in his cabin. Tom McCabe was the same," said Dillman, "though I had to listen to the tale of how he got a birdie on the final hole to win before he'd let me out of there. Two nice, friendly, trusting people, who assumed that everyone else lived by the same rules."

"Did you learn anything of value?"

"Not from our golfer. He's told all and sundry about winning that big tournament and having the cup on display in his cabin. In fact, he actually took it with him into the lounge one day."

"What about the Frenchman?"

"He was more cautious," said Dillman, "though he did talk about his clock to the man who sat opposite him at his table."

"Who was that?"

"Philip Agnew."

"That name has cropped up more than once."

"Yes, Mr. Rutherford, I may need to have another talk with him. But there's a second name that caught my ear as well. According to M. Fourier, he was chatting to someone in the smoking room who expressed an interest in seeing the clock. The man said that he might make an offer for it," Dillman reported, "but M. Fourier refused to part with it. The man in question was Frank Spurrier."

There was a knock on the door and Dillman opened it to let Genevieve in. She gave Rutherford a smile of recognition.

"I'm sorry I'm late."

"You came at the perfect time," said Dillman.

He recounted what he had just told the purser about his interview with Jean-Paul Fourier. Genevieve was not surprised.

"I don't see anything sinister there," she said. "Mr. Spurrier does all the buying for his auction house. He's always looking for bargains."

"He was aware that the clock was in that cabin."

"So was Philip Agnew," Rutherford put in.

"What use would he have for a French Empire carriage clock?"

"I don't see Mr. Spurrier as a thief either," said Genevieve.

"Neither do I," Dillman agreed. "In his position, he has to look and sound like a pillar of respectability. But it's not beyond the bounds of possibility that he has an accomplice aboard. If he can't acquire certain items by fair means, perhaps he resorts to illegal ones." Genevieve looked doubtful. "It's only a suggestion."

"Follow it through," she said. "If he was involved in one theft, Frank Spurrier must have been involved in them all. How would he dispose of the stolen items?"

"In the case of the carriage clock, it would be easy. He'd sell it at auction when M. Fourier would be safely out of the way in France."

"What about the diamond necklace and the tiara? If he advertised any of those in his catalog, there's always the chance they'd be recognized by their owners. I know, from having just talked to her, that Mrs. Nettlefold frequents auctions."

"Spurrier would have a means of disposing of stolen goods," said Dillman. "He deals with jewelers all the time, so he must be aware of the ones engaged in shady practices."

"Wait a minute," said Rutherford, trying to piece it together in his mind. "Why has Mr. Spurrier become a main suspect? I thought you told me that the murder and most of the thefts were the work of Edward Hammond. Are you hinting that the two men are working together? One steals, the other picks out the targets?"

"It's an idea we ought to look at, Mr. Rutherford. But we're jumping ahead of ourselves," said Dillman, turning to Genevieve. "We haven't heard about the visit to Griselda Nettlefold."

"She was utterly charming," said Genevieve.

The purser gulped. "Really? I thought she'd eat you alive."

"You were unlucky. Mrs. Nettlefold expended most of her bile on you, Mr. Rutherford. She regrets that now and asked me to pass on her apologies."

"My scars still show."

"Well, she didn't attack me," said Genevieve. "Her only concern was to get the tiara back. It's been in the family for three generations. What annoys her is that she was warned to keep it in the safe whenever she was not wearing it. One of her dinner companions told her, in so many words, that it would be stolen."

"A prediction?"

"Yes."

"From whom?"

"Thoda Burbridge, the medium who held the séance I went to."

"Does she have a crystal ball or something?"

"Psychic gifts."

"I'd say that it was plain common sense," said Dillman. "Anyone with a diamond tiara that valuable is going to tempt a jewel thief."

"Only if we have one aboard, Mr. Dillman," added the purser, "and I've never had that misfortune on previous voyages. It looks as if I'm paying for all those trouble-free crossings now. The *Celtic* has been hit by an outbreak of serious crime."

"The murder still comes first. If we can solve that, we can solve all the other crimes. Apart from the theft of Sir Arthur's book, that is," said Dillman. "I see that as quite separate."

"So do I," said Genevieve.

"Where's that list of names that Mrs. Lowbury gave you?"

"Right here, George." She took it from her purse and passed it to him. "I haven't had time to take a close look at it."

Dillman unfolded the paper. "It will repay study," he said. "When I heard that Edward Hammond might be aboard, I thought it unlikely that he'd travel in first class. I was wrong. He's here under a false name." He held up the list. "Somewhere on here is the man who killed David Lowbury. All that we have to do is to unmask him."

"You had no right to set him onto me," protested Leonard Rush.

"That's not what I did," said Saul Pinnick.

"Then why did he come after me?"

"He was interested that you slept on deck."

"So do a few other people. Did he hound them as well?"

"All I did was to point you out to him, Mr. Rush."

"You should be grateful to Saul," said Miriam. "At least he's shown sympathy for you. Nobody else on this ship has. They've got none to spare. I know I haven't."

"Stay out of this, Mirry," advised her husband.

"I'm not having anyone shouting at you."

"Mr. Rush is entitled to voice his opinion."

"That doesn't mean he can threaten you."

They were in the lounge in steerage. Pinnick and his wife were seated, but Rush was standing over them and he had been gesticulating at the old man. He was chastened by Miriam's comment. He had not meant to intimidate Pinnick, merely to make a complaint. When he spoke again, his voice was quieter and more measured.

"I just want to be left alone."

"That's what you think now," said Pinnick sagely, "but that will change. Believe me, I've seen it happen so many times."

"Seen what?" asked Rush.

"Grief. Unhappiness. Pain."

"I know only too well what they feel like," Miriam grumbled.

"When someone you love dearly passes away, you're in a daze for weeks afterward — months, in some cases. You can't see the point of going on without them."

"That's how we were when Sharan died."

"Our eldest daughter. Sharan was only nine at the time."

"It broke my heart," said Miriam, eyes moistening.

"But we had to go on," explained Pinnick. "People depended on us — our other children, relatives, friends, neighbors, customers. We had to go on until we eventually managed to come out of that daze. You're still in it, Mr. Rush. That's why we want to help."

His wife nudged him. "It was your idea, Saul, not mine."

"We both know what bereavement is, Mirry."

"I've had over fifty years of knowing what it is."

"It's not the same," bleated Rush. "You had your problems and I'm sorry for that, but it's not the same as me."

"Why not?"

"I had nobody else but my wife."

"No children?"

"Two were stillborn. We lost the third."

"You must have friends and relatives."

"We left," said Rush. "We cut off all our ties. We wanted to start that new life in America that we'd heard so much about. It was our last chance of a little happiness."

"You think this wasn't *our* last chance?"

"I can't go back home in disgrace."

"That's what we're doing," said Pinnick, "and there's plenty more in steerage doing the same. America didn't want us. So," he went on resignedly, "we go back to England and pick up our old lives somehow. Let people laugh at us, if they wish. We did at least get to sail across an ocean and see New York."

"Only from a distance," said Miriam.

"It was an experience, Mirry."

"I hated it."

"You'll forget it in time."

"Well, I won't," said Rush soulfully. "Being turned away told me the truth about myself. It was like looking in a mirror. I'm finished. I've got nothing to offer anymore. I might as well be dead."

"But you're not, are you?" said Pinnick with a smile. "You think about it but you've got too much sense to do it. You're still with us, Mr. Rush, and I'm glad that you are. So is Mirry."

"Yes," she muttered, responding to his prod.

Rush swallowed hard and shifted his feet. Nobody else in steerage had taken the slightest notice of him. It was churlish to get angry with the two people who did bother about him. Mourning his wife so compulsively, he had ignored the fact that others had their own share of anguish and disappointment. They coped with their grief somehow. Leonard Rush had not yet learned to do so.

"Keep that man away from me," he pleaded. "I don't want to talk to anyone. I simply want to be alone with my thoughts."

Philip Agnew was not inclined to hide his emotions. When he learned that George Dillman was a detective, his anger swelled immediately.

"Is that why you talked to me the other day?" he demanded.

"Yes, Mr. Agnew."

"Then why didn't you tell me? I hate being lied to."

"I didn't lie to you, Mr. Agnew," said Dillman. "Not in the way that you imply. I just wanted to talk to you about that séance."

"You were spying on me."

"Do you have anything to make you feel guilty?"

"Of course not!"

"Then you have nothing to worry about, do you?"

Dillman was glad that the conversation was taking place in the other man's cabin. Agnew's raised voice would have ignited too much attention in a public room. Unlike their previous meeting, this one had perforce to be more private.

"There was something you didn't tell me about the séance," said Dillman. "You left earlier than anyone else."

"Out of sheer disgust. That woman was useless. She did nothing at all for me. Mrs. Burbridge doesn't have any psychic gifts at all."

"Other people would disagree."

"Misguided fools!"

"A second séance, by all accounts, was much more successful. Since I wasn't there, I can't verify that. What is certain is that the lady definitely has some powers. She can sense things about people," said Dillman. "Private things that they'd rather keep to themselves. I think that you know what I'm talking about, Mr. Agnew."

"No, I don't."

"Were you ever involved with the Mormon Church?"

"Who told you that?" he retorted.

"Mrs. Burbridge was certain of it."

"Don't believe a word that fake medium tells you."

"She made extremely accurate observations about other people. They had the courage to admit that she was right. For some reason, Mr. Agnew, you can't do that."

"There's nothing to admit."

"Are you quite sure of that?"

"Look," said Agnew, squaring up to him, "I want to know what's going on here. You've got no call to come banging on my door so that you can ask me a lot of questions."

"I feel that I have, sir."

Agnew thrust out his jaw. "Prove it!"

"Very well," said Dillman calmly. "During the séance in which you were involved, something of considerable personal value was stolen from the stateroom belonging to Sir Arthur and Lady Conan Doyle. The thief must have known they were absent. You, Mr. Agnew," he continued, "left that séance early, having had a row with Sir Arthur about his attitude toward killing animals."

"What he did on that whaling boat sickened me."

"That's irrelevant. The stolen item was a book that, quite apart from anything else, contains a virulent attack on Mormon doctrines. I have to examine the possibility that it may have been taken in the spirit of vengeance by someone of that religious persuasion."

Dillman expected a vigorous denial. Instead, Agnew became sullen and took a pace backward. As he weighed his words, he studied the detective resentfully. Dillman pressed on.

"Since then," he said, "your name has come to my attention more than once, and never in the most flattering circumstances. Mrs. Lowbury informed a colleague of mine that she found your manner quite objectionable, and she's not a lady to make such a complaint lightly." He waited for a reply but none came. "Do you agree that you met Jane Lowbury?"

"Yes," said Agnew. "I met her. She is a pretty woman."

"You managed to upset her somehow."

He scowled. "What am I supposed to have done?"

"I'm investigating the theft of a carriage clock from Jean-Paul Fourier," Dillman resumed. "I believe that he mentioned the fact that it was kept in his cabin."

"So? Does that make me a thief?"

"Let's go back to Thoda Burbridge. Why did she upset you?"

"She cheated me, Mr. Dillman, that's why."

"I think it was because she found you out."

"No!"

"You did have a connection with the Mormons, didn't you?"

"Don't keep on about it."

"Why are you so ashamed of the fact?"

Agnew's temper flared up and he bunched his fists. For a moment Dillman thought he was going to have to defend himself but the danger soon passed. Turning away, Agnew slumped into a chair, his hands clasped, his elbows resting on his knees. After lengthy contemplation, he looked up.

"If I tell you the truth," he said wearily, "it goes no further than this cabin. Is that understood?"

"Yes, Mr. Agnew."

"Then I want a second promise from you. When I finish, you get out of here and stay clear of me for the rest of the voyage."

"That depends on what you have to tell me."

"Sit down."

Dillman obeyed and waited while Agnew collected his thoughts.

"I did not steal a book from that animal hunter," said Agnew. "I wouldn't touch anything that man has written. And I didn't steal a clock from that funny little Frenchman either. Yes, he told me about it because all he could talk about was his collection of clocks. Has he accused me?"

"Of course not."

"He'd better not, Mr. Dillman."

"I'm not accusing you either. I'm just pointing to certain facts."

"I can see how it looks," Agnew conceded, "but you're on the wrong track. I left that séance because I felt let down. I came straight back here and did some damage to a bottle of brandy I always keep at hand. Are you a drinking man, Mr. Dillman?"

"Now and then, sir."

"I drink to forget. I drink to forget that my wife died. I drink to forget that we lost both our children. I drink to forget that my first business venture almost crippled me. But most of all," he confessed, "I drink to forget that I grew up in Utah in a family of Mormons."

"Are the memories so painful, Mr. Agnew?"

"Sometimes," said the other. "Sir Arthur Conan Doyle attacked Mormon beliefs in his book — is that right?"

"He was particularly critical of the doctrine of polygamy."

"Not every man has a string of wives — my father didn't."

"Sir Arthur also censured the power of the elders."

"Then he obviously never lived with Mormons," said Agnew. "There are people in charge, but that's true of every community. They set the standards and enforce control."

"That's why you broke away, isn't it?" Dillman guessed. "You wanted more freedom. You rebelled against control."

"No, Mr. Dillman. I left because I couldn't measure up to what was asked of me. I lived among people who led good, decent, honest, industrious lives that served a common purpose. I could never match up to them," said Agnew sadly. "I had urges I shouldn't have had. I wanted to see the world. I wanted to enjoy a drink whenever I chose to. And I wanted to be able to look at a pretty woman the way I looked at Jane Lowbury. In other words," he concluded, "I wasn't fit to be a Mormon. I just couldn't climb high enough."

Dillman was interested to hear praise of the Mormons. It came in sharp contradistinction to what Conan Doyle had had to say about them in *A Study in Scarlet,* though it had to be borne in mind that the novel referred to the early days of Mormon settlement in Utah. Looking at the religion from outside, the writer had been appalled. Trying to practice it within a devout Mormon family, Philip Agnew had been unequal to its demands. He had run away from home but he could not outrun the guilt he felt at having betrayed his heritage. Dillman could now see why Thoda Burbridge's claim about his background had enraged Agnew so much.

"Thank you for being so honest with me,"

said Dillman.

"That's more than I can say about you."

"My job depends on a certain amount of deception."

"Then go off and do it somewhere else," said Agnew, getting to his feet and opening the door. "As for Mrs. Lowbury, I didn't mean to cause offense. It won't happen again."

"Good-bye, Mr. Agnew," said Dillman, rising to his feet.

"Just get out of my life."

Lady Conan Doyle stood still while her husband fastened the clasp on her necklace. He took the opportunity to place a gentle kiss on the back of her neck.

She laughed. "Your mustache tickles me."

"You've never complained before."

"It wasn't a complaint," she said, facing him. "I liked it."

"And what about the trip to America?" asked Conan Doyle. "Now that you've had time to see it in perspective, what's the verdict?"

"I loved every minute of it, Arthur."

"Even the traveling?"

"Even that. I know that you forewarned me, but I just wasn't prepared for the sheer size of everything. When I first saw New

York I was completely overawed. The whole trip was inspiring," she said. "It's such a pity that our memories of it are clouded by the theft of your book."

"And by that other embarrassment, Jean," he said. "I'm sure that Nobby Ruggles is a competent barber, and he's clearly a man with all the right instincts, but — oh dear! — I do wish he hadn't recited that poem at the concert. I felt as if I were being roasted on a spit."

"It's a good poem. He did very well."

"Too well. People have been congratulating me ever since."

"At least we didn't have to watch Ruggles doing it again."

"I couldn't have sat through another concert knowing that he'd spring a second poem on me. The worst of it is," he said, straightening his bow tie in the mirror, "that he insists on giving us a private performance."

"Tell him we're too busy, Arthur."

"I don't want to hurt the man's feelings."

"Would you rather he hurt yours?" she replied, squeezing his arm. "Don't worry. I'll find an excuse to put him off."

"No, no. It's my responsibility."

She looked at her watch. "We must go. They'll be wondering where we are. Lady

Bulstrode did ask us to be punctual. It will be amusing to see who else has been invited."

"As long as it's not Nobby Ruggles."

Lady Conan Doyle pulled on her evening gloves and took a final look at herself in the mirror. She was wearing a pink evening gown with a matching stole and gloves. Every time she moved her head her earrings glistened. She spoke over her shoulder.

"Do you think it will ever be found?"

"What?"

"A Study in Scarlet."

"I sincerely hope so, Jean," he said. "That book is my talisman."

"Mr. Dillman has had no success so far."

"Give him time."

"What has he actually been doing?" she said.

"Getting on quietly and efficiently with his job."

"I expected him to retrieve it long before now."

"George Dillman won't let us down."

"How can you be so confident about that?"

"It's easy," said Conan Doyle, taking her by the shoulders to turn her round. "I know a good detective when I see one."

■ ■ ■ ■

It was a small but convivial gathering. Lord and Lady Bulstrode were attentive hosts, welcoming each newcomer warmly and introducing them to everyone else. A steward served drinks. Genevieve was not surprised to find that she was the youngest person in the room. What did astonish her was that neither Frank Spurrier nor Joshua Cleves tried to talk to her. Though they each gave her a smile of acknowledgment on arrival, they drifted off to engage others in conversation. Spurrier took the opportunity to compliment Lady Conan Doyle on her jewelry while Cleves paid court to the wife of the American ambassador to France. Genevieve found herself monopolized by a grinning Brazilian who bred champion racehorses and a dour Scotsman who owned a whiskey distillery.

Drink flowed and the chatter became increasingly louder and more animated. When she tired of hearing about the wonders of Brazil and the delights of single malt whiskey, she excused herself and went across to Spurrier, who had been talking earnestly to Lady Bulstrode. He detached

himself politely so that he could face Genevieve.

"A lovely party," she remarked.

"I feel privileged to be invited."

"Did I see you give Lady Conan Doyle
your business card?"

"Have you been watching me, Miss Masefield?" he said with a note of challenge. "If
you have, you'll have seen that I've parted
with four business cards and acquired three
in return."

"Was that by way of advertisement?"

"Of course. One can never have too many
customers. If a lady wears fine jewelry the
chances are that she might like to bid for
some of the items at one of my auctions.
While I'm crossing the Atlantic in either
direction I'm always looking to recruit new
customers."

"I didn't know you had such an interest
in jewelry," she said.

"I'm fascinated by it," he told her, face
impassive, "and even more so by the ladies
who wear it. Some — like you, for instance
— select brooches, necklaces and earrings
that are both tasteful and appropriate. They
heighten your beauty. Others," he went on,
lowering his voice, "wear unsuitable jewelry
that is either distracting or tending to vul-
garity."

"I hope that nobody here is guilty of that."

"No, Miss Masefield."

"I'm glad that we all pass your test, Mr. Spurrier."

"I'd never presume to set a test," he said. "Do excuse me," he went on, seeing that Conan Doyle was helping himself to a drink from the tray, "I must have a word with Sir Arthur."

Genevieve was mystified. A man who had gone out of his way to speak to her on previous occasions had now apparently lost interest in her. Her feeling of relief was edged with a slight sense of pique. It was disconcerting to be studiously ignored. Lord Bulstrode came across to her with Cleves at his elbow.

"Were you there, Miss Masefield?" he inquired.

"Where?"

"At the concert this afternoon."

"No," she said. "I wasn't able to get there."

"Joshua says that I missed a special treat."

"Yes," said Cleves, "it was a delight for anyone interested in horses. One of the ship's barbers recited a poem by Sir Arthur called 'the Groom's Story.' I laughed all the way through."

"I'd like to see a copy," said Lord Bulstrode.

"Oh, it won't mean so much on the printed page. Ruggles — that's the name of the barber — turned it into a real drama."

"I'm sorry I wasn't there," said Genevieve. "That wasn't all I missed, Joshua. Where were you at lunchtime?"

"I had business to discuss with an associate of mine."

"I see."

"Agnes and I kept her diverted while you were away," said Lord Bulstrode. "And the four of us will be back together at dinner."

"I'm hungry," announced Cleves, "and I always play my best game of chess on a full stomach. Be warned, Rupert."

"I'll be ready for you."

Cleves broke away to talk to the grinning Brazilian, leaving Genevieve alone with her host. It was ironic. Having come with the intention of fending off Spurrier and Cleves, she was feeling oddly neglected by both of them. Lord Bulstrode gazed around.

"I do like to be in the same room as kindred spirits," he said.

"I'm glad that you consider me one of them."

"We needed a sprinkling of pulchritude among all the hoary old buffers like me. Not that you're here solely for decorative purposes," he added quickly. "You'd light up any assembly. Agnes and I are both very fond of you, Miss Masefield. We hope that you'll be able to come down and see us in the country one day."

"Thank you, Lord Bulstrode. I'd like that."

"Joshua has promised to visit us as well."

"Has he?"

"Yes," said Lord Bulstrode. "It would be altogether splendid if the pair of you could come together."

Genevieve did not reply. When she glanced across at Cleves, his back was to her but she no longer believed that he was now indifferent. In securing an invitation to visit his titled friends, Cleves was trying to ensnare her by other means. Her eyes flicked across to Spurrier. She wondered what his next maneuver would be.

In the interest of pursuing his investigation, George Dillman elected to miss dinner that evening. Wearing an overcoat and scarf, he also took a hat with him when he stepped out onto the main deck. There was a blustery wind and the sea was quite choppy. It was the sort of weather when few passengers would venture outside. Dillman nevertheless expected to find one of them on deck. Since there was none of the stately ritual followed in first class, dinner in steerage was served earlier and quicker. Leonard Rush had left immediately afterward.

Dillman found him sitting in a corner with a blanket around his shoulders. Rush was no more than seven or eight yards from the lifeboat from which the discarded frock coat had been retrieved.

"Is this where you always sleep?" asked Dillman.

"Go away!"

"I need a word with you, Mr. Rush."

"Stop haunting me!"

"The only way to get rid of me is to help me," said Dillman with authority. "What I didn't tell you when we last met is that I'm working as a detective on this ship. I'm investigating the disappearance of a passenger."

"It's nothing to do with me," said Rush, retreating farther into his blanket. "Why bother me?"

"Because I think you might have been a witness."

"No, Mr. Dillman."

"Answer my first question: Do you always sleep here?"

"Yes," replied the other. "It's out of the wind."

"It also happens to be close to the place

where an item belonging to the missing man was found. If you were lurking here in the shadows you could well have seen something."

"I was fast asleep."

"How do I know that?"

"Because I'm telling you."

"I think you're lying."

"I don't give a damn what you think!"

He tried to turn away but Dillman grabbed his shoulder to prevent him from doing so. He crouched down beside Rush and spoke with quiet intensity.

"I don't think you quite understand," he began. "A serious crime was committed last night and I fancy that you're in a position to help me solve it. Perhaps I should warn you that I have powers of arrest aboard the *Celtic.* If you persist in holding back crucial information, I'll have no alternative but to have you locked up by the master-at-arms. Do you want to spend the rest of the voyage behind bars?"

"No!" yelled Rush. "I've done nothing wrong."

"You're withholding evidence. That's a crime."

"I don't *have* any evidence."

"When we reach Southampton you'll be formally charged by the police. Unless you stop lying to me, that is. I've been doing this job long enough to know when someone is not telling the truth, Mr. Rush. I know the smell of dishonesty and I'm catching a distinctive whiff of it right now." Rush looked cornered. Dillman changed his tack. "It may be that you don't think it was your business," he said reasonably. "Or that you misunderstood what you saw. I appreciate that, Mr. Rush. But even the tiniest scrap of information can be valuable in a murder inquiry."

Rush sat up. "It wasn't a murder, Mr. Dillman."

"Then what was it?" Realizing that he had given himself away, Rush took refuge in silence. Dillman lost patience. "Right," he said, getting up and hauling the man to his feet, "let's get you safely locked up where you belong, shall we?"

"No!" protested the other.

"You're impeding the investigation."

"It wasn't murder."

Dillman released him. "Go on. I'm listening."

"It was suicide," said Rush, wrestling with his memories. "He had the courage to do what I should have done. But I had nobody to help me do it. That was the difference. All I had to do was to throw myself over the side but I couldn't manage it. I was too scared."

"Tell me what you saw."

"He had a friend. When I woke up, I saw two of them over there by the lifeboat. His friend was lifting him over the rail, Mr. Dillman. I heard him say something. He sounded very sad."

"What did you hear?"

"He said, 'I'll miss you, David.' That's all. It wasn't murder. He was helping someone take his own life. I don't know who David was but I understand how he must have felt. I *envied* him, Mr. Dillman."

"How can you envy a man like that?"

"I wanted someone to do that kind of favor for me."

"That was no favor. It was cold-blooded murder."

"His friend was showing kindness."

"Can you describe this friend?"

"It was dark. All I could see were blurred shapes."

"Didn't it occur to you to intervene?"

"Why?"

"It's what anyone else would have done," said Dillman. "It's what Mr. Pinnick would have done, I'm certain."

Rush gave a mirthless laugh. "Don't mention Saul Pinnick."

"Why not?"

"I detest the man."

"From what I hear, he's been your only friend on the ship."

"That's why I can't abide him," said Rush vehemently. "I want someone to help me die and all that Mr. Pinnick is interested in is keeping me alive."

"Why didn't you report what you saw?"

"I told you. It's no concern of mine."

"Someone was pushed overboard. That's a crime."

"Not if the man wanted to die. It was an act of mercy."

"I don't think there was any mercy involved," said Dillman, "and you might have realized that if you'd woken up a little earlier. Thank you very much. You've confirmed what I feared."

"Does that mean you'll leave me alone?"

"Yes, Mr. Rush. You can go back to sleep now."

Even by the high standards that had already been set, the dinner that evening was exceptional. Genevieve Masefield began with a delicious *consommé d'Orléans*, then she chose sirloin for her main course. It was served with green peas, rice, cauliflower à la crème and exquisite *pommes de terre châ-*

teau. For pudding, she selected *gâteau Mex-
icaine.* While she enjoyed the meal, her mind
was inevitably grappling with the problem
of solving the various crimes. Somewhere in
the room, she believed, was the man who
had killed David Lowbury and been responsible for a series of thefts. It took an effort
for Genevieve to conceal her deep unease.

Joshua Cleves sat beside her but he had
been unusually subdued during the meal.
Genevieve had to endure none of his cus-
tomary shrewd glances and gentle innuen-
dos. He was clearly adopting a new approach.

"Joshua had a lovely idea," said Lady Bulstrode.

"I'm a man of lovely ideas," said Cleves
genially.

"He suggested that we all go to the Derby
together this year. Can you think of a more
pleasurable way to renew our friendship?"

"We'd have our own box, of course," said
her husband.

"You must come, Miss Masefield. Please
say that you will."

"I'd love to come, Lady Bulstrode," said
Genevieve, trying to sound as if she would
accept an invitation she was certain to
refuse. "Thank you for asking me."

"We're minded to ask Sir Arthur and his

wife to join us."

"It would make up a very jolly party," said Lord Bulstrode. "All six of us together. We can eat, drink and be merry."

"And place a few well-judged bets," Cleves insisted.

"I have a knack of making a tidy profit out of the Derby."

"I'll be glad to see how it's done, Rupert."

Genevieve was aware of the manipulation that lay behind the invitation. Though Cleves was no longer engaged in a subtle courtship of her, he had carefully set up two events — visits, respectively, to the Bulstrode country seat and to the Derby — that would draw Genevieve and him closer together. She had no doubt that he would attempt to devise other schemes before the end of the voyage, and that Frank Spurrier would do the same as well. The time would come when they would both have to be firmly rebuffed.

Having finished his meal, Spurrier made a point of coming across to their table and standing behind Genevieve so that she could not see him properly. He thanked Lord and Lady Bulstrode for including him in their private party earlier on, then exchanged a few words with them.

"Shall I see you in the smoking room,

Josh?" he asked.

"I'll come with you right now," said Cleves, getting up and excusing himself from the others. "There's something I want to discuss with you, Frank."

Genevieve was convinced that she would be the main subject of their discussion and they had gone off for a tactical debate. It was demeaning for her to be fought over by two men who were more interested in the tussle itself than in her. Evidently she was the designated prize and it made her seethe with anger. She decided that it was the last meal she would share with Joshua Cleves. Hiding her annoyance behind a smile, she took her leave of her other dinner companions and walked toward the door.

As she left the saloon, someone stepped out from behind a pillar and beckoned her across. Thoda Burbridge was patently worried. Her face was etched with concern and her voice trembled.

"I must speak with you, Miss Masefield," she said.

"Of course."

"Your husband is in danger."

"You told me that before," said Genevieve, "and I passed on the warning. My husband pointed out, quite rightly, that the job we do is bound to have its hazards."

"I'm talking about *now.*"

"What do you mean?"

"I have a very strong feeling that something is about to happen to him," explained Thoda. "Where is he — still in the dining saloon?"

"No, Mrs. Burbridge. He had work to do elsewhere."

"Find him, Miss Masefield."

"Why?"

"Find him at once," urged Thoda, taking her by both shoulders. "Go in search of him now — before it's too late."

After his visit to the main deck, George Dillman spent a long time trying to work out how the killer could have taken his victim from the first-class area to the point where he shoved him overboard. He went through a maze of corridors and up and down a confusing series of companionways. The most direct route was one used only by the crew and Dillman timed the journey from David Lowbury's cabin to the lifeboat on the main deck. If he had been held at gunpoint, Lowbury could have been hustled quickly from first class to steerage and beyond. The only person to see them was Leonard Rush.

As he tried to envisage the scene once

again, Dillman retraced his steps. He was soon walking past the cabin to which Lowbury had returned when he was sent to fetch some pills. Jane Lowbury would still be inside and Dillman was tempted to knock on the door to see how she was, and to tell her what he had learned from Rush. In the end he decided against it, not wishing to disturb her and needing to have more complete evidence of what had actually occurred before talking to her. He walked on past and turned a corner.

Dillman did not hear the footsteps behind him. The first hint he had of trouble was when something hard struck the back of his head. Dazed by the blow, he stumbled forward but managed to steady himself by putting both hands out wide against the wall. His attacker was on him in a flash, holding him tight with one arm while clamping the other against his throat and applying pressure. Too groggy to respond at first, Dillman was revived by the sharp pain in his neck. All the breath was being slowly choked out of him and he started to splutter. Time was rapidly running out for him.

With a supreme effort he turned sideways, then flung himself backward with all his might, ramming the other man against the wall and forcing him to weaken his hold.

Dillman pummeled fiercely with both elbows and heard his adversary grunt in pain. Then he got both hands on the arm around his throat and slowly pried it away. The man changed the point of attack at once. Grabbing the detective by the shoulders, he hurled him against the opposite wall, then delivered a punch to the ear that sent Dillman reeling.

Someone came into the corridor at the far end and walked toward them. There was a witness. The attacker had to get away. Using both fists, he clubbed Dillman to the floor, kicked him a few times, then fled in the opposite direction and vanished around the corner. Blood streaming down the back of his head, and limbs feeling like lead, Dillman drifted slowly into oblivion.

Twelve

Lord Bulstrode was so shocked by what he had just seen that he came to a sudden halt. He was scandalized. A man had just been violently attacked in front of him. Such things simply did not happen in first class on ocean liners. The victim clearly needed help. Lord Bulstrode forced himself into action. Moving as fast as his body would allow on a full stomach, he hurried along the corridor and with great difficulty lowered himself to one knee. He stared down at Dillman with dismay.

"Are you all right, old chap?" he asked.

He saw the blood for the first time and blanched. Taking a white handkerchief from his pocket, he held it against the scalp wound. Lord Bulstrode was made painfully aware of his age and of the fact that he had drunk far too much that evening. His back and legs were hurting because of the unaccustomed position in which he had put himself, and his mind was fuzzy. Unsure what to do, he hovered uncertainly over Dillman and uttered unheard words of sympathy.

"You just lie there, my friend. You'll be fine when we get some help. It looks far worse than it really is. I'm sure it's nothing serious. Hold on. I'll fetch a doctor."

With a supreme effort he got to his feet and winced at the tremors he felt in his left knee. His head was starting to pound and his eyesight was blurred. While he gathered his strength he leaned against the wall, panting noisily and wishing that he were in better physical condition. When a young woman came into the corridor at the far end, he did not immediately recognize her. It was only when she came running toward him that he realized it was Genevieve Masefield. She flung herself down beside the body.

"What happened?" she gasped.

"He was beaten to the floor by some blackguard," said Lord Bulstrode. "The coward ran away when I came along. I was about to go in search of a doctor."

Genevieve was relieved to see obvious signs of life in her husband. Dillman was breathing normally and his eyelids were starting to flicker. Apart from the scalp wound she could see no other injury. Holding his face tenderly in her hands, she spoke to him.

"George," she whispered. "Can you hear me?"

"You know the fellow?" asked Lord Bulstrode, touched by the affection in her voice.

"Very well."

"Who is he?"

"A friend of mine — George Dillman."

"I'm glad that I arrived when I did, Miss Masefield, or that rogue might have finished the poor man off. Murder on the White Star Line!" he exclaimed, waving his arms. "It's unthinkable."

"He's coming round," said Genevieve, bending over Dillman.

"Feel free to use my handkerchief. We don't want any blood on that lovely dress of yours."

"He's far more important than a dress."

"Of course."

"George," she said. "It's me, Genevieve."

Dillman struggled to open his eyes. "Where am I?"

"Someone attacked you. Lord Bulstrode was a witness."

"I was," attested the peer. "He was a real brute."

As he regained consciousness, Dillman

was acutely aware of the searing pain at the back of his skull. He put a hand to his head and felt the handkerchief that Genevieve was now using to stem the flow of blood. Memories began to come back. He chided himself for having been caught off guard.

"I was hit from behind," he said, trying to master the pain. "When I came around a corner, someone must have followed me."

"He did," confirmed Lord Bulstrode.

"You saw him?"

"As large as life."

"Did you get a good look at him?" said Genevieve.

"Afraid not, Miss Masefield. He was too far away."

"But you can tell us something about him, surely?"

"I think so."

"How old was he?" asked Dillman, sitting up with Genevieve's help. "And how tall?"

"I only got a brief glimpse of him," explained Lord Bulstrode, "but I'd say that he was somewhat older than you, Mr. Dillman. And he was nowhere near your height."

"What sort of build did he have?"

"Thickset."

"What else do you remember?"

"Very little. It was over so quickly. I was appalled to think that such an unconscionable thug could be employed on the *Celtic*."

Dillman was perplexed. "He's a member of the crew?"

"Yes," said Lord Bulstrode confidently. "It's one thing I do recall. The man who attacked you was dressed as a cabin steward."

Sir Arthur and Lady Conan Doyle did not linger in any of the public rooms. Now that everyone was aware of their presence on the ship, they were under constant surveillance, either watched in admiration from afar or approached directly by those wishing to boast to their friends that they had met a famous British author. Sir Arthur yearned for the privacy of their stateroom. As they walked along the corridor toward it, he thought he had shaken off his devotees for the night when the most fanatical of them suddenly stepped out of an alcove to confront him. Nobby Ruggles stood to attention.

"Good evening, Sir Arthur," he said.

"Oh — hello there, Ruggles."

The barber bestowed an obsequious smile on Sir Arthur's wife. "Good evening to you, Lady Conan Doyle."

"Good evening," she said with some misgiving.

"I know that it's late," said Ruggles, "but I wondered if you'd like to round off the evening by listening to my rendition of 'the Groom's Story'? It was much appreciated at the concert."

"No doubt about that, Ruggles," said Sir Arthur. "We've heard glowing reports of your performance."

"I'd be happy to re-create it for you."

"Not now."

"It won't take long, sir."

"We're both feeling very tired," said Lady Conan Doyle, "and it's a poem that deserves a larger audience than two."

Ruggles was persistent. "Then why not invite some friends into your stateroom?" he suggested. "You could all enjoy a glass of brandy while I recite the work of the greatest poet since Shakespeare."

"Heavens above!" cried Sir Arthur with embarrassment. "Let's not exaggerate. Compared to Shakespeare I'm a crude versifier. And there are many better poets among my contemporaries. I can't hold a candle to Kipling," he admitted frankly. "On my first visit to America I played golf with him and told him how his work had inspired me. Rudyard Kipling is a true poet. I'm really a novelist who strayed into verse by way of experiment."

"Well, it was a very good experiment, Sir Arthur."

"That may be so, Mr. Ruggles," said Lady Conan Doyle, gracious yet firm. "However, this is neither the time nor place to discuss the matter. My husband and I simply wish to retire to bed, so I fear that we must decline your kind offer."

"Oh, I see." Ruggles was deflated. Reviving quickly, he held up the book that had been tucked under his arm. "Then perhaps you'll favor me with your signature, Sir Arthur. You did promise."

"Yes," agreed the other wearily. "I suppose I did."

"That, too, can wait," said his wife, determined to rescue him. "When Sir Arthur is ready, Mr. Ruggles, *he* will contact you."

"But it would only take a second," argued Ruggles.

"That second will be of my husband's own choosing."

"Tomorrow, perhaps," said Sir Arthur.

"Why not now?"

"I've already told you," said Lady Conan Doyle.

"Yes, you have." There was a flash of resentment in the barber's eye, then the obsequious smile returned. "I seem to have come at a bad time," he said, taking a step backward. "Tomorrow it shall be — or any other time Sir Arthur chooses. And we must arrange a private performance of 'the Groom's Story.' I recited it in tribute to you. If you wish, I can give you an encore of 'Corporal Dick's Promotion' as well."

"That won't be necessary," said Sir Arthur.

"Then we'll stick to the groom. He always gets a laugh."

"Another time, Ruggles."

"Of course, Sir Arthur. Good night to you both."

"Good night," they caroled.

Tucking the book back under his arm, Nobby Ruggles walked off smartly as if on the parade ground.

Sir Arthur used the key to let them into the stateroom. After switching on the light, he shut the door behind them.

" 'The Groom's Story,' " he said with a remorseful roll of his eyes. "I'm beginning to wish I'd never written that blessed poem."

"It's a lovely poem, Arthur — light, humorous and diverting. What I regret," said Lady Conan Doyle, removing her stole with a flourish, "is that it ever fell into the hands of Nobby Ruggles."

■ ■ ■ ■

George Dillman recovered quickly. When they had helped him back to his cabin, the ship's doctor had been summoned by Lord Bulstrode to treat the wound. Having cleaned away the blood, he inserted sutures and urged the detective to take to his bed. The advice was instantly disregarded. As soon as the doctor had left, Dillman was eager to return to work.

"It must have been Edward Hammond," he declared.

"Working as a steward?" asked Genevieve with disbelief.

"No, that was a convenient disguise to allow him to move freely around the ship. He'll have discarded it by now. Tonight's little episode may have been painful, but it's also encouraging."

"*Encouraging?* He almost killed you."

"He proved that we're on the right track, Genevieve. The reason he attacked me is that I'm breathing down his neck."

"I'm only interested in saving *your* neck," she said.

"I'll be more careful in future," he assured her, "and I won't be taken unawares again." He unlocked a valise and took out a revolver. "Mr. Hammond and I can fight on equal terms now."

"Take care, George!"

"We must both do that from now on."

Dillman's head ached unrelentingly but his brain was crystal clear. After listening to what Genevieve had done in the time they had been apart, he related his conversation with Leonard Rush and was convinced that what the miner actually saw was the body of David Lowbury being pushed into the sea. Instead of being an assisted suicide, it was a calculated act of murder.

"We still haven't found a motive," Genevieve observed.

"Then you must go in search of one."

"Me?"

"Yes, Genevieve," he said. "There's something we should have done earlier and that was to mention a certain name to Mrs. Lowbury."

"And what name was that?"

"Horace Pooley."

"Wasn't he the man killed by Hammond in New York?"

"Exactly. I want you to find out if Jane Lowbury had ever heard of him. Pooley was a wealthy financier. He and Lowbury were birds of a feather. They may have been friends. And while you're at it," he told her, "bring up the name of Edward Hammond."

"Why?"

"Because there's an outside chance she may know it."

"I don't see how, George."

"Hammond's victims had a similar background. The connection between the two crimes must lie somewhere in the financial world."

"Perhaps it does," said Genevieve, "but Mrs. Lowbury is unlikely to lead us to it. She and her husband haven't known each other all that long. How much will she have picked up about his business affairs in that time?"

He crossed to the door. "Ask her."

"Now?"

"There was a light in her cabin when I went past earlier," he said, "and she deserves to know what I discovered on the main deck. Since her husband was definitely thrown overboard, it's unfair to let her go on thinking he's still alive and on the ship."

"What will you do, George?"

He grinned. "Keep looking over my shoulder."

While they were in the lounge together, Frank Spurrier was unable to express his full anger to Joshua Cleves. He was obliged to take part in a conversation with two elderly Swedish passengers and a London impresario. Cleves had arranged to play cards that evening in the cabin of an acquaintance. When he excused himself, Spurrier also got up from his chair. Once the two of them were outside, the pretense of affability could be cast aside. Spurrier was simmering.

"Why the hell did you do it, Josh?" he demanded.

"Do what?"

"Tell Genevieve Masefield that we had that argument."

"It wasn't exactly a state secret, Frank."

"You should have kept your mouth shut."

"I'll do as I choose fit," said Cleves angrily. "I certainly won't ask *you* what I can and can't divulge. It's good that Genevieve should know the truth about you and not mistake you for the English gentleman you pretend to be."

"By the same token she recognizes you as a Polish Jew who tries to conceal his background out of a sense of shame."

"You're the person who's ashamed, Frank."

"No, I'm not."

"Then why are you so annoyed that I told Genevieve about the quarrel we had with

David Lowbury — and where *is* the man, anyway? Have you hidden him away somewhere?"

"Don't be ridiculous!"

"There's some strange link with Lowbury and you didn't want Genevieve to hear about it." His stare transfixed Spurrier. "What's going on?"

"Nothing," said Spurrier evasively.

"I'm bound to find out sooner or later."

"There's nothing, I assure you."

"Where is he?"

"I have no idea, Josh."

"Tell me the truth."

"That *is* the truth."

"I smell something fishy."

Spurrier held back the retort he was about to make. Instead, he inhaled deeply and took a moment to compose himself. Joshua Cleves would not be easily deceived. He knew Spurrier too well to be fobbed off with a lame excuse. It had been a mistake to argue with him.

"This is nothing to do with Lowbury," said Spurrier at length. "I couldn't care two hoots about the man. I just think it was unfair of you to give the impression to Miss Masefield that I had a bad temper." Cleves laughed. "When he told us we were wasting our time pursuing her, you were as angry as

I was, Josh. Did you mention that to her?"

"No," said Cleves, "but then I also omitted to tell her about the rest of your failings. You, on the other hand, couldn't wait to stick the knife into me."

"She was entitled to know the facts."

"Selected facts. Chosen to blacken my reputation."

"Chosen to fill out the picture."

Cleves chuckled. "Have it your way, Frank," he said. "Whatever you told Genevieve, it hasn't put her off me. We had a very amicable time over dinner this evening."

"I think she has your measure."

"Yes, I'm a friend of the British aristocracy."

"A friend or a performing bear?" asked Spurrier with a thin smile. "The simple fact is that, with all your advantages, you've failed to win the bet. I'll have to show you how it's done, Josh."

"Time is rapidly running out."

"When the moment comes, I move very fast."

"I'll still be ahead of you."

"Miss Masefield may have other ideas."

"She'll choose the better man," said Cleves, "and that has to be me. Excuse me, Frank," he went on, easing him aside. "The card table awaits me and I'm in the mood to win lots of money."

In the circumstances, Jane Lowbury took the news well. Genevieve had expected her to dissolve into tears when she heard what had happened to her husband, but she held them back. She had had time to prepare herself for the worst. Though she recoiled in horror, she also seemed relieved to have information about her husband's death instead of being kept in the dark.

"Who could want to *do* such a thing to David?" she asked.

"We have one possible suspect, Mrs. Lowbury," said Genevieve.

"Who is he?"

"Let me ask you a question first. Have you ever heard of a man named Horace Pooley?"

Jane looked surprised. "Why do you ask that?"

"It could be relevant."

"Then the answer is yes. Horace Pooley is a financier. He's very famous in New York. Because he's involved in all sorts of big projects, his photograph is often in the newspapers."

"I'm afraid that the only thing people will have been reading about him recently is his obituary."

"I didn't know that he'd died."

"He was killed, Mrs. Lowbury, by a man who burgled his house."

"That's dreadful!"

"Did you ever meet Mr. Pooley?"

"I didn't," said Jane, "but David knew him. They were about to make a deal at one point but it fell through. David always spoke highly of him. I can't believe that he was murdered."

"There's something else I must tell you," said Genevieve. "We've come to the conclusion that his killer is on board and that he was involved in the death of your husband."

"Are you sure?" gasped Jane, a hand to her mouth.

"Almost certain."

"What's the man's name?"

"Edward Hammond — but that's not the name under which he's traveling. He's sailing with a false passport."

Jane frowned in concentration. "Edward Hammond?"

"Does that name mean anything to you?"

"It could do," she answered. "David used to employ an Ed Hammond but he had to dismiss him. I don't know the full details except that David was tempted to call in the police."

"I don't suppose that you ever met Hammond?" said Genevieve.

"No."

"Did your husband tell you anything else about him?"

"Not really. He never talked much about his business."

"If Mr. Lowbury dismissed the man, Hammond might well have borne a grudge against him. He was clearly connected with the financial world in some way. When he realized that your husband was aboard, he took his revenge." Genevieve gave a shrug. "That's how it's starting to look."

"And this man is still at liberty?"

"I'm afraid so."

"Then why don't you arrest him?" said Jane anxiously. "If he's already killed two people, he's a danger to everyone."

"We know that, Mrs. Lowbury. Earlier this evening he attacked my partner, George Dillman."

"Goodness! Was he hurt?"

"Yes," said Genevieve, "but he was very fortunate. Someone came along and disturbed Hammond. He ran away."

"This is terrible! The man is a menace."

"That's why we're doing all we can to catch him. Our problem is that we don't know which name he's hiding behind or in which class he's traveling. He obviously has access to first class. When he attacked my partner, Hammond was disguised as a cabin steward."

"Can't you just search the ship from top to bottom?"

"We could if we knew who we were looking for, Mrs. Lowbury, but we don't. The description we have of Edward Hammond is very general. It could fit dozens of people."

"But while he's free," said Jane, "none of us is safe."

"It's the reason you must take no chances, Mrs. Lowbury. Since this man has never met you, he should have no call to be hostile toward you, but he seems to have a warped mind. He might decide that revenge against your husband would only be complete if he added you to his list of victims." Jane gave a cry of alarm. "That's only a remote possibility, but it's one we have to take seriously. To that end, I'd advise you to remain in your cabin."

"Oh, I will, Miss Masefield. I won't stir from here."

"Don't let anyone in unless you know who it is."

Jane gave a shudder. "I feel so vulnerable."

"We'll arrange for someone to patrol the corridor outside at regular intervals," said Genevieve to reassure her. "And we'll be taking a closer look at anyone in the uniform of a cabin steward."

"What about you?"

"I don't follow."

"This man is a ruthless killer," said Jane, "If you go after him, you're risking your life. Do you have any kind of weapon?"

"No, Mrs. Lowbury."

"Then how can you hope to capture him?"

"My partner is armed."

"Oh, I see." She sat down on a chair and tried to take in all that she had heard. Eventually, she looked up. "What about David?" she said piteously. "Will there be any kind of funeral?"

"We can't have a funeral without a body."

"He deserves *some* kind of service, Miss Masefield."

"I'll speak to the chaplain."

"No, no, don't do that. Let me think about it first. I'm not sure that I'm strong enough to go through with it just yet."

"Would it make a difference if we caught Edward Hammond?"

"Oh, yes!" said Jane with feeling. "It would make all the difference in the world."

"What makes you think he has an accomplice?" asked Rutherford.

"It's the way he can disappear with ease,"

said Dillman thoughtfully. "I feel that someone is sheltering him."

"Who?"

"It may be a member of the crew. Someone provided him with a steward's uniform, after all. It was good camouflage."

"I'd hate to think that a member of our crew is working with Hammond," said the purser worriedly. "The White Star Line is very careful about the people it employs, even at the lowest level. If we have a villain on the payroll, he must be weeded out immediately."

It was early morning and they were in Rutherford's office. He had been flabbergasted to hear of the assault on Dillman, and sorry that the detective had sustained a nasty head wound. Though it was largely concealed by Dillman's hair, it still smarted. The purser was baffled by something.

"Why did Hammond pick on you, Mr. Dillman?"

"Because I'm on his trail."

"Yes, but how did he know that you're the ship's detective?"

"He must have seen me conducting my search," said Dillman. "Unless, of course, he was tipped off by this accomplice of his."

"But almost nobody apart from me knows that you and Miss Masefield were hired as detectives. The vast majority of the crew think that you're simply passengers."

"And we want them to go on thinking that. It's the same with everyone else. When I was attacked last night, we didn't tell Lord Bulstrode that we had an official role on board. All that he knows is what he saw."

"A first-class passenger being beaten up by a cabin steward."

"Hammond had more on his mind than grievous bodily harm."

"Yes," said Rutherford, swallowing hard. "But for the timely arrival of a witness, I could now be attending your funeral."

"I'm not ready for that just yet," warned Dillman with a grin.

"If he's tried once, he may well try again."

"That's why I'm carrying a weapon, Mr. Rutherford."

"What about Miss Masefield? Is she a target as well?"

"Hopefully, she's not. But I've told her to exercise additional care and to stay in public areas. She's perfectly safe there."

"Shouldn't you be doing the same?"

"Not if I want to catch him. I need to be seen in order to draw him out of cover again. Don't worry," he said, patting the revolver under his coat. "I'm not a tethered goat. I'm armed. So, I fear, is Edward Hammond."

"What about this accomplice of his?"

"I can't even guarantee that he exists, Mr. Rutherford. I'm relying on instinct. The reason that Miss Masefield came looking for me last night was that she'd been warned by Mrs. Burbridge that I was in imminent danger."

"Thank goodness she did!"

"I lack that kind of prescience but I have learned to pick up some vibrations. Experience tells me we're looking for Edward Hammond and an unnamed accomplice."

"Who could or could not be in the crew."

"Yes," said Dillman. "In case he isn't, then I need to ask a favor of you. I want to borrow your master key."

"Why?"

"To get into the cabin of Mr. Frank Spurrier."

"Do you think that *he's* involved in some way?"

"Let's just say that I'd like to investigate him a little. Give me five minutes in his cabin and I'll find out if he's the person he professes to be."

Rutherford was cautious. "I can't authorize the search of a cabin unless it's in exceptional circumstances."

"I would have thought the murder of one passenger and an assault on another might qualify as exceptional. And I'm not only depending on my own judgment here. Miss Masefield also has cause to suspect Frank Spurrier."

"Five minutes, you say?"

"Less, probably."

"You'll need someone to act as a lookout."

"I'll take Wilf Carr with me," said Dillman. "Nobody will look twice at a cabin steward waiting in a corridor." He gave a grim chuckle. "I found that out last night."

As an insurance against a further ambush, Sir Arthur Conan Doyle decided to honor his promise at the earliest opportunity. Immediately after breakfast he went to the men's hairdressing salon and signed the book of poems belonging to Nobby Ruggles. Because the barber was about to shave a customer whose face was already covered in white lather, the conversation was necessarily brief.

"Thank you, Sir Arthur," said Ruggles.

"My pleasure."

"I carried this all the way through the Boer War."

"I'm relieved to see that it survived intact."

"The poems are so easy to learn."

"You proved that," said Conan Doyle.

"When would you like me to perform 'the Groom's Story'?"

"When we have time."

"And when would that be?" pressed Ruggles, turning to give an appeasing smile to his customer. "I work long hours here, so evening would be best."

"I'll be in touch."

"It's well worth hearing. Everybody said so."

"I'm sure they did, Ruggles," said Conan Doyle, "but you're not sailing on the *Celtic* in order to recite my poetry. You're here to cut hair and shave off beards. We must keep things in proportion."

"Nothing is as important as your work, Sir Arthur."

"It is if you're sitting in the barber's chair."

"Shall we say this evening after dinner?"

"No, Ruggles."

"Before dinner, then?"

"We'll let you know," said Conan Doyle easily. "Meanwhile I'd be grateful if you didn't keep popping up like a jack-in-the-box. My wife and I are rather tired of it. Is that understood?"

"Of course," replied Ruggles.

"Thank you. Good-bye."

"Good-bye, sir."

Ruggles gave him a salute, but the moment Conan Doyle turned his back, he dropped his arm and glared at the author. Putting the book aside, he picked up his razor and began to sharpen it on the leather strop.

Wilfred Carr was thrilled to be called upon to act as a lookout. While the steward lurked outside the cabin, Dillman let himself in with the master key and began a rigorous search. Before coming, he had taken the trouble to ensure that the occupant was otherwise engaged. In the unlikely event that Spurrier returned unexpectedly, Carr had been told to bang hard on the cabin door so that Dillman could make his escape in time. As it was, no signal came. He was safe.

The detective was swift and methodical, working his way through every drawer, cupboard and item of luggage. Frank Spurrier was a man of taste, buying his suits from a Savile Row tailor and his hats and overcoats from Jermyn Street, also in London. Nothing in his effects suggested cheapness or lack of discernment. A first search revealed nothing incriminating. Dillman therefore began a more thorough exploration, looking at places he had ignored before. He felt under the bath, he went through the pockets of each garment and he peered into every last corner of the cabin.

His tenacity was eventually rewarded. Under the table, invisible from above, was a small box that had been neatly taped to the wood. Even the cabin steward would not have known that it was there. Taking a penknife from his pocket, Dillman slit the tape so that the box fell into his hand. He stood up and flipped open the lid of the box. Inside was a copy of *A Study in Scarlet.*

The game was afoot.

Genevieve was not looking forward to his company, but she knew how crucial it was to keep Frank Spurrier occupied while his cabin was being searched. She found him in the lounge, reading a magazine.

"Do you mind if I disturb you?" she said.

"Not at all," he replied, tossing the magazine aside and rising to his feet. "Please take a seat. I'm delighted to see you."

"Thank you."

They sat down opposite each other. As he appraised her Genevieve was conscious once more of the strange power that he seemed to exude. There was a fixed smile on his face but she had no notion of what he might be thinking.

"It's good to see you without Josh in tow," he began.

"Mr. Cleves is not my traveling companion."

"He boasted that you were on first-name terms."

"That's a permissible informality on a voyage," she said.

"Does that mean I can take advantage of it?"

"If you wish, Mr. Spurrier."

"I do, Genevieve, and you know what I'd prefer to be called."

"I believe I do, Frank."

"That's better," he said, relaxing. "I had the feeling that I'd never get past your outer fortifications."

"Have you been laying siege to me, then?"

"Perish the thought!"

"Then what have you been doing?"

"Taking a natural interest in the most beautiful young woman aboard. There you are, Genevieve, I've given you a straight answer."

"Frank by name and Frank by nature."

"Give or take the occasional white lie," he added. "But I'm so glad of this opportunity to put the record straight on one small matter. Whatever Josh told you, I didn't lose my temper with David Lowbury. I simply took exception at something he said about you."

"Me?"

"He passed an unpardonable remark. Let's leave it at that."

"Are you telling me that you were defending my honor?"

"That's what it amounts to."

"In that case, I owe you my thanks. However, I'm surprised at Mr. Lowbury. I obviously misjudged him."

"We all did, Genevieve."

"You got to know him and his wife quite well, didn't you?"

"As well as one can when dining together."

"I don't recall seeing either of them around recently."

Spurrier smiled. "They are on honeymoon, after all."

"Yes," said Genevieve, thinking of the ordeal that Jane Lowbury was suffering. "I suppose that's the explanation." She looked up to see Joshua Cleves descending upon them. "Ah, we have company."

Beaming away, Cleves lowered himself into a seat beside them.

"My two best friends," he announced.

"I thought your closest friends were Rupert and Agnes," said Spurrier, pronouncing the names with a sarcastic edge. "What's happened, Josh? Has the British aristocracy dropped you?"

"No, they've clutched me to their bosom. Am I right, Genevieve?"

"They do seem to like you," she agreed.

"I'm a very likable man. Now," he said, "what bunkum has Frank been telling you about me this time?"

"Your name hardly entered the conversation," said Spurrier. "Genevieve and I were just having a quiet chat. It's what English people do on transatlantic voyages."

"Thanks for reminding me that I'm an American — or, if you prefer, the son of Jewish immigrants from Poland. In both countries, oddly enough, a quiet chat is not unknown."

"I was asking about David Lowbury," said Genevieve.

"I've no time for the man."

"He seems to have vanished."

"You won't find me complaining about that, Genevieve."

"What do you have against him?"

"Nothing," said Spurrier, jumping in before Cleves could speak. "Lowbury is a disagreeable fellow. Why don't we order coffee and talk about someone more palatable?"

"Yes," consented Cleves amiably. "We can talk about *me.*"

■ ■ ■ ■

Sir Arthur Conan Doyle was overjoyed to have his copy of *A Study in Scarlet* returned to him. When Dillman called on him in his stateroom, he pumped the detective's hand by way of thanks.

"Where on earth did you find it?" he inquired.

"I'd rather not say until the full facts have emerged. Collusion is at work, Sir Arthur. The man in whose cabin I found the book is not the thief. He had a confederate."

"Well, I trust that they'll both be punished," said Lady Conan Doyle. "This whole business has been very distressing."

"It's over now, Jean," her husband declared, opening the book to look inside. "My lecture notes are all here — splendid!"

"I must ask two things of you, Sir Arthur," said Dillman. "First, please deposit the book in a safe so that I don't have to hunt for it again." Conan Doyle signaled agreement. "Second, don't mention the fact of its theft and retrieval to anyone else."

"I wouldn't dream of it, Mr. Dillman."

"We owe you profound gratitude," said Lady Conan Doyle, "and I must add an apology for doubting you. My husband was convinced that you would find the book in time, but I did not share his faith."

"I'll let you in to a secret, Lady Conan Doyle," said Dillman. "Neither did I at first. The point is that book and author have been happily reunited. By the way," he went on, "I hear that we have an expert on your work aboard, Sir Arthur. One of the barbers has been reciting your poems at various concerts."

Conan Doyle sighed. "His name is Nobby Ruggles."

"And he's a confounded nuisance," added his wife.

"Oh, he's not that bad, Jean."

"Yes, he is. He keeps snapping at your heels like a terrier, desperate for you to autograph his book of poems."

Dillman was alerted. "A book of poems?"

"It is called *Songs of Action.*"

"And would it be a first edition?"

"I'm sure that it would," said Conan Doyle. "Ruggles has been sitting on it for years like a mother hen on her eggs. He claims to know every poem by heart."

"What an extraordinary compliment to you, Sir Arthur."

"That's what I thought at first."

"Mr. Ruggles overstepped the mark," said Lady Conan Doyle. "He doesn't seem to know the difference between hero-worship and polite conduct. He did everything he could to wheedle his way in here."

"Into your stateroom?"

"Yes, Mr. Dillman. It was so intrusive."

"The fellow is too eager to please," said Conan Doyle, adopting a more tolerant tone. "Because we missed his performance of one of my poems, he wanted to recite it to us in private."

"In *here?*"

"That's right, Mr. Dillman. He was most insistent."

"Thank you for telling me," said Dillman. "I may need to talk to this barber myself. What manner of man is he, Sir Arthur?"

"An old soldier who misses the excitement of army life."

Nobby Ruggles was allowed a mid-morning break of fifteen minutes. Instead of enjoying his usual rest and refreshment, he slipped out of the salon and hurried to the nearest companionway. Making sure that nobody saw him, he climbed the steps that led to the promenade deck. At the top he inched the door open and checked that nobody was in the vicinity. Then he darted out and made his way along a corridor. When a passenger came out of a cabin ahead of him, Ruggles gave him a deferential smile and went past. He turned a corner, walked another five yards, then stopped to look in both directions. Relieved to see that he was alone, he rapped on the door.

"Who is it?" asked a voice from inside the cabin.

Genevieve was astounded by the revelation about Frank Spurrier. When she met up with Dillman she had not expected such a dramatic development. Her jaw dropped.

"You found the book in his cabin?" she said incredulously.

"Cunningly concealed beneath the desk."

"I'd never have accused him of being a thief."

"Oh, I don't think he stole the novel," said Dillman. "Someone else did that and sold it to him. Spurrier is a receiver of stolen goods."

"That still makes him a criminal, George. Why should he want to buy the book? He runs a respectable auction house. It's not an item that he could sell openly without causing suspicion."

"That's why it will go to a private collector. He would never accept something like that unless he knew exactly where to place it. I'm sure that he knows people willing to pay a high price for a unique copy of *A Study in Scarlet* — people who don't ask questions about how he acquired such an item. I had a glimpse into that world when I was a Pinkerton agent," said Dillman reflectively. "If a famous painting disappeared, it never turned up on the open market. It was offered to private collectors with no scruples about buying stolen property."

"Is Sir Arthur's book that valuable?"

"It doesn't compare with an Old Master, but it would certainly tempt a bibliophile. The longer he keeps the book, the more its value would grow. It's always possible, of course, that Spurrier intended to keep it himself until it could command a higher price."

"Are you going to arrest him?"

"I thought that you might like that honor, Genevieve," he said with a twinkle in his eye. "I've an idea how we should go about it."

"Where's the book now?"

"Restored to its grateful owner."

"Frank Spurrier will have noticed that it's missing, then."

"I hardly think so."

"Why is that, George?"

"Because it was hidden in a box that was

taped to the underside of the desk. All I had to do was to replace the box in the same position. If he chances to look under the desk, he'll think that his booty is intact."

"I look forward to confronting him," said Genevieve with relish. "Arresting him is the best way possible to stop him pestering me."

"I feel that Joshua Cleves should be there as well. Then you'll be able to rid yourself of his attentions at the same time. I think he'll be shocked to learn that he's been pursuing a ship's detective all this while. Invite them both here, Genevieve."

"To my cabin?"

"What better place?" he said. "They'll both come running."

Genevieve was intrigued by the notion. She could make an arrest and reject her self-appointed suitors at the same time. She told Dillman about the conversation she had had with the two men in the lounge, and how they had been vying for her favors.

"I'm glad that all that will come to an end," she said. "But if Frank Spurrier didn't steal that book, then who did?"

"That's the first question I'll ask him, Genevieve. I thought it was an isolated crime, completely detached from all the other things that have happened on the ship. I've revised that judgment now."

"All the crimes are the work of the same man?"

"The same man and his accomplice. There are two of them."

"Do you have any idea who they are?"

"Not yet," he said, "but I'm hoping that Frank Spurrier will be able to point us in the right direction." He winked at her. "Perhaps you should send him a little note, Genevieve."

Thoda Burbridge was strolling along the promenade deck when she was accosted by one of her admirers. Sophie Trouncer was delighted to have a moment alone with her.

"Oh, Mrs. Burbridge," she said, "I can't thank you enough."

"All I did was to pass on a message to you."

"But it's one that I desperately needed to hear. I've been so immersed in mourning the death of my husband that I felt guilty if another man aroused my interest in however casual a way. It was as if I was betraying Geoffrey."

"Not at all," said Thoda.

"Mother always urged me to marry again, but it seemed wrong."

"Each of us mourns in a different way, Mrs. Trouncer. In your case, you allowed

403

much more than a decent interval, so you should have no qualms about countenancing the idea of a second husband."

"But I needed to be given permission."

"I'm glad that I was able to help."

"I needed Geoffrey to release me," Sophie went on. "We were so close that life with another man was never an option. Now, it is."

"Good."

"More to the point, I believe that I've met him."

"Oh?"

"We've shared the same table and got to know each other very well. He's a little younger than I am," she confided with a giggle, "but Mother dismisses that as a mathematical quibble."

Thoda laughed. "Mrs. Hoyland has a robust attitude to life."

"She's always been so forthright and full of energy."

"Does she approve of your choice?"

"In every possible way."

"Then I wish you well, Mrs. Trouncer," said Thoda. "When we sat around that table in my cabin, I can assure you that I did not set out to act as a matchmaker. If that is what I turned out to be, then I'm happy for you."

"I'm hoping that you might help."

"In what way?"

"You sense things about people, Mrs. Burbridge. You knew about the circumstances of my birth and you guessed that that odious Mr. Agnew had been involved with a Mormon community at one point."

"That wasn't a guess, Mrs. Trouncer — I was certain of the fact."

"I wondered if I could trespass on you," said Sophie impulsively. "I know that's it's a misuse of your gift and that I should be ashamed to ask this, but I'm finding it hard to contain my excitement. I want you to tell me if this particular gentleman is really the one for me."

Thoda was insulted. "I'm not a fortune-teller in a booth at a funfair," she said haughtily. "I'm an acknowledged medium. I do not predict people's marital arrangements."

"Would you at least agree to meet Mr. Dillman?"

"No, Mrs. Trouncer. What I will tell you is this, however. If you do marry again, I can promise you that it will not be to anyone who is sailing on this ship." She swept off. "Good day to you!"

When the steward brought him the note,

Frank Spurrier was still in the lounge. Genevieve Masefield wanted to see him in her cabin as soon as possible. Leaping up, he went off to obey the request at once, convinced that his subtle wooing was at last about to pay dividends. The feeling of elation lasted all the way to her cabin door. It was then dispersed by the arrival of Joshua Cleves.

"What the devil are *you* doing here?" Spurrier challenged.

"I was about to ask you the same question, Frank."

"Genevieve sent me a note."

"I had one as well," said Cleves, taking it from his pocket. "She wanted to see me here. Ah, I think I know what's going on," he continued smugly. "The day of decision has come. Genevieve is going to choose between the two of us and that means you'll be ousted."

"You're the one to be rejected, Josh."

Before they could debate the issue the door suddenly opened and Genevieve beckoned them in. Cleves went boldly over the threshold but his confidence faltered when he saw that George Dillman was already in the cabin. Spurrier followed him in. After shutting the door, Genevieve went to stand beside her husband.

"I believe that you've both met George Dillman," she said, taking his hand. "What he forgot to mention is that we're married."

Cleves spluttered and Spurrier goggled. Both were crestfallen. Two men who prided themselves on their instinctive knowledge of women had been completely fooled.

"You're married to a ship's detective?" said Cleves, agog.

"It's worse than that," explained Dillman. "Genevieve is both wife and partner. She, too, is employed by the White Star Line as a detective."

Spurrier was fuming. "Then why didn't she have the grace to tell us?" he said vehemently. "And why drag us here to watch this absurd little charade?"

"It's no charade, Mr. Spurrier. You were invited for a specific reason and Mr. Cleves is here as an observer."

"And what am I supposed to observe?" said Cleves grumpily.

"The arrest of your friend."

"Frank Spurrier," said Genevieve, taking over, "it's my duty to arrest you on a charge of receiving stolen goods. A copy of a book that was taken from Sir Arthur Conan Doyle was found in your cabin. As a result you'll have to spend the rest of the voyage in the custody of the sergeant-at-arms."

Cleves was rocked. "Is this true, Frank?"

"No," retorted the other. "There's been some grotesque mistake here. I know nothing about a stolen book."

"Then why was it found by my husband," said Genevieve, "hidden in a box that bore your name?"

"It must have been planted there by someone."

"And I'm looking at the person who planted it."

"Frank — a crook!" said Cleves with a guffaw. "This is priceless! I'm so glad I was here to witness the arrest."

"Shut up, Josh!" snarled Spurrier.

"Yes," said Dillman, "I think we can dispense with your presence now, Mr. Cleves." He shepherded him out of the cabin. "Good-bye."

Dillman shut the door but they could still hear Cleves's laughter as he walked off down the corridor. Frank Spurrier's humiliation was intensified. As he stared at Genevieve, his eyes blazed.

"You'll need a lot more evidence to convict me," he said.

"We'll have it when we arrest your accomplice."

"I *have* no accomplice, Mr. Dillman."

"Do you confess to the theft of Sir

Arthur's book?"

"No, of course not!"

"Then you worked in league with a professional criminal," said Dillman. "The disappearance of *A Study in Scarlet* was only one of a number of thefts on board this ship, and the spate of crimes culminated in murder."

"Murder!" yelled Spurrier. "I had nothing to do with that."

"What about the other thefts?"

"All I did was to buy one item that was offered to me and I did so in good faith. I didn't ask where it came from and was quite unaware that any crime had taken place."

"Then why did you feel it necessary to hide the book?" asked Genevieve. "If there was nothing improper in the transaction, you had no reason to go to such lengths to conceal it." Spurrier looked uneasy. "I think you knew that you were being offered stolen property."

"I deny that."

"You can do so again in court," said Dillman. "The point is this, Mr. Spurrier. One man is responsible for all the crimes committed on the *Celtic,* but he needed a confederate."

"Well, it was not me — I swear it!"

"You accepted stolen goods from him."

"That was a foolish error."

"How many other foolish errors did you make?"

"None!" howled Spurrier. "I was involved in one small deal with him, that's all. I'm not his confederate. I don't even like the man."

"What man?" asked Dillman.

"David Lowbury."

Luncheon in steerage was the same clamorous event to which they had all become accustomed. Saul Pinnick, however, noticed that it had a different feature this time. Armed with sheaves of paper, members of the crew were working their way along the tables.

"It looks as if they're doing a head count, Mirry," he said.

"What?"

"They seem to be checking off names."

"I can't see anybody," said his wife, screwing up her eyes. "Unless something is happening right in front of me, I can't see it."

"That's why you've got me, my love. I'm your eyesight."

She popped a chunk of bread into her mouth and chewed it hungrily. A man soon came level with them. He consulted his list.

"Names, please?" he invited.

"Saul and Mirry Pinnick," said Pinnick. "Mirry as in Miriam."

The man put ticks on his list. "Thank you."

"What's going on?" said Miriam.

"We think someone may be missing."

"It'll be *him,* Saul. I know it."

"My wife means Len Rush," said Pinnick. "He lost his wife on the voyage to America, then got turned back. He was in despair. He was talking about throwing himself overboard."

"What was that name, sir?" asked the man.

"Len Rush — that's Len as in Leonard."

After working his way down the list, the man flicked over the page to study the next one. Pinnick was saddened by the thought that Rush might have committed suicide and he reproached himself for not doing more to revive the man's spirits. Rush had not been seen all morning. It looked as if he had finally fulfilled his threat.

"No," said the man, tapping the page. "Leonard Rush is here. I met him on deck only five minutes ago. He's not the missing man."

"That's good news," declared Pinnick.

Miriam was contentious. "Is it?" she said through a mouthful of food. "I don't see why."

She knocked hard on the cabin door and waited. When it was heard, Jane Lowbury's voice sounded timid and cautious.

"Who's there?" she said.

"It's Genevieve Masefield."

"Has something happened?"

"I need to speak to you, Mrs. Lowbury."

The door was unlocked and Jane opened it. Her expression of suffering changed to one of surprise when she saw that Dillman was standing there as well. Without waiting for an invitation, they went into the cabin and closed the door behind them.

"We're going to move you from here," said Genevieve.

"But I'd rather stay," insisted Jane.

"This is not for your safety, Mrs. Lowbury, it's for *ours*."

"Yes," said Dillman pointedly. "As long as your husband is on the loose, we're both in danger."

"On the loose?" Jane's face registered puzzlement. "What are you talking about? David was murdered. You told me so yourself. He was pushed over the side of the ship."

"That's what you both wanted us to

believe, Mrs. Lowbury, and the trick worked very well at first. But there were always worrying aspects to your story."

"I don't understand."

"Oh, I think you do," said Dillman. "Take that nonsense about your pills, for instance. I don't believe they ever existed. If you really needed important medication, you'd be certain to carry it with you."

"You'd also have asked for some replacement pills from the doctor," Genevieve pointed out, "yet you refused to take anything at all. We know why now — your husband was still alive."

"Except that we don't believe he was your husband. The man with whom you've been sharing your cabin is known to the police as Edward Hammond." Dillman loomed over her. "He's wanted for the murder of Horace Pooley and for that of a steerage passenger who died in his place. Mr. Hammond deliberately left his coat in that lifeboat to deceive us. It was a clever ruse but it had some fatal flaws." He gave her a cold smile. "That's why we're here."

Jane tried to brazen it out. "I don't know what you're talking about," she said with righteous indignation, "and I'll be certain to complain to the purser. I'll thank you both to leave my cabin at once."

"You've nothing to hide, then?"

"Nothing at all, Mr. Dillman."

"Then you won't object if I search the cabin, will you?"

"Wait!"

Jane lunged forward to stop him but she was grabbed from behind. Genevieve held her in a firm grip. Dillman did not have to look far. Opening a leather chest, he rummaged through some clothing and produced a sparkling gold cup. He read the inscription on it.

"When did you win a golf tournament, Mrs. Lowbury?" he asked.

Jane's scream of rage reverberated around the cabin.

Edward Hammond congratulated himself on his success. Having shed one false identity, he had acquired another in its place and it did not involve sustained pretense on his part. The man whom he had killed and pushed overboard had been a lone steerage passenger who preferred to sleep on deck. All that Hammond had had to do was to rob him of his clothing and his passport, and he had the perfect disguise for the remainder of the journey. He might have to endure days of boredom in steerage, but his nights were spent in the arms of his lover in first class. Posing as a heartbroken widow, Jane had been looking after the property he had stolen from various people. It was, Hammond reasoned, the last place that the ship's detectives would ever think of looking.

He had another cause for contentment. When the names of all passengers were being checked, he was able to give that of Ronald Coveney. In his ragged clothes and with his unshaven face, he easily passed for the man he had murdered nights before. Avoiding meals in the saloon, he subsisted on food that Jane saved for him. When he saw her that evening, he knew that a delicious meal would be waiting in the cabin. His return was carefully timed to coincide with dinner in first class. After changing into the steward's uniform he had stolen, he hid his clothing in steerage and went up the companionway reserved for the crew. By the time he reached the first-class areas, cabin stewards had finished turning down the beds. The coast was clear.

Hammond moved swiftly to his cabin and knocked three times. Two knocks came in reply to confirm that Jane was alone. Hammond tapped on the door once more to complete the agreed code. As the door opened, he dived in and turned to embrace

Jane. But she was no longer there. In her place was George Dillman.

"Good evening, Mr. Hammond," he said. "Remember me?"

"Where's Jane?" demanded Hammond.

"Where she belongs — under lock and key."

Hammond did not even try to talk himself out of the situation. The game was up and his only chance of escape lay in overpowering the detective. Launching himself at Dillman, he tried to grab him by the throat, but the latter was ready for him this time. He moved smartly sideways and delivered a left hook that caught Hammond on the ear and made his head ring. Hurt and enraged, Hammond swore and rushed in again. Dillman knew how strong he was and gave him no chance to grapple. With a well-aimed kick, he caught Hammond in the crotch and made him double up in agony. Hammond expelled a string of expletives like a blast of hot steam. Before the man could recover, Dillman felled him with an uppercut to the chin.

"Now, then, Mr. Hammond," he said, standing over him with his revolver in his hand, "I think you have a little explaining to do."

■ ■ ■ ■

Nelson Rutherford was far too excited to sit down. He jumped around behind his desk as he congratulated Dillman and Genevieve.

"Now I know how the real Nelson felt when he won a battle," he said happily. "It's exhilarating. Except that I didn't actually win this battle. You were kind enough to do it for me."

"It was something of a Pyrrhic victory," admitted Dillman, putting a gentle hand to the back of his head. "We had casualties. I still have the scars by way of testimony."

"But you and Miss Masefield succeeded in the end."

"We were determined to do so," said Genevieve. "We knew that Hammond had to be on the ship somewhere."

"It just never occurred to us that he was traveling under the name of David Lowbury," said Dillman. "He and his partner were very convincing. Jane Lowbury has obviously had acting experience. That was how she met Horace Pooley, you see."

"Was it?"

"Yes, Mr. Rutherford," said Genevieve. "I got the whole story out of her. He saw her on the stage, contrived an introduction and showered her with gifts. She quickly became his mistress and enjoyed all the trappings that went with it. Then he found someone else and dropped her like a stone."

"No wonder she wanted revenge."

"She wanted Pooley hurt but not killed. Since she'd visited his house often while his wife was away, she knew exactly where he kept his valuables. When she teamed up with Hammond," said Genevieve, "she was able to give him precise instructions about where to go."

"He claims that Pooley disturbed him during the burglary," said Dillman, "but I'd question that. My feeling is that Hammond killed him out of spite, having already set up his escape on the *Celtic.* They brought a small fortune on board with them."

"And added to it while they were here," noted the purser. "The captain sends you his warmest congratulations. You not only solved a murder, you returned every item of stolen property to its rightful owner. Sir Arthur Conan Doyle has been singing your praises ever since," he went on, "though he is sad about Ruggles."

"The barber who recited Sir Arthur's poems?" said Genevieve.

"That's him. He was sorely tempted. Ruggles was so guilt-ridden that he confessed to Sir Arthur. It all started when he gave David Lowbury a haircut."

"Edward Hammond," corrected Dillman.

"He knew him as Lowbury at the time. Nobby Ruggles yields to none in his worship of Sir Arthur, so he naturally began to talk about him to his customers. Lowbury was very interested, especially when Ruggles told him that he kept an album of cuttings about his hero."

"I bet that Lowbury — Hammond, that is — asked to see it."

"He did," said Rutherford. "And there were several photographs of Sir Arthur. Some of them showed him holding his copy of *A Study in Scarlet*. The captions always explained that he never gave a lecture on Sherlock Holmes without it."

"In other words," Genevieve remarked, "Hammond knew that the novel would be in his cabin."

"And having talked to Frank Spurrier, he had some idea of its value. When he mentioned a figure to Ruggles, the barber was amazed. He has a first edition of *Songs of Action,* it seems, an anthology of Sir Arthur's poems. Since he left the army," continued the purser, "Ruggles has fallen on hard times. Barbers are not well paid. Having heard that an author's signature added to the value of any book, he got his copy of *Songs of Action* autographed, then took it to Lowbury's cabin to offer it to him."

"But he wasn't there," said Dillman. "He was skulking in steerage. And I doubt if Jane Lowbury opened the door to him."

"She didn't, Mr. Dillman. She told him to go away. Ruggles was chastened. That book of poetry is the only thing of value he owns, yet, in a weak moment, he had been ready to part with it. He felt ashamed."

"Is that why he owned up to Sir Arthur?"

"Apparently."

"Then it was very noble of him."

"Sir Arthur felt the same," said Rutherford. "He even invited him in to recite one of the poems. Nobby Ruggles will brag about that for the rest of his life. I, of course, would prefer to brag about the way that George Dillman and Genevieve Masefield cleaned up the crime spree on the *Celtic.*"

"That won't be possible," said Dillman seriously. "Trumpet our success and we'd never be able to work for the White Star Line again. Every villain would know who we were and take steps to avoid us."

"I accept that. It's such a pity we can't divulge details of the crimes to Sir Arthur. Think of the novel he could write about it."

"That's exactly why he must never know," said Genevieve.

"No," added Dillman. "As far as he's concerned, this voyage was all about two séances, a performing barber and a missing copy of *A Study in Scarlet*. There's enough material there for a good author."

ABOUT THE AUTHOR

Conrad Allen is the author of seven previous mysteries in this series featuring sleuths George Porter Dillman and Genevieve Masefield investigating murder aboard some of the most famous luxury liners of the early twentieth century, including the *Lusitania, Mauretania, Minnesota, Caronia, Marmora, Salsette,* and *Oceanic.* He lives in England.

ML